THE ABOLITION OF DEATH

Also by James Anderson

The Alpha List

JAMES ANDERSON

The abolition of death

Walker and Company
New York

First published in the United States of America
in 1975 by the Walker Publishing Company, Inc.

ISBN: 0-8027-5316-7

Library of Congress Catalog Card Number: 74-21911

Printed in the United States of America.

10 9 8 7 6 5 4 3 2 1

THE ABOLITION OF DEATH

.

PROLOGUE

'I can live for ever.'

Thomas Mehler said the words aloud to himself. But still he couldn't really take them in. It wasn't that he disbelieved them. On the contrary. He was sure now the drug would work. It was just that his imagination simply could not grasp the concept of immortality – of living for hundreds of years. It would take time to free oneself from the old ideas.

Years . . . Time . . . The very words had taken on new meanings.

He said it again: 'I can live for ever.' Then he checked himself. *Could* would be better than *can*. Because he wouldn't be immune to accidents. Or, for that matter, to disease.

However, a careful man ought to be able to avoid accidents. And most diseases would be under control before the century was out.

He'd need luck, of course. But given that, there had to be a reasonable chance that his life – and the lives of millions of others – really would be everlasting.

He had discovered something for which mankind had been searching throughout history. Just by chance.

He'd always been sceptical about stories of chance scientific discoveries. A few months before he'd have said they were so rare as to be almost non-existent. But now he knew better.

It had been incredible luck. He couldn't really claim much credit.

And yet –

He *had* seen the significance of that first laboratory result. Not everyone would have done so. And not everyone would have had the knowledge and the ability to follow it up.

He remembered the hours of intense thought. The tentative experiments, privately, almost furtively, carried out. The sense of disbelief

5

when they'd proved positive – disbelief so strong that he had repeated them all, with variations, again and again.

Until now he was sure.

Not that the work was over. Far from it. Months, perhaps years, of it lay ahead. But it should be fairly straightforward work. The road was clear. All he needed was time, money, and assistants. And to get these things he had to have official backing. Here the procedure was clearly laid down. Government grants were always available for important scientific work.

Theoretically . . .

For suppose the civil servants didn't grasp the implications? Or simply disbelieved him and didn't give him a chance to prove his point? Suppose he got tied up with pretty officials or bogged down in ponderous committees? He'd known it happen to colleagues of his.

Could he somehow bypass the usual channels? Go straight to the top? Dare he even go straight to the Chairman himself?

It would be an audacious thing to do. But if *he* couldn't get away with it, with a discovery like his to put across, who could?

If he could once get an audience he could, he knew, convince the Chairman. Once he'd done that, he'd be bound to get what he asked for.

It would be so little, really, he'd be requesting. His own private laboratory . . . somewhere quiet . . . in the country . . . with a nice house attached . . . perhaps the 45th District . . . there was a part of it he'd always loved. Freedom from all other work and distractions . . . no more teaching . . . that would be bliss. Three or four full-time assistants. And adequate funds. That was all. So little, really – considering that his was the greatest discovery in scientific history.

And then, eventually, he would publish his findings. They would mean overnight fame. In the annals of science his name would rank with Galileo, Newton, Einstein. As a benefactor to humanity above Pasteur, Lister, Fleming, Salk. There would be awards. The Nobel, of course, and every other honour the world had to offer. As well as riches . . .

Thomas Mehler dreamed.

1

From the street the bar looked cheerless, shabby, and none too clean. But that suited Petros. He wasn't in the mood for strip-lighting, stainless steel, and piped music. He opened the door and went in.

There were about a dozen customers inside, including a group of long-haired, leather-jacketed youths noisily drinking beer at one end of the counter. Petros went to the other end. He didn't notice a shifty-faced little man, sitting with a fat woman at a table just inside the door, look up, stare at him, nudge the woman, and whisper.

Petros ordered a double Scotch and stood moodily drinking it. It was a long time since he'd tasted whisky, but he didn't enjoy it much. He had been a heavy drinker at one time, but except for the occasional glass of beer that prisoners were allowed, he hadn't had access to alcohol in jail. He'd been surprised how little he'd missed it.

The first glass did nothing for him at all. He ordered another, carried it across to a table against the wall, and sat down. There was a juke-box, blessedly silent, next to his chair, and he leaned up against it and tried to work out a course of action – anything at all that would improve the situation.

There had to be something he could do. Because he certainly wasn't prepared to follow Paula's advice and just sit back and wait for matters to take a turn for the better. They weren't going to. That was clear to him now. He was permanently branded.

A hired assassin. That was how people saw him.

And the fact that the only payment he'd received had been the chance to go on living didn't matter.

It had been the latest batch of anonymous letters which had brought it home to him. He remembered the first of them almost word for word. Strange, really, because it had been mild compared with most of the others he'd received in the past.

TO A MURDERING RAT

This is just to let you know that there are some people what get sick when they think that the stinking foreigner who shot President Kauffman is walking round free less than five years later. You admitted you killed him. You should have been strung up. Instead they let you out of jail after four years. But don't think you're going to get off so lightly, Petros. We're going to get you so you'd better look out.

That was all. No obscenities. No gory details about just how they were going to kill him. And no threats to Paula.

'I feel quite insulted,' she'd said.

But Petros hadn't been able to joke about it. Because it meant that after six months the letters still hadn't stopped. Before this, nearly three weeks had passed without one arriving, and both he and Paula had thought there weren't going to be any more. Then it had come. Out of the blue. So although he'd been getting five or six of them a day after he'd first been released, this one had been a greater blow than any of them.

With the next postal delivery two more letters had arrived. Petros had been bewildered. Eventually Paula had enlightened him: there had been another magazine article about Kauffman and him two days ago. The letters were probably the outcome of that. She hadn't mentioned it before – had hoped he wouldn't find out.

Why now? he had asked, baffled. Why on earth did they want to rehash the story again at this particular time?

Then she had told him: it would have been Kauffman's sixtieth birthday this week. That was why he was in the news again.

At that moment Petros had realized that the affair was never going to die. For next year would be the fifth anniversary of Kauffman's death. The year after, the Kauffman Institute would be opening. So it would go on. There would always be new reasons for publicity: TV programmes, newspaper features, books. Every one dragging in his name; and Paula's too.

'Meanwhile, Kauffman's assassin, 39-year-old Mikael Petros, is living peacefully with his attractive schoolteacher wife, Paula, and is working as a petrol pump attendant at Rostein's Garage, a filling station situated on . . .' That was roughly how they went, as a rule.

Petros was so deep in thought that he hardly noticed one of the long-haired youths come slouching across the room and put a coin in the juke-box. The sudden blast of noise brought him out of his reverie with a start. He looked up angrily.

'Can't you ask?' he snapped.

Two lack-lustre eyes swung slowly round to rest on him. 'What d'yuh mean?'

The youth's skin was dotted with pimples, he had a long pointed nose, thick lips like two slices of liver, and lank hair to his shoulders.

Petros looked at him with distaste. 'You know what I mean.' He had to shout to make himself heard above the increasing noise of the record, and most of the heads in the bar turned in his direction. 'Couldn't you have had the common courtesy to ask if I minded before you started that thing bellowing in my ear?'

The liver lips parted in a slow grin. 'That's what it's for, innit?'

'Not if other people object.'

'Oh yes it is. Ask the guy behind the bar. The box is here so anyone what wants to can play it. If you don't like it, clear out.'

He was right, of course. A complaint would have achieved nothing. But Petros was in too ill a mood to admit this. In a sudden temper he jumped to his feet, within a split second of slamming his fist into the repulsive face. In the nick of time he remembered that he was on parole. The youth took a step back and his hand went to his pocket. Petros clenched the edge of the table and cast round for a cutting reply, but just then the shifty-faced little man by the door called out: 'Hey, boy, you want to watch out with him. He's a killer, he is.'

Immediately every voice in the room was hushed. The only sound was the continued blaring of the juke-box. Pleased with the effect he'd made, the little man shouted: 'That's Mikael Petros. That's the man who killed Kauffman.'

Petros stood motionless, paralysed by a wave of anger and humiliation. He sank down onto his seat, clenched his fist, and under cover of

9

the table punched his thigh two or three times in sheer frustration. He stared down at the grimy table top. He was aware of the youth stepping closer and standing over him.

'Is that right?'

Petros neither moved nor spoke.

'I said are you Mikael Petros?' The voice was louder this time.

'What if I am?'

'Well of all the bloody cheek!' He turned to the room at large. 'This murdering bastard comes in here and starts telling us what to do. A paid killer! He should have swung years ago.' He bent over and put his head close against Petros's, breathing beerily over him. 'Listen, mate. I don't like foreigners. Especially I don't like foreign spies, who come over here and knock people off. Most of all I don't like foreigners who try to boss me around. So if you know what's good for you, get the hell out of here. Now.'

Petros looked up. He spoke very quietly. 'I will get out when I'm ready. Which is not yet. If you're thinking of starting something, let me remind you that, in your own words, I am a paid killer, so you might get more than you bargained for.' He picked up the glass and drained it, then shot out his other hand and grabbed the youth's wrist. 'Now, if you don't want this glass smashed against your pretty face, shut your mouth and get away from me.'

He released the wrist and leaned back. At that moment the record on the juke-box came to an abrupt end. There was complete silence in the bar. The youth straightened up, gave a scornful laugh, then turned and swaggered slowly back to his companions. Petros remained quite still. Every eye in the place was on him. For a few seconds the atmosphere was tense. Then the door opened and three teenage girls tumbled in, laughing and screeching. A second later conversation started up again. Petros lit a cigarette. For some minutes various people continued to throw glances in his direction, but as more customers entered and others left, he gradually ceased to be the centre of attention. He went to the counter and ordered another whisky. The barman eyed him curiously, but served him without comment.

Petros remained standing at the counter. He had a couple more drinks and began to feel light-headed. Perhaps he was overdoing it, after such a long lay-off. Anyway, he'd stayed long enough. His self-respect would let him leave now. He finished his drink and walked to the door. The group of youths was still gathered at the far end of the counter. As Petros went out to the street, the leader said something to the others and thirty seconds later they put down their glasses and followed Petros out.

The barman watched them go. He caught the eye of the shifty-faced man and gave a shrug. The shifty-faced man grinned.

In the street, Petros again fell into a reverie. It was getting dark, but he just trudged on, hardly conscious that he was leaving behind the streets of shops and bars and houses, and that he didn't know where he was.

The time in the bar had done nothing to improve his state of mind. On the contrary, it had only emphasised what an impossible position he was in. And he could see no way out. Paula had talked of moving to a different part of the country, changing their name, him changing his appearance. But that was out of the question. The only effective way to change your appearance was plastic surgery, which cost a fortune. Then, what would they do about jobs? Paula was naturalized and a qualified teacher. But she wouldn't be able to give references, or say where she'd been working, without revealing who she really was. And he himself was an alien with no qualifications. He'd never be given anything but the most menial work. He'd only got the job at the garage because Rostein had thought it would be a good sales gimmick to give his customers a chance to get their petrol from the man who'd killed the President. There wasn't the remotest prospect of advancement there. And now the novelty had worn off Rostein would be quite glad of an opportunity to get rid of him.

So the future was grim. There was nothing he could think to do. There was nowhere he could go. He was stuck in this country, among people who hated him, for the rest of his life. For of course, he could never return to his homeland. He'd face certain execution. And there wasn't a hope of any other nation in the world being willing to take him in.

Petros suddenly came to himself in a dimly-lit road, flanked by big silent buildings. Factories, he supposed, or warehouses, though it was now quite dark and he could see very little. He was lost. He swore out loud and halted.

It was then that he heard the footsteps behind him. He held his breath. They stopped and he heard a little laugh. He felt his heart miss a beat. A voice, not far away, called softly: 'Petros. Oh, Petros.'

Petros licked his lips and peered back into the gloom. By the faint light of the nearest lamp post he could just see a long-haired figure, standing quite still in the centre of the road about thirty metres away. As Petros watched, the figure raised its hand and beckoned, and one by one four other silhouettes came from behind the first and formed a line spread across the road. They must have been following in single file, some distance apart, so that he wouldn't hear their footsteps. His own, echoing back from the high walls each side, had effectively drowned the sound of the leader's.

Petros looked ahead again. The road stretched into the distance, a black tunnel, punctuated at intervals by feeble haloes of light from the street lamps. There was not another person, not a vehicle, not one illuminated building, not a telephone box. He'd walked right into trouble.

There was another laugh, and he heard footsteps coming towards him. There was only one thing to do.

Petros ran.

With whoops, they came after him.

He didn't stand a chance. He'd drunk a lot of whisky on an empty stomach, had already been on his feet a long time, was nearly forty years old, and out of condition after four years in jail. Within seconds he knew they were gaining. He desperately tried to increase his speed, stumbled, and went crashing down. He lay still, eyes closed, feigning unconsciousness. Perhaps if they thought he was badly hurt they'd panic and run away. But when a boot crashed against his ribs he couldn't keep back a gasp of pain. Then they hauled him to his feet and stood round him in a tight circle.

The spotty-faced leader stood right in front of him and leered into his face. 'Well, killer?'

Petros said: 'Well?'

12

He seemed to have no answer to this and just stood, leering idioti-
cally. At last he said: 'I don't like killers.'

'You're just jealous, that's all,' Petros said.

'And I don't like cheeky foreigners. Lousy swine – coming over
here and killing our President and then trying to boss me around. You
got off too easy. They should have topped you.'

'Is that what you intend to do now?'

'Ain't got no rope. There's better ways, though. Slower and more
fun.'

'I thought that was coming. So let's get it over with, shall we?
Would you like me to start?'

Petros drew back his fist and smashed it with all his strength into the
liver lips. The lout staggered back. Before Petros could attempt
another punch the others had his arms pinned to his sides.

Then they set to work on him.

They were amateurs, but they made up for that by enthusiasm. The
blows and kicks rained on his body from every direction. After the
first few seconds he could make no attempt to fight back, but merely
went limp and prayed for oblivion. But it wouldn't come. Dimly,
through the pain, he knew they didn't intend to stop for a long time
yet.

But then they did stop.

Suddenly he was just conscious that they'd released him and that he
was sinking to the ground. He hardly heard the shouts or the running
footsteps. He only vaguely knew that a figure was bending over him,
was just aware that he was being raised to his feet and led away, and
after that was conscious of nothing.

Later, but not all that much later, there was a bright light; blurred
glimpses of faces; a familiar voice, questioning and anxious; another
voice, giving reassurance. He was lying on something soft, capable
hands were examining him, warming liquid was running down his
throat. Everything swung back into focus. He was on the settee in his
own sitting-room and Paula was kneeling beside him, her hand
behind his head, a glass in her hand.

13

'Hullo,' he said.

'Hullo, darling. How do you feel?'

'I – I don't know. How did I get here?'

'These gentlemen brought you home.'

Petros moved his eyes and saw a young man standing behind Paula. He was tall and well-built with thick dark hair, and was in the act of bending over to put something into a black bag that lay on a small occasional table. He glanced up at Petros out of very deep-set eyes and gave a smile. 'How do you feel?'

'Sore.'

'Yes, you will do for a couple of days. But there seem to be no bones broken and there's no evidence of internal injuries – just severe bruising.'

Petros said: 'Are you –'

'I'm a physician. Your wife says you don't have a regular doctor of your own.'

'No.' It had been slack, but he'd never got around to signing on with Paula's doctor after getting out of prison.

'Then I'll come and see you again tomorrow afternoon. But I think all you need is rest.' He straightened up and handed Paula a small pill box. 'Give him a couple of these before he goes to bed. They'll make sure he sleeps.' Then he looked across Petros to someone behind the settee. 'Will you be wanting me again tonight?' he asked, and there was a subtle change in the tone of his voice.

'No,' said the voice of another man.

Petros slowly turned his head upwards over the back of the settee and saw the man who had spoken.

He's old, was his first thought, for the man's hair was white. Then he noticed the unlined face and the clear blue eyes, and he changed his mind. But you couldn't call the man young. And 'middle-aged' would somehow have been a word even more wrong.

'Then I'll leave you now, if that's all right,' the younger man said, and the white-haired man gave a nod.

Petros turned his head back to the physician. 'Thank you very much,' he said, 'I'm very grateful.'

'I've done very little. There's the one you should thank.' He

14

nodded towards the white-haired man. 'Good night.'

'I'll see you out,' said Paula, getting to her feet. They left the room.

Petros turned back to the white-haired man. 'I'm extremely grateful, sir. But I'm afraid I don't exactly know what it was you did. I can remember hardly anything after they set on me.'

The white-haired man walked round to the front of the settee. He said: 'Some friends of mine and I saw you being attacked by those young men, so we drove them off and brought you home.'

'Well please thank your friends for me as well. It was a miracle your turning up.'

'Not really.'

'Well, Mr – er, may I know your name?'

'My name is Pelli.'

'Well, Mr Pelli, I'm most grateful. I don't know what would have happened if you hadn't come along.'

'They would have killed you.'

Paula, coming back into the room, gave a little gasp. Petros was silent for a few seconds. Then: 'Yes, I believe you're right,' he said soberly.

'They would not have meant to. But they had lost all control.'

'So – I owe you my life.'

Mr Pelli didn't answer, just gave the slightest of shrugs.

'If there's ever anything I can do in return . . .' Petros tailed off.

'Yes, there may well be something.'

Petros had spoken purely conventionally, and the reply took him slightly by surprise. 'Oh? Of course – anything. Please tell me.'

'Not now. If you are agreeable, I will come and see you when you feel better. Shall we say the day after tomorrow – Friday? For perhaps half an hour.'

'Yes, certainly.'

'Very well. Incidentally, your employer, Mr Rostein, has been informed of the attack and that you will not be working tonight or tomorrow night.'

Petros stared at him. 'You did that?'

'I had it done.'

Petros didn't know what answer to make to this. It was left to Paula

15

to say: 'Thank you very much. But you shouldn't have bothered. I could have done that.' There was the slightest tinge of resentment in her voice.

'You would not have been able to notify him for some time yet,' Mr Pelli said. 'As it is, he has had a much longer period to make other arrangements. And the man on the eight to twelve shift will not now be stranded without a replacement.' As he spoke, Mr Pelli looked directly at Paula for the first time. Surprisingly, she appeared to find this disconcerting. Her eyes dropped and for a moment she seemed somehow younger.

'Now your husband must rest,' Mr Pelli said to her. 'You will stay home with him tomorrow?'

'Yes, of course.'

'Good.' He looked at his watch. 'I must go.'

Petros said: 'Thank you again – for everything.'

'I did only what was necessary. Till Friday, then. Will three o'clock suit you?'

'Fine.'

Paula said: 'I don't know whether you'll want to see me, but for once I shall be here at that time. As it happens, I have the afternoon off.'

'I know. Otherwise I would not have suggested that hour. You will be affected by what I have to ask, so I want you to hear it.'

Thirty seconds later Paula came back into the sitting-room, having seen Mr Pelli out. She gazed at Petros blankly. 'Who on earth was that?'

Petros shook his head.

'And how did he know so much about us?'

'Oh, I'm quite famous, remember?'

'Not that famous. He could find your name and address in your wallet, and he could know from the publicity that you worked at Rostein's Garage. But how did he know that you're on the night shift, and that you start at twelve? How did he know that I've got Friday afternoon off? Those things haven't been in the papers.'

'Why didn't you ask him?'

'I don't know, really. I didn't like to, somehow. Did you notice,

16

too, how respectful that doctor was – almost as though Pelli was his boss?'

'Perhaps he is.'

'And what on earth can he want you to do for him?'

'I don't know. And honestly, darling, I don't really care much at the moment. I'm just damn grateful he and his friends were there. All I want to do now is get to bed.'

'Oh, sorry. I'll give you a hand. But I don't like it, Mike. For some reason, that man frightens me.'

The tablets did their job and gave Petros a sound sleep that night. In the morning he was still stiff and sore, and he stayed in bed. Paula sat with him for much of the time, and he gave her an account of just what had happened the previous night. When he'd finished, he said: 'It's all the fault of that blasted magazine.'

'Oh, Mike, you can hardly blame the magazine for your getting beaten up!'

'It was that article which triggered off the latest batch of letters, wasn't it? If it hadn't been for the letters I wouldn't have been in the mood I was – probably wouldn't even have gone to that bar at all.'

'Well, there is that,' she said. 'The ironic thing, though, is that it's not at all a bad piece, really. It's fair to you, doesn't condemn you at all – and it's got its facts reasonably straight.'

'Got a copy of it?'

She nodded.

'Let's see it.'

'Sure you want to?'

'Yes.'

She went out of the room and came back carrying a folded magazine. She opened it and handed it to him. He took it and gave a wince. There were photographs of Kauffman and Petros himself, and a big black headline: THE DREAM OF PRESIDENT KAUFFMAN. Petros started to read.

'Alexis Kauffman was born sixty years ago this week. Fifty-

17

three years later he became President of the Republic. Nearly five years ago he was killed by an assassin's bullet. He died because, unknown to all but a handful of his associates, he had a dream.

He wanted this country to break off all trade and diplomatic relations with its nearest neighbour and closest ally.

Economists would have said he was mad. And he knew that in the short term things would be tough. He believed, though, that in the long run the country could only benefit from such a step.

However, it wasn't this prospect that made him want to break off relations. His motive was a deep sense of shame that our economic support was helping to keep a cruel and corrupt regime in power.

Kauffman believed that the withdrawal of this support would be a body blow to that regime and to its Chairman, and that as a result it would eventually fall.'

Petros looked up. 'Surely everybody knows this. It was only five years ago. They're writing as though it were ancient history.'

'I think that magazine's aimed largely at the teenage market. Their readers would mostly have been kids at the time. To them it practically *is* ancient history.'

Petros read on.

'President Kauffman was destined never to see his theories put to the test. For the Chairman found out about his plans. He foresaw the same outcome to them that Kauffman anticipated. And he marked Kauffman down for death.

At that time in one of the Chairman's prisons an ex-army officer called Mikael Petros was awaiting execution for murder. The regime's espionage organization put into operation a plan they had often used before when the Chairman had wanted a particularly dirty or dangerous job carried out.

They offered Petros a reprieve.

On condition he assassinated President Kauffman for them.

To Petros it was a miracle. It seemed to him that all he had to do was agree to make the attempt to kill Kauffman. He would then be

18

released from prison and sent out of the country – when he could simply forget all about his task and just disappear.

But there turned out to be a snag.

Petros was warned that if he accepted the assignment he would be given an injection. That the substance injected into him would be a poison. And that it would kill him in three months unless he received a shot of a secret antidote. He would be given that shot only when Kauffman was dead.

Petros accepted the assignment.'

Petros gave an exclamation of disgust.

'What's the matter?'

'They make it all seem so casual. "Petros accepted the assignment". Just as though I were accepting a – a cigarette. I had about ten hours to live! This makes me sound completely cold-blooded.'

'Oh, I don't think it does, really. I don't suppose they had the space to go into your state of mind. The piece is chiefly about Kauffman, after all.'

'And I'm just one of the supporting cast. I know.' He started reading again.

'Petros came south, ostensibly an ordinary tourist, as in those days thousands of his countrymen used to every year. And eventually, as all the world knows, he did succeed in assassinating the President.

The Chairman must have thought that he had averted a great threat to his regime and that once more he was secure.

But Petros was arrested. And he talked. Our own intelligence services knew about the system of 'injection blackmail' and were able to confirm that Petros's story could well be true.

Moreover, Kauffman himself had suspected that an attempt would be made on his life, and had prepared for such an attempt succeeding. After his death a film he had made was shown on television. In it, he exposed the Chairman's regime for the evil thing it really is, accused its members of plotting his murder, revealed his plan for severing relations between the two countries, and nominated as his successor Roland Manson, then a little-known Parliamentary Delegate, but a man who fully supported the severance policy.

Overnight, Kauffman became a martyr. A tremendous revulsion of feeling against our former allies swept the country. At the ensuing presidential election Delegate Manson was returned to power with a huge majority on a platform of putting Kauffman's policy into immediate operation.

The Chairman's plot had backfired on him disastrously.

Mikael Petros did not die as a result of the injection. His story of how he had been pressurized was generally believed and there was widespread sympathy for him. President Manson himself recommended he be dealt with leniently. He was sentenced to eight years imprisonment. By all accounts he was a model prisoner and was released on parole six months ago.

Now thirty-nine, he is working as a petrol pump attendant and living with his wife in a new apartment building called Riendett House. He has had to put up with many insults and anonymous letters — even threats to his life and that of his wife —

Petros swore. 'Oh, this is great, isn't it?' He re-read the last paragraph aloud. 'They practically suggested people should send us anonymous letters. Even gave our address!'

'Yes, I thought that was unkind. There isn't anything more about you, though. The rest is all economics and politics.'

'They couldn't have done much more damage than they've done in that one paragraph if they'd devoted every page of the damn rag to my life story.'

'Well, cheer up. I expect it'll be the last one. The story's sure to wear thin soon. People will forget all about you, then. They'll just ignore you.'

'Want to bet? Ask yourself if Lee Harvey Oswald would be ignored if he were alive and at liberty in the States today — and then think how long it is since John Kennedy was assassinated. No, as long as I live I'll be the Man Who Shot the President. I won't even be able to go into a bar without expecting a repeat of what happened last night.'

Later, when she brought his lunch in, he said: 'I've been thinking. Do you reckon Manson would help?'

'He's helped already, hasn't he?'

'You mean speaking up for me before I was sentenced? Why shouldn't he do that again now? After all, he wouldn't be President if it wasn't for me. And as he is practically the only other person to know the full truth about Kauffman's death — '

She interrupted. 'We agreed never to speak about that. It's the only way to be sure of keeping the secret.'

'I never have spoken about it. But it's important to remember it, all the same. Manson, together with just one other man, whose name I was never told, knows why I really killed Kauffman, and that morally I'm less guilty than even my Counsel maintained. He knows I deserve help. And he knows that he's almost the only person who *does* know it. So don't you figure he's got a duty to help me?'

'What do you expect him to do? Go on television and make a "Don't be beastly to Petros" speech? Let himself be photographed with his arm round your shoulder?'

There was so much sarcasm in her voice that he was shocked. She looked rather abashed. 'I'm sorry, Mike. But honestly I just don't agree with the way you've been talking for the last few days. I don't know what's come over you. You did what you did with your eyes open. Manson helped you in every way you could reasonably expect. He saw that you got the medical attention you wanted so desperately. He said publicly that you'd been put in an intolerable situation and that he hoped the courts would deal lightly with you. They did. You got eight years. You've been released on parole after four. You're being allowed to stay in this country. I'm sure Manson was responsible for that, too — you might have been deported. You can't expect him to take up cudgels on your behalf just because of a few cranks — which is all that the letter-writers are. Now whatever you say, the letters *are* getting fewer, and I say they'll stop altogether soon. I don't think the trouble last night was anything to do with you being the man who shot the President. You picked a quarrel with a gang of

21

yobboes. They'd have probably beaten you up anyway – the fact that you'd killed Kauffman was just an excuse. Now, I know things have been going badly the last few days, but I'm sure it's only a phase. So I still say the same thing: stick it out a bit longer; just carry on as you have for the last six months – and see what happens.'

'See how many times I get beaten up, is that it? How many do you suppose it will take for the excuse to wear a bit thin?'

2

Elsa Vandar stood inside the garden gate, staring out over the rolling moorlands. Then she turned to her brother.

'It's a lovely place, Thomas.'

'I'm sorry you haven't been able to see it before.'

'I *was* a bit hurt when the months went by and you never asked us. Then I realized that there had to be a reason.'

'It wasn't only you, my dear. I've had hardly any visitors since I've been here. I knew that anyone who called would have to undergo all sorts of security checks. I didn't want to put you and Martin through that. I only found out a few weeks ago from Vort, the Chief of the section in charge of security here, that the mere fact that you are my sister, and we've been writing to each other, meant that they'd screened you both a long time ago.'

'We never knew anything about it.'

'If they didn't need to question either of you personally, you must have first-class security ratings.'

'So I should hope.'

'Anyway, there was no trouble at all when I put your names forward as potential visitors. I'm sorry Martin wouldn't come.'

'He will next time. I think he thought we'd like to have some time alone just once, after – how long is it exactly, now?'

'I've been here two and a half years.'

She stared. 'Never!'

'I have, you know. It seems every bit of that to me, too.'

'I was thinking it was about eighteen months,' she said slowly. 'I remember it so clearly – that evening when you came and told us you'd resigned from the university to do special government work. I just couldn't believe it when you said they were going to give you your own private laboratory, your own country house in the 45th, and assistants and everything. It seemed too good to be true.'

'Unbelievable that old Thomas should actually have lived up to expectations at last, was it?'

'I didn't mean that! You've always lived up to expectations as far as I'm concerned.'

'I know. I'm sorry.'

'It was just so unexpected. And you were so secretive about it all. Even now I still don't know what it is you're working on.'

'Nobody does. Not even the lab assistants — at least in theory. They're changed every so often, just so none of them will be able to get any real understanding of what the work is.'

'Goodness, it must be secret. Are you sure *you* know what it is?'

He smiled. 'Sometimes I doubt it.'

'When are you going to be able to tell me?'

'The day before I publish. That's a promise.'

'And when will that be?'

'Within months, I hope.'

'Really? Oh, Thomas, that's wonderful! And then you'll be famous, will you?'

'Famous? Oh yes, I'll be famous all right.'

'How famous? Just among other scientists? Or among people at large? Will you be as famous as Professor Berrog was, for instance?'

'More so. Much more.'

'No! Goodness, I can hardly believe it.'

'Oh, you'll be proud to have been born a Mehler, Elsa. You'll be tacking it on in front of your surname: Elsa Mehler Vandar. Bit of a mouthful, I'm afraid.'

'It'll be terribly exciting. I only wish mother and father were still alive to know about it. And — ' She broke off.

'Go ahead. "And Christine", you were going to say, weren't you? It's all right. I've got over Christine's death now. I can talk about it.'

'Good,' she said. 'Christine wasn't the sort of wife who'd want you to go on grieving for ever.'

'I didn't say I'd stopped grieving.'

'Well, you should try, Thomas. You've been living alone far too long.'

'And I should get married again? Is that what you're saying?'

She flushed slightly, then said: 'I don't want to be tactless. But why not? It *is* six years since she was killed.'

'I know. I've got no particular desire to get married again, though. Not yet, anyway.'

'Well, don't leave it too long. You *are* thirty-seven, remember. You haven't got forever.'

'Don't you be too sure that –' He stopped short, smiling.

'What's the matter?'

'Nothing. Just a thought. Don't worry about me, Elsa. Perhaps when this job is over I'll get out into society again.'

'I shouldn't imagine you'll be able to avoid it, you'll be so famous.'

'That's a nice thought.' He paused. 'Listen, try to forget a lot of what I said about my work. I got a bit carried away. I don't get much chance to show off. I *think* all I said will come about. But there is one more important experiment to do before I know finally.'

She looked at him closely. 'You're a bit worried about it, too, aren't you? I thought there was something.'

'A little worried. Theoretically, everything should be OK. But one can never be absolutely sure with practical experiments. Still, I'll know soon enough.' He gave a sudden shiver.

'It's getting cold,' she said. 'Let's go indoors.'

They turned and walked back to the house, past the new red brick extension jutting out from the back of the old stone building. Through the windows white-coated figures could be seen moving about.

'Sorry I can't show you around in there,' Mehler said.

'Don't be. You know it wouldn't mean anything to me.'

They entered the house. Mehler took a few steps towards the kitchen and called out: 'Could we have some tea now, please, Mrs Shenkar.' Then they went into the sitting-room.

'How do you spend your days?' Elsa asked. 'Do you work normal hours?'

'No mornings and evenings mostly. I try to keep the afternoons free.'

'What do you do in the afternoons?'

'Go out on the moors usually, if it's fine. Just walk – for hours, sometimes – or sit and read or write. Other times I watch television. About once a week I go into Township N, do some shopping and see a film. Occasionally I go to the District Capital and stay on for a concert or play in the evening, but not very often.'

'And you're always on your own?'

'Oh no, I'm never on my own.'

She looked puzzled for a second, then said: 'Oh, you mean the guards?'

He nodded.

'They really go with you everywhere?'

'Everywhere. Oh, they let me have the impression of being on my own as far as they can. But when I'm up on the moors they're never more than ninety or a hundred metres away, if I go into town they keep about ten paces behind, and if I go to the cinema they sit near me.'

'Doesn't it get on your nerves?'

'It used to. But I've grown accustomed to it now.'

'Don't the government trust you?'

'Oh, they trust me all right. I mean, they've more or less got to. I went straight to them when I first hit on – first *made* my discovery; which I wouldn't have done if I'd been a potential traitor. And having been a protégé of Berrog meant I wasn't unknown to them even before I made this breakthrough. No, I think they want to discourage anybody from trying to kidnap me – or just approaching me and attempting to bribe me to defect. Not that there would be much point in that, really. I mean, my discovery's not a weapon, or anything like that. Everybody in the world will benefit from it eventually.'

'I suppose this country will be the first, though, won't it? There might be people in other countries who wouldn't want to wait for it. Does that make sense?'

'Yes, it does. It makes very good sense.'

'Oh, Thomas, is there any chance of somebody kidnapping you? I mean, could two men do much to protect you?'

'Come over here.' He walked across to the window. She joined him. Outside the front of the house ran a narrow country road. Just to the left of the front gate as they looked out the road started to climb. About a hundred and fifty metres up the hill, on the other side of the road and sideways on to it, so that it faced straight down the hill, stood another house. Mehler pointed to it. 'That's where they hang out. My guards. Six of them. At this moment one will be sitting in the front window watching this house. He'll see if anyone comes within half a kilometre of it. At night I'm protected by a highly sophisticated system of burglar alarms, infra-red rays and the like. If a fieldmouse tried to get in here, they'd know about it up there. And do you know what they keep up there in a shed behind the house?'

Elsa shook her head.

'A small helicopter. They've also got the very latest radio equipment. If I go walking on the moors the two guards detailed to follow me wear miniature, bullet-proof morse transmitters locked to their wrists. At predetermined but irregular intervals they send a simple variable signal. Then –'

'What does that mean?'

'Well, before they leave, it's decided, say, that they'll transmit three dashes at 2.45, four dots at 3.10, treble dot dash at 3.25, and so on. I'm over-simplifying a bit, but that's the principle. No outsider can possibly know what the next signal is to be, or what time it's due. They won't even tell me. If the right call didn't come in on schedule, the chaps at the house would know straight away something was wrong, and they'd be on their way in seconds to where the last call came from. Also, they'd alert the nearest army post, and if I'd really vanished they'd get the whole area cordoned off. The guards have an emergency button on each of their transmitters, too. They've only got to press it for it to emit a homing signal it would be virtually impossible to stop. Then, of course, both of them are armed, and they close in on me like a couple of guided missiles if anyone else comes within twenty metres of me. If I go into town the same kind of radio routine applies, but because the wrist transmitters haven't got the range to reach here from Township N. a radio car always follows a couple of kilometres behind, to pick up the signals, and parks in the town all the time I'm there.'

'All this for my brother,' she said wonderingly. 'I had no idea.'

'It's purely routine, so they tell me. All Catagory A people get basically the same kind of treatment.'

'Catagory A?'

'The most important service chiefs, politicians, and scientists.' There was a note of pride in Mehler's voice.

The door opened and a tall, gaunt woman came in, wheeling a trolley which bore a teapot, jugs and cups, and plates of biscuits and cakes.

Mehler said: 'Ah, thank you, Mrs Shenkar.'

The woman nodded and went out without speaking.

Mehler said: 'Even Mrs Shenkar's armed.'

'What?'

'Yes, she and her husband are both on the security police payroll. They've had special training in this sort of thing and they work together, doing nothing else. When my job here is finished, they'll go on to somebody else, perhaps a government minister.'

'I see.' Elsa went across to the trolley. 'That was her husband who met me at the station, was it?'

'That's right. He acts as my chauffeur and as general handyman as well as bodyguard: ferries the lab assistants about, fetches any scientific equipment I need, does the household shopping, and so on.'

'Is that your car?'

'No! Can you imagine my buying an unwieldy great thing like that – even if I did drive these days? No, it's a government car – official issue.'

'It's very comfortable.'

'Oh, I have the best of everything, my dear. No one could be better looked after. The government seem determined to keep me perfectly happy – and safe.'

3

Petros got up after lunch, and was relaxing in an easy chair when Paula showed the physician into the sitting-room at about three o'clock. He came across to Petros's chair and looked down at him out of his deep-set eyes. 'How are you?' he asked quietly, and it seemed to Petros that he really wanted to know.

'Not too bad.'

'Really? Good.' He appeared genuinely pleased. 'Let's have a look.'

Paula went out and the physician proceeded to give Petros a most surprisingly comprehensive examination. It was a complete going-over rather than a mere checking on the injuries he had received. At the same time, though, it was remarkably quick – yet did not give the least impression of being rushed. The physician was deft, gentle, unhesitating, and apparently absolutely confident. He asked no questions, and apart from the standard brief instructions given to any patient, didn't speak at all. After the first few seconds Petros, to his surprise, found himself not only quite relaxed, but even contented.

In a very short time the physician straightened up, saying: 'You'll do.'

'Yes?'

He nodded, and started putting his things away in his bag. 'As I said, no serious injuries – just bruising. Here's some stuff for that.' He placed a small bottle on the table. 'You can start work in a day or two. You'll be glad to know that, apart from being a little out of condition, you're very healthy.'

In spite of the brevity of the examination, it didn't occur to Petros to doubt this. He felt quite sure that if this man said he was healthy, healthy he was. 'That's fine,' he said. 'Thank you very much. That was quite an examination. I didn't expect a complete check-up.'

'Not really complete yet.' He had finished packing his bag, but he

29

made no attempt to leave. Instead, he moved across to a chair facing Petros and sat down. 'Now I want you to tell me what's worrying you.'

'What makes you think anything's worrying me?'

'I know there is. Tell me.'

Petros had never been one to talk much about himself and he knew that his problems were not those that a doctor could do anything about. He opened his mouth with the intention of saying 'It's nothing,' but as he did so he caught the physician's eye and instead, unintentionally, came out with the words: 'It's a long story – ' He broke off.

'I have plenty of time.'

There was something strangely compelling about his manner. Reluctantly, Petros said: 'It's just that I can't see any decent future for myself. I hate my job – '

'Why?'

'Oh, a number of reasons. In the first place, I don't like night-work. My wife and I are back together again after nearly ten years apart, and most of the time we're having about six hours together out of the twenty-four. I leave for the garage before she goes to bed, and get home in the morning after she's left for school. And at weekends I'm falling asleep all day.'

'Can't you transfer to day work?'

'I could ask. But the trouble is that it was only three months ago I applied to be put on nights.'

'What was the reason for that?'

'I was sick of being a walking tourist attraction. Do you know why I got that job in the first place?'

'I imagine as a sort of advertising stunt.'

'Precisely. During my trial Rostein read that my last job in the old country had been manning petrol pumps. So when I came up for parole he wrote offering me work. I was very grateful. I might not have got parole if I hadn't had a job waiting for me. I knew he was doing it mainly for publicity – but I didn't bargain on him getting quite so much of it. The day I started, the place was swarming with TV and press men. You must have seen the pictures.'

'It was difficult to miss them. I imagine Rostein did well out of it.'

'It was incredible. People came from all over town, and from farther afield, just to be able to say they'd got their petrol from me. There were queues at my pump for weeks. I didn't mind at first — even the insults some of them would call out, even being spat at once or twice. But after a time it began to get on top of me. So I asked Rostein to put me on nights.'

'Which he did — even though you were doing his sales so much good?'

'Well, the big boom had dropped off by then. People were still coming, but he was losing customers, too — regular, account customers, mostly conservative businessmen and retired people. They didn't like having to queue and then perhaps eventually be served by a murderer. And they told Rostein so. So he was glad enough for me to hide myself away in the dark. The next week he got another gimmick — started giving away ball-pens with his name on. I was happier, too, at first. Nearly all the night trade is through-traffic and the drivers don't know me from Adam. All the same, I have been thinking of asking to switch back to days. I thought people might have forgotten about me by now. But after being recognised last night I'm not so sure.' He explained what had happened in the bar. Then he said: 'Besides, I doubt very much if Rostein would be willing to move me back. So I just don't know what to do. It seems I can't win either way.'

'Is there no other work you could get?'

'Who'd give me a job? I'm not trained for anything.'

'You were a soldier, weren't you?'

'Yes. Centuries ago. A good one, too. I was a major at twenty-nine.'

'How did you come to give it up?'

'That was my fault.' It was Paula who spoke as she came into the room, carrying a loaded tray. She put it down. 'You'll have some coffee?'

'Thank you. Why was it your fault, Mrs. Petros?'

'It wasn't, Petros said. 'Don't believe her. I didn't resign my commission until two years after we were divorced.'

31

'But you would never have had to if I hadn't left you.'

The physician smiled. 'I'm afraid I'm getting rather out of my depth.'

'Sorry. It's simple enough.' She passed him a cup of coffee. 'Cream? Sugar?'

'No thank you. Please go on.'

'I hated army life. I nagged Mikael to get out. Naturally he didn't want to. It was his career. I should have accepted that. But I wouldn't. That led to friction all round and eventually I walked out.'

'Hundreds of men's wives leave them,' Petros said. 'Mostly with much less reason, incidentally. All those men don't go to pieces, start boozing – or turn up blind drunk at a regimental dinner and interrupt a speech in order to give their candid opinion, among other things, of the ancestry, personal appearance, and habits of the Commanding Officer.'

'Oh. Is that what you did?'

'So they told me afterwards.'

'I can see why you resigned. What happened then?'

'It's rather like one of those nineteenth century moral tracts: more and more booze and a succession of ever more miserable jobs and ever cheaper digs.'

Petros took a cup of coffee from Paula himself, added sugar, and stirred it. He took a sip. 'Then,' he said, 'one day I committed a murder. I was arrested straight away, tried, and condemned to death. In this country I'd have probably done two or three years for it, but that's by the way. What happened after that came out at my next trial – the one that actually was in this country.'

The physician nodded. 'You were offered a reprieve – on condition you killed Kauffman.'

Petros nodded. 'What choice did I have but to agree? I was taken to a big country house, the HQ of a special government unit which regularly organized that sort of thing. The head of it was a man called Marcos. I was given the injection – the injection which they promised would eventually kill me if I didn't get a shot of the de-activator, as they called it. I was briefed, instructed how to obtain money and guns when I got here, and given all the necessary papers. Then I flew to this

32

country. The arrangement was that if I succeeded in killing Kauffman I should go on to Amsterdam, where someone would give me ten thousand American dollars, another set of false papers, and a plane ticket to any country in the world I chose.

'Well, of course, in the end I did shoot Kauffman. But I never got to Amsterdam. I was caught. I'm quite good at killing, you see, but not so good at getting away afterwards.'

'You were given eight years originally, weren't you?'

'Yes. But I was paroled after four. You could say I've been lucky. The only trouble is that all the nice, kind liberals who wrote sympathetic articles and made sympathetic speeches four or five years ago, saying I should be treated leniently, seemed to forget about me when I came out. Whereas the hard-liners, and the lunatics, haven't forgotten. And they let me know what they think.'

'How did the two of you get together again?'

'Oh, that was sheer coincidence,' Paula said. 'After we split up I managed to get permission to emigrate to this country. I was very lucky, because only about a hundred exit visas a year were issued. Then when Mikael came here on his assignment we happened to run into each other. We succeeded in patching up our differences. We remarried while Mikael was serving his time.'

'It can't have been easy for you – you, personally, I mean,' the physician said, looking at her keenly.

'Oh, it's not been too bad.' Paula gave a shrug.

'It's been ghastly for her,' Petros said. 'Can you imagine what she went through: the wife of a notorious political assassin – and at the same time a schoolteacher? Pressure being put on her employers to sack her – which only a very influential lady on the board was able to prevent. 'Having to face the other teachers, parents, and, worst of all, the children. *I* couldn't have stood it.'

Paula gave an embarrassed laugh. 'Oh, he's exaggerating. It was unpleasant at one time. But that's all in the past now.'

'Completely?' the doctor said quietly. 'What about the beginning of the academic year, for example? Aren't things still awkward then?'

She looked at him with a sudden, new respect. She nodded. 'Yes, you're quite right. I don't look forward to the new intake each year.

33

Within a couple of days every one of them will have heard all about me from the older children. Then sooner or later I know one of the bolder ones is going to mention the subject of murder, or ask an apparently innocent question about how loyal a woman should be to her husband, or something. Then again, I teach languages and literature, and it's a bit embarrassing sometimes with certain of the set books.'

He nodded. 'Such as *Macbeth* among the English ones, for instance?'

'Precisely,' she said.

The physician nodded thoughtfully. He looked from one of them to the other, then: 'Thank you for telling me,' he said, and stood up.

They'd both been waiting for something more than this and were a little taken aback. Then Paula stood up, too.

Petros said: 'Before you go – that gentlemen you were with last night: do you know him well?'

'Yes.'

'Who is he?'

'Didn't he tell you his name?'

'Yes, but I mean *what* is he? What does he do?'

'He has a number of interests. You could say he arranges things.'

'Oh, I get the picture,' Petros said. 'In other words, you're not prepared to talk about him.'

'I would gladly talk about him. But I understand he is coming to see you tomorrow, and I do not wish to influence your opinion. It will be best for you to get to know him yourself.'

'He seemed to know a lot about *us*,' Paula put in.

'I'm sure he did.'

'Were you with him and his friends when they rescued me?'

'No, he called me and said my services were needed, and asked me to meet him here. I arrived in time to help him upstairs with you.'

'He says he wants me to do something for him. Do you have any idea what it might be?'

'You'll have to hear that from his own lips, I think.'

'I see. Fair enough.'

The physician stood up. 'Now I must go.'

Petros said: 'Thank you again for everything – including your interest. About your account –'

'There's no charge. But take my advice and sign up with a doctor as soon as you can.'

'Could I sign up with you?'

'No, I'm sorry, I'm not in general practice. Good-bye.'

Paula went with him to the front door, then came back into the sitting-room. She raised her eyebrows. 'Well?'

'That's – quite a guy,' Petros said.

She nodded. 'Mm.'

'You felt it, did you?'

'What?'

'Well – ' He laughed. 'I don't know. But something.'

'Yes. Definitely something. Neither of us have ever talked like that to anyone before. We were positively garrulous.'

'I thought *he* would have said more after we'd finished our story. He kept on for me to tell him everything.'

'What did you expect him to say?'

'I'm not sure, really. Offer to help, I suppose. But then, what could he do?'

'Nothing. He's just a doctor. He's already done more than he was called upon to do.'

'True. But I expected him to express some sympathy, at least – say he was sorry for us.'

'Did he really need to say that? Wasn't it obvious in every gesture – every expression on his face? I don't think anyone's ever felt sorrier for me than he did. Or made me feel less sorry for myself.'

4

Thomas Mehler sat at his desk staring at the wall and tried not to feel apprehensive.

He had known it would come to this sooner or later. He had avoided thinking about it. But he could avoid it no longer.

The drug worked on animals. It slowed their ageing by a factor of anything up to five. And with the latest batch there had been none of the side-effects – the horrible side-effects; he shuddered – suffered by the subjects of the earlier tests. The two four-month puppies in his private section of the annexe had shown only as much physical development in the eight weeks after receiving their initial doses as their brothers and sisters from the same litter had in twelve days. Yet they had apparently sustained no mental impairment of any kind. He had learnt all he could from them. Tomorrow he would arrange for them to be given away – but to somebody who did not know their real age.

So the next subject had to be human. A baby would be ideal: a baby's ageing process was so much faster than an adult's that it was possible to determine much sooner whether ageing had been retarded. Besides, babies didn't talk. There would be no trouble getting one – or a dozen, for that matter. He'd only have to apply. But he didn't feel happy about the idea. He didn't want it said that in developing his discovery he had been responsible for causing death or harm to a human being. It wouldn't be a good start for the drug's life.

Because there *were* risks, even for an adult. Theoretically they were small. But there could never be certainty a drug was harmless to man before it had been tested on man. As, he suddenly thought, old Berrog had known well when he'd opposed those experiments ten years ago. There might be some substance in the body, some chemical that had been taken in food over the years and had built up in the tissues, which might conflict with the drug. Or it might cause brain damage of a kind that would not be evident in an animal.

But the test had to be made.

Because he had to know what the drug would do. However great the risk, he had to know.

Mehler reached into his desk drawer, brought out a small, flat case and took from it a hypodermic syringe. On the desk-top was a small glass phial containing a pinkish liquid. Mehler picked it up. Just thirty millilitres. Representing how many thousands of man-hours? Thirty millilitres on which floated the future of mankind.

Damnably difficult to calculate the dose. But better to play safe.

Carefully, Mehler transferred five millilitres of liquid to the syringe. No more. Not a single drop could be wasted. He turned back his shirt-cuff and quickly, before he had time to think, inserted the point of the needle in his arm and pressed the plunger. He withdrew the needle, let it fall onto the desk, and sat back.

He stayed quite still for ten minutes, waiting. Then he realized he was being foolish: he knew there was no question of the stuff being a quick-acting poison; and that if, there was anything wrong, it would take time for the symptoms to appear. He had already decided that if he took another six shots at weekly intervals without ill-effects, he personally would be satisfied. How long the medical profession would later require for its own clinical trials before passing the drug he didn't know. Perhaps years – unless it was overruled by public demand.

But that wasn't his worry. In six weeks he could test the drug on a baby. A few weeks after that he would know finally if it was completely effective. Then he could publish.

Until then there was nothing to do except wait – and observe himself. He could send the lab assistants away and relax for a bit – read, go for some long walks, take in some plays or concerts in the District

Capital, perhaps even get himself a girl again — it had been a long time . . . He would enjoy himself.

As much as he could under the circumstances.

5

As the time approached for Mr Pelli's visit on the Friday afternoon, Petros and Paula both found themselves feeling unaccountably nervous. There was no rational reason for this. But they couldn't throw it off.

When it was nearly three o'clock they both stopped what they were doing and waited quietly. They were quite certain Mr Pelli would be absolutely prompt. Sure enough, the bell went exactly on time.

Paula answered the door and brought Mr Pelli into the sitting-room. Petros shook hands with him. Paula offered coffee and Petros a drink, both of which he refused. They all sat down. Petros took out his cigarettes and proffered them.

'I do not smoke, thank you.'

'You don't mind if I – ' He broke off, stuffed a cigarette into his mouth, and lit it. Dammit all, it was *his* flat! He inhaled deeply and said: 'I'd like to thank you again for all you did the other night. It was very good of you.'

'How do you feel now?' Mr Pelli asked.

'Oh, better, thanks, much better.'

'I am glad.'

There was silence for a few seconds. Then Petros said: 'I hope that I can oblige you in whatever it is you want me to do for you.'

'It is not merely a question of your obliging me. If you agree to my suggestion, I believe it will be to your own benefit, to your wife's, and to the benefit, in addition, of a great many other people.'

'Oh. Sounds interesting. Perhaps you'd better tell me what it is you have in mind.'

Mr Pelli didn't speak immediately. He just looked at Petros. It was a long, searching, unblinking look, and it made Petros feel even more uneasy.

Then: 'I want you to go home,' Mr Pelli said deliberately.

Petros felt himself go pale. For seconds he couldn't speak. When he managed to get words out, they came as a whisper. 'Home? You mean –'

'I mean to your own country and your own people.'

So he'd been wrong, quite wrong in all his ideas about who and what Mr Pelli was. Petros felt panic seizing him and he fought it off, telling himself that there was no danger, no real danger at all. He said hoarsely: 'So that's it. You're just another of the Chairman's agents. You've been sent here to take me back, with a cock and bull story about it being for my own good. I used to expect this at one time.'

'You are wrong. I have no connection with your country or its government.'

The words had a strong ring of truth and Petros felt a fractional easing of tension. 'Then what –'

'I don't understand.'

He and Paula spoke together, then both broke off.

'Who the hell are you?' Petros asked. 'Who *are* you working for? The government of this country?'

'All I can answer to that is that you will not find my name on any list of government servants.'

'That's no explanation. I want to know –'

'It would be best if you were simply to accept that I am, as they say, on the side of the angels. You have nothing to fear from me. I shall not attempt to force you to do anything against your will.'

Puzzled, but now more relaxed, Petros asked: 'Then why do you want me to go? What for?'

'There is an important task to be undertaken in your country. I wish you to be the one to undertake it.'

'But don't you realize I'd be committing suicide if I went back home? I'm a wanted man there – a traitor. I nearly brought the government down.'

'Nearly but not quite. I'd like you to help complete the job.'

'*Me?* You can't be serious!'

40

'Perfectly serious.'

Paula spoke, her voice tense and angry. 'This is a cruel thing to ask. You've obviously no conception of what Mikael's been through.'

'I assure you I have every conception of it – more so, in fact, than anybody else. I know the pressures he was put under – on both sides of the frontier.' He looked directly at Petros. 'I know the full circumstances of Alexis Kauffman's death, and why it was you were caught and tried.'

Petros's eyes widened. '*What* do you know?'

Mr Pelli told him.

Petros drew in a deep silent breath. 'So that's who you are!'

Mr Pelli raised his eyebrows.

'I've always known there were two people alive who knew the whole truth: Manson – and one other man. You're that man. You were a friend of Kauffman?'

'Yes.'

'And you know Manson?'

'I do.'

'He sent you to me?'

'No.'

'No, I bet he didn't. He wouldn't ask me to go home. He knows I'm a dead duck if I'm caught there. He was behind my getting permission to stay in this country.'

'I assure you that if Manson knew you were undertaking this assignment he would be delighted.'

'But why, for heaven's sake? I don't understand.'

'Let me try to explain. First, however, I should like you to tell me just how much you know about the political repercussions of the assassination and of your arrest and trial.'

'Why do you want to know?'

'It is important that you should understand these matters. Otherwise you can never fully appreciate the implications of this task I spoke of. So give me an account of the public and political events that followed your trial. I will then know precisely how much I have to explain.'

It was on the tip of Petros's tongue to refuse to discuss the subject

41

any more. He had no intention of undertaking this task, so Mr Pelli's request was pointless. Then he looked at Paula and saw her give a small nod. He realized at once what was in her mind. Pelli had, after all, saved his life. The least he could do was play along for a bit, not turn down the request too abruptly. So he gathered his thoughts for a few seconds, then said:

'Well, naturally, my own government denied everything I said at the trial. First of all they claimed I wasn't Mikael Petros at all, but an imposter — because, of course, the execution of Mikael Petros had been officially announced months before. Later, they admitted that I was Petros, but said that the prison governor had been bribed by what they called "foreign agents" to let me escape, and that with the collaboration of the medical officer and the warders, a fake execution was staged, and that the foreign agents had then smuggled me out of the country and forced me to kill Kauffman simply in order to drive a wedge between our two peoples. It was a terribly weak story, and obviously nobody believed it. I've sometimes wondered since what happened to the governor.'

'He was removed from his post. So were the two warders who were in charge of you. None of them has been heard of since.'

'Is that so? Well, I'm not disposed to feel sorry for them. Where was I?'

'Nobody believed the government's story,' Paula said.

'Oh yes. There was a tremendous revulsion of feeling against them here. Manson succeeded Kauffman on a platform of breaking off all relations between the two countries. I was in prison by then, but I gather it led to a lot of economic difficulties here at first. The long-term effects have been pretty good, though, haven't they?'

'Yes. This country had always been highly dependent on yours economically — dangerously so. After the break she was forced to diversify her economy and to make fresh trading agreements. The advantageous effects of this are beginning to show. Politically, too, she has benefited. Her standing in the world has never been higher than now.'

'Well, that's fine, but I still — '

'What do you know of the effects on your own country?'

Petros sighed. 'Well, it hit them, didn't it? I mean, they were revealed to the world as blackmailers and assassins. Several other countries severed diplomatic relations. They lost markets for their exports, I believe, and obviously they had to find other sources for the things they used to buy from this country – meat and grain and dairy produce and wool, etc. – presumably at much higher prices. Look, you clearly know much more about this than I do. I'd far sooner you told me anything I ought to know.'

'As you wish,' said Mr Pelli. 'But all you have said is quite accurate. In addition, though, the regime had been working for years to gain influence among the neutral and developing nations. This influence was lost almost overnight. They dared not risk being implicated in any further outrages such as the Kauffman assassination, so they were forced drastically to curtail espionage and spying. Therefore they have fallen back industrially and scientifically. A revolution they had hoped to foment in South America, and which would have put a puppet government controlled by them in power in a country rich in mineral resources, did not take place. All these factors have led to economic hardship – inflation, unemployment, shortages – and civil unrest. The government has been brought to its knees. The Chairman is close to being overthrown; he is still clinging to power, but if circumstances do not radically improve the government will fall.'

'Well, I've no cause to love the regime,' Petros said. 'I'll lead the cheering when it goes.'

'I said only that it would fall if circumstances do not radically improve. Unless the task I mentioned is successfully performed, your government will regain all the power, wealth, and influence that it once had – and much, much more. The Chairman – who, remember, can trace all his troubles directly to you – will become the most powerful tyrant the world has ever known.'

Paula drew her breath in sharply. Although it took an effort, Petros did no more than stir in his chair. 'I'll risk that,' he said. 'I'm not a coward, but I'd be taking an insane gamble if I went back. Sorry, but I'm staying here?'

'Why?' Mr Pelli asked unexpectedly. 'Are you so very happy here?'

43

'Happier than I'd be back in the condemned cell.'

'But do you think you will ever feel you are at home here — that you will live down your past and be accepted as a normal citizen?'

Incredulously, Paula said: 'Are you suggesting he could somehow earn people's good opinion by doing something for the country? That's crazy! Assignments like that are kept top secret. Ordinary people would never even know about it.'

'Not the details. But it would be reported that your husband had undertaken a dangerous mission on behalf of the government. Later, he would receive an official honour — an award. Finally, when he was accepted for naturalization—'

Petros gave a start. 'You could arrange that?'

'Yes.'

'You're trying to bribe me?'

'Not at all. I am pointing out the legitimate rewards you would receive. At present you are an outcast here — distrusted and disliked. But once it was officially acknowledged that you had served the country, you would find yourself treated quite differently. Patriotism here has grown stronger since Kauffman died.'

'Naturally, I want all that,' Petros said. 'To be naturalized and accepted. If it was anywhere else you were asking me to go, I'd say yes like a shot. But I can't go home. They'd kill me. I'm sorry, but I daren't risk it.' He spoke decisively.

Mr Pelli didn't say anything for some moments. He looked from Petros to Paula and seemed to be trying to make a decision. Then: 'Don't you realize that you are in just as much danger from them in this country as you would be if you went home?' he said.

Petros went cold. Somehow he kept his voice steady. 'Just what do you mean by that?'

'Well, surely you do not imagine that the Chairman has forgiven or forgotten what you did to him — or that he ever will? I can tell you for a fact that he has personally ordered your death.'

6

For ten seconds after Mr Pelli's words nobody moved. Then, while Paula still sat as though frozen, Petros got to his feet, crossed to the sideboard, took out an old bottle of cognac, and poured himself a large glass. He took a swig and turned round to face Mr Pelli again.

'It occurred to me long ago that they'd want revenge,' he said. 'After I was released I went to see one of your Intelligence people. He said what you said just now – that the regime's image had taken such a hammering that they were having to tread very carefully, and that they wouldn't risk trying to get back at me, because if they did it would be obvious who was responsible, and they just couldn't afford any more bad publicity. So he told me not to worry.'

'He was right in that probably you do not face immediate danger. I do not say that the threat is necessarily imminent. Years may pass before they act. They will be prepared to wait until they can kill you in such a way that it will seem an accident. But sooner or later, do it they will.'

Petros returned to his chair. He sat down, then said: 'You're telling me that I'm doomed.'

'No.'

Petros felt a flutter of hope. 'What do you mean?'

'If you undertake this assignment and successfully carry it through you will be safe.'

'Why?'

'Part of the assignment is to obtain certain papers. The possession of those papers will guarantee protection from any act of revenge.'

Petros had to ask. He didn't want to, but having gone so far, the next question was inevitable. He looked down at his glass and spoke in a flat voice: 'What is this assignment?'

'To approach a certain man, deliver a message to him, and bring him back to this country, with the papers in his possession. You will be provided with ample funds and all the necessary documents for yourself and the other man. You will not be out of pocket, as a sum equal to the wages you receive from Mr Rostein will be paid to your wife for as long as you are away.'

'But suppose I didn't come back at all?'

'I said it would be paid for as long as you are away.'

'You mean if I was killed, Paula would continue to receive the money always?'

'Yes – with suitable increases from time to time.'

'I'd have to chuck my job. If I got back I'd be out of work. And I wouldn't qualify for unemployment pay.'

'I promise to find you satisfactory employment, with wages at least equal to those you are now receiving.'

Paula had been listening silently for some time. Now she suddenly burst into angry speech. 'Mikael, what's the matter with you? Sitting there calmly discussing terms – as though you're really considering going! Are you out of your mind?'

'I've got to consider it. If I don't, I'll have the threat of being murdered hanging over me for the rest of my life.'

'I just don't believe it. I believe the security man you saw before. The Chairman won't dare harm you.' She turned to Mr Pelli, her eyes blazing. 'You've not produced one scrap of evidence to support a word you've said. I think you're just trying to use Mikael, like Marcos and his lot did before. I daresay your motives are better, since you're working for a decent government, but the principle's exactly the same. You men have all got one-track minds. It's a game with you. An individual life means nothing if it gives you a temporary advantage. I'm just thankful we now live in a country where you can't force him to go.'

'I can understand how you feel,' Mr Pelli said. 'But I assure you that you are quite wrong. I'm as sensible as you are of the danger Mikael will face if he goes back. But he will face just as great a threat if he remains here – and one with no time limit. I wouldn't have asked him if I did not believe he had a better chance than anyone else available to succeed in the assignment – and, moreover, the right to be given the first chance to go.'

'What do you mean – "the right"?' She sounded scornful.

'It will be only fair that the man who carries out this task is given the benefit of the papers. Your husband is a man who has a particular need of their protection. I am, therefore, not only asking him to go, but *giving him the opportunity* to be the one to go.'

She was taken aback for a moment, then rallied. 'If you believe, as you say, that he's got a better chance than anyone else to pull off this job, you must have had him marked out for it for some time. Because you certainly didn't pick him on the basis of what you saw the night before last.'

'True.'

'So it wasn't just a coincidence you were there when those thugs attacked him?'

'I never claimed it was.'

'In other words, you and your so-called friends had been watching him?'

'One of them had.'

'Why?'

'Because of possible danger. Your husband has had several threats made against him from within this country. Moreover, though it is likely that the danger he faces from the Chairman's agents is a distant one, no one can know this for certain. I therefore thought it advisable that he should be guarded.'

'So you had a man watching him all the time the other night – well before he was attacked?'

'Yes.'

'It must have been obvious to this man that those thugs were out to get Mike.'

'As soon as it became obvious, my friend requested assistance.'

'Which conveniently arrived just after they'd started on Mike – not quite in time to prevent them attacking him at all, but before they'd had a chance to do him any serious injury.'

Petros looked at her curiously. 'What are you getting at, darling?'

'Just this: he could have set the whole thing up – arranged for them

47

to attack you.'

'Why should I do that?' Mr Pelli asked.

'As a way of underlining to Mike the wretchedness of his position in this country – so that afterwards he'd be in a mood to consider anything that would help him. And as a dramatic way of introducing yourself and establishing yourself in his mind as a protector and friend – so that he'd trust you and be prepared to listen to you. As he has done.'

'An ingenious theory, but not true. Those young men were nothing more than they appeared to be. And nobody influenced them to attack your husband. I give you my word on that. I will admit that afterwards I did not altogether regret that the incident had taken place. It did, as you say, provide me with a good opening. But I set up nothing. And our intervention came at the earliest possible moment.'

Mr Pelli looked straight at Paula. She met his gaze unblinkingly for a few seconds. Then she looked away. 'All right,' she said in a quiet voice. 'I believe you.'

'And do you also believe the rest of what I told you?'

'I suppose so.' Her voice sounded flat and dull. 'I don't know why I should. But I do.'

Mr Pelli turned his eyes on Petros. 'And you?'

Petros hesitated. Then he sighed and nodded.

'So do you wish to hear more about the assignment? Or shall I leave now and never trouble you again?'

Petros glanced at Paula, but she wouldn't meet his eye. He said: 'I'm not promising anything. But you might as well carry on a bit longer.'

'What do you wish to know first?'

'Well, with the border closed, how would I get into the country – and out again afterwards?'

'You will fly yourself in by helicopter at night.'

'Helicopter? But I haven't flown one of those for ten years!'

'It is a skill once learnt never forgotten. You will be able to have adequate practice before leaving. I have a friend called Alex, a qualified helicopter pilot, who can instruct you.'

'But how on earth could I fly a chopper in secretly? Every metre of the frontier is patrolled. And there's blanket radar coverage.'

'The idea is simple. Do you know of the MAS?'

'No, I don't think so.'

'The letters stand for Medical Air Service. It is an international organization formed a few years ago, its function being the rapid transporting of emergency medical supplies. Virtually every nation in the world is now a member. It is unique in that it operates between countries irrespective of the political relationship between them, and its aircraft are able to ignore national frontiers. It could not operate effectively without this concession, and as no country wished to be excluded from the service, all were forced to accept this provision.'

'Very interesting. But I don't see the relevance.'

'The relevance is this: MAS aircraft are constantly criss-crossing Europe at every hour of the day and night, carrying drugs, vaccines, rare blood, special machines, and so forth. The European headquarters of the service are at Geneva, and from there they notify each country of the movements of MAS aircraft across their frontiers; each country then notifies its own ground observers and radar operators that an MAS machine will be crossing a certain point of the frontier at a certain time. This has now become purely routine.'

Petros frowned. 'I still don't see it. You're not suggesting I should steal an MAS helicopter and cross in that?'

'No, simply that you should use one for cover – fly close to it, so that the sound of your engine will not be heard on the ground, and the two machines show up as a single image on the radar screen. Once you have crossed the frontier, another friend of mine will shine a beacon light for you to land by.'

Petros took a deep breath. 'I see.' He nodded appreciatively. 'Clever.'

'Alex will go into the exact details of the flight with you,' Mr Pelli said. 'How you leave the country after completing the assignment will be for you to decide. It may be possible to do so quite openly. You and the other man will have all the necessary documents. Should this not be possible, however, the helicopter will have been well hidden in a remote area, and you may decide to use it again.'

Petros was silent, assimilating this. Then he said: 'I'm sometimes recognised in the street even now, you know. If that should happen when I'm on the assignment . . .'

'You are less likely to be recognised there than practically anywhere else in the world – unless, of course, you should happen to meet someone who knew you before. It is one of the very few countries where your picture was never published.'

'Oh, I see. I didn't know that. Well then, tell me more about the assignment itself. Who is the man I'd have to bring out? Where does he live? Not near any of my old homes, I suppose?'

'No, he lives in the 45th District. His name is Thomas Mehler. He is a scientist, a biochemist. He is currently engaged upon a course of government-sponsored experiments, arising from a certain scientific discovery he has made. You will deliver to him a letter from a very old friend of his, a man now known as Herschel, whom Mehler believes to be dead. It will warn him that when he has completed his present experiments, the Chairman intends to have him murdered. Mehler lives in a country house with a private laboratory attached, and is closely guarded by the security police. His mail is read before being delivered, his telephone calls are monitored, and he never goes out alone. He communicates with nobody without the authorities knowing of it.'

'Then how the devil am I supposed to deliver the letter?' Petros said.

'It's absolutely impossible,' Paula added.

'No, not impossible. I would not ask anyone to undertake an impossible task. Mehler can be approached secretly—given ingenuity and care.'

'But that's only part of the job,' Petros said. 'Afterwards, I'd have to get him out of the country. And you haven't yet explained why you want him brought out.'

'Because it is imperative the Chairman should not gain control of Mehler's discovery to use for his own ends.'

'And where do these papers come in?'

'They actually have no connection with Mehler's discovery. He simply happens to have access to them. If published, they would do grave damage to the Chairman and his regime. You must persuade Mehler to bring them with him. You will be safe once the government know that publication of these papers will follow should any harm befall you.'

'I'd be quite on my own, would I?'

'For most of the time. But I have friends there and help will be available if you need it. I will give you a telephone number to call in an emergency.'

Beams of the afternoon sun had started to stream dazzlingly in through the window. Paula stood up, crossed the room and adjusted the curtains. She turned round, her back to the window, and looked at Mr Pelli. 'Surely this a job for a professional spy. Why do you want Mikael?'

'Because he is a native of the country, speaks the language, and knows the people and customs as only a native can. Because the threat he faces means he will have a very strong incentive to succeed. Because he can pilot a helicopter. And because he is a man of great courage and resource.'

The words seemed spoken sincerely with apparently no element of flattery, and Petros felt himself blush. It was years since anyone other than Paula had said anything nice about him, and he didn't know how to take it. He muttered: 'Thanks,' and looked away.

'Well, I'm glad you realize that,' Paula said.

'I would not want him otherwise.'

'This discovery Mehler has made: why is it so essential the Chairman shouldn't get hold of it? What is it? I think Mikael ought to know that. He'd be risking his life; he has the right to know what for.'

'He would be risking his life on behalf of the well-being of the entire human race for as long as it continues to exist,' Mr Pelli said.

There was complete silence in the room. Petros just didn't know what to say. What sort of answer could one possibly make to a remark like that? He cleared his throat. 'I don't doubt it's important, but surely . . . I mean, you must be pitching it a bit high.'

'No.'

'Could you explain, please?' Paula said helplessly.

Mr Pelli leaned back in his chair, put the tips of his fingers together,

51

and fixed his gaze on the ceiling. 'What do you understand by the word "elixir"?' he asked.

7

The night was inky black and quite quiet. The only light was the glowing end of Petros's cigarette, the only occasional sound the distant rumble of an unusually heavy lorry on the freeway. There was no fog and hardly any wind. Conditions were ideal. This Saturday night had been a good choice.

For the tenth time in as many minutes Petros looked up through the perspex top of the cockpit. He craned his neck and peered towards the south-west, to where the MAS helicopter would come from. But there was still no sight of its lights, nor sound of its engine. 'Come on, come on,' he muttered.

Alex said: 'It's only just 11.45.'

'You're quite sure the call from the hospital did go out?' He'd asked the question before and it had been unnecessary then.

'Yes,' said Mr Pelli.

Alex said: 'You've got a perfect night for it.' He'd said that before, too. Why *he* should be nervous Petros couldn't think. He grunted in reply.

Petros was sitting in the cockpit, with the door open. Mr Pelli and Alex were standing near. They'd been like this now for ten minutes, just waiting.

Petros opened his mouth to say something else, then closed it again. He took a puff of his cigarette and threw it out onto the grass, half-smoked. It glowed scarlet on the grass. Alex put his foot on it.

Petros had seen a lot of Alex in the last hectic week since finishing work at Rostein's. He had turned up first at the flat with Mr Pelli the previous Monday morning – a tall, ungainly-looking young man of about twenty-eight, with a round, cheerful face, and wearing an oil-stained leather jacket. It hadn't taken Petros long to find out that he was more than simply a helicopter pilot, but in effect Mr Pelli's right-hand man in all the practical arrangements connected with the assignment.

Now he said sharply: 'Listen!' He swung round to the south-west, staring into the sky.

Petros's heart gave a leap. He said: 'Is it – ?'

'Ssh.' Alex lifted a pair of field-glasses to his eyes. Petros held his breath. Then he heard the drone.

Alex said: 'I've got it.'

'Will it pass overhead?'

'Not quite. It'll be a little to the west. About seventy-five degrees high. You'll see it all right, though. Better start up again.'

'I hope this precious machine of yours works.'

'She'll work. Good luck.' He held out his hand, groped for Petros's in the dark, shook it briskly, and stepped back.

Mr Pelli said: 'Go in safety.'

Then he too stepped back, Petros closed the door, switched on the dim panel light, and pressed the starter. For a second he thought the engine was going to fail him, then it spluttered and fired. Petros revved up and looked upwards over his shoulder, towards the point in the sky where the light should appear. He waited, his eyes fixed, unblinking, until the sky itself seemed to be pulsating before his eyes. Still nothing. He felt himself start to panic. He'd missed it. It had passed overhead without him seeing it. He'd never pick it up now.

But even as he thought this the flashing, orangey-red anti-collision beacon of the MAS helicopter floated almost lazily into his vision, just where Alex had said. This was it.

Petros pressed the button of the stop-watch, engaged the clutch, and with his left hand moved the collective lever upwards, at the same time turning the twist-grip throttle on the end of it. The note of the engine grew louder, the machine gave a momentary shudder, a lurch, and he was in the air. He rose swiftly, his eyes fixed on the dancing light above him. He continued climbing straight up until the MAS machine was several hundred metres in front of him. Then he pushed the cyclic stick forward with his right hand and pressed the left rudder

54

pedal. The light of the helicopter grew brighter as he rose towards it. Soon he could make out the silhouette of the machine itself against the speckled backcloth of the sky. Now he could clearly see both its flashing beacon light and its white tail light, and was able to calculate his distance from it quite accurately. Closer and closer he went, until it seemed that the other pilot was bound to hear him.

At last he reached the position which he and Alex had worked out in advance: about twenty-five metres behind, and three or four metres below the other machine. Just here he was clear of the downwash of air from its rotor blades, and would not be visible to the pilot; yet he was close enough to it to make it impossible for the frontier guards to distinguish the sound of two helicopters passing over them – or, of course, for the radar operators to define two aircraft on their screens.

Petros glanced at his air-speed indicator. It showed 130 km/h. Which was a relief, because all their calculations had been based on the assumption that this would be the speed. It meant they'd cross the border about twenty-two minutes after take-off.

If all Alex's figures had been right.

'Here's the frontier,' Alex had said, running his finger along a wavy red horizontal line on the map he had laid out on the table. 'And here are the three southernmost Districts of your country adjoining it to the north – the 43rd in the west, 44th in the centre, 45th in the east. You can't cross directly into the 45th, because the MAS doesn't operate regular flights there. And the 44th is a bit too populous; so you'll cross from the north-west of this country into the 43rd and make your way east to the 45th by rail or road. Now, fortunately, one of the largest blood banks in this country is attached to a hospital up here' – he tapped a point on the map – 'in the north-west, just ninety kilometres south of the frontier. Next Saturday night an urgent call for supplies of a rare blood group will go out to the MAS from the 43rd District Capital Hospital, 120 kilometres north of the frontier. The MAS are sure to call on this blood bank for it. The hospital is in the centre of the city, a good way from an airfield, and the MAS always use choppers, not conventional aircraft when they deliver urgent supplies for it. With me?'

Petros nodded.

'Taking a straight line from the blood bank to the hospital, you'll see that the flight path crosses the frontier just *here* – which is about the most desolate stretch of it. It's mostly forestry land to the north – the only really extensive timber-producing area in the whole of your country, I'm told – plus a few farms. The actual frontier consists of two wire fences with a narrow strip of no man's land between. It's extensively patrolled by troops on the north, and there are observation towers with searchlights and towers every five hundred metres. On this side, of course, it's less closely guarded. You'll be sitting in your own machine immediately under the MAS helicopter's flight path just here – 48 kilometres south of the frontier. Then you'll take off as it passes overhead, come up behind it, and fly below and to the rear of it, and as close to it as you can safely get.'

'Why do I take off so far from the border?'

'Because you don't want to fly too near the frontier without the cover provided by the other chopper. There might be a short period after take off while you're climbing and manoeuvring during which you'll be visible on the radar screens as a separate aircraft.'

Petros nodded. 'I see.'

'There'll be no moon, so no one will be able to see you from the ground, and your machine has a specially muffled engine, so it won't be heard over the MAS chopper. Stay within, say, eight hundred metres of it, and the radar boys won't spot you either.'

Then had come the figures.

'I estimate your landing point at 104 kilometres beyond the frontier, making the overall distance roughly 152. The MAS machine will probably be cruising at 128 or 130 km/h. So altogether the trip should take about seventy or seventy-two minutes.'

'You're not allowing for wind speed at all.'

'Right. I've assumed there won't be any wind. High winds are rare in the area at this time of year. But if there should be a wind, I can easily change your flight plan accordingly at the field before take-off.'

'Now,' Alex had continued, 'before you reach your landing point you've got to throttle back and let the MAS helicopter get ahead of you again.'

'Why?'

'So that the pilot won't see the landing light which Mr Pelli's friend is going to light for you – if he did, he might report it. It'll be switched on immediately the other machine has passed overhead. Now you mustn't be more than eight hundred metres behind it, remember, or you'll show up as a separate blip on the radar screens. But at that speed you're going to cover eight hundred metres in about twenty-two seconds, so there's not going to be a lot of leeway. If you were too close, and the light was switched on a few seconds late, you could overshoot it, and then you'd be in a bit of a mess. So I recommend that some time after you cross the frontier, say round about *here*' – he put his finger on the map again – 'over forestry land, where it's unlikely there'll be anyone underneath to hear your engine, you reduce speed by 20 km/h for about a minute and three quarters. The other pilot will then automatically draw approximately six hundred metres ahead of you. After one and three quarter minutes accelerate again to your original speed. When you get to the landing field you'll be sixteen or seventeen seconds behind him, so the people on the ground will be able to let him get well past before switching on.'

'And I should spot the beacon after about seventy minutes or so?'

'If he keeps to 130, yes. You'll need to add or subtract about one minute to or from that for every two kilometres per hour slower or faster he goes. I'm fixing a stop-watch to your instrument panel. Start it when you take off, and you'll know at any time how long you've been airborne without having to keep looking at your wrist watch and making calculations.'

'Thanks.'

'I've written down all the figures – distances, compass bearing, times and speeds. You'd better learn them.'

He had handed Petros a piece of paper covered with scrawled figures. And Petros had learnt them.

He glanced now at the stop-watch. Any moment he'd be crossing the frontier. He tensed, waiting for the dazzling blaze of light which would mean that his mission was over practically before it had begun.

Minutes passed. And nothing happened. He relaxed fractionally. He had to be across by now. The ruse seemed to have worked. The first stage of the assignment had been successful. The next move would be the drop back from the MAS machine. After that the landing. And then . . . ?

'Land within twenty metres of the beacon light,' Alex had said. 'You'll find yourself in the centre of a field, near an old deserted farmhouse. Mr Pelli's friend will meet you, help you get the helicopter under cover, take you to a place where you can spend the rest of the night, and in the morning drive you to the nearest town, Township 43/S. From there you can get a train or coach to the 43rd District Capital, and from *there* east to the 45th. There's no reason why the cops should go anywhere near the farmhouse, so with ordinary luck the chopper will still be there if you need her to get out of the country again.'

'And suppose I don't? What happens to her then?'

'I shouldn't worry about that if I were you.'

Did that mean that Mr Pelli was prepared to abandon her? A pity, if so. She was a lovely little job. Not new – and this was a good thing, because he wouldn't have wanted a machine too advanced compared with those he'd flown before – but beautifully maintained. He had been impressed the first time he'd seen her.

Alex had driven him out to a small deserted airfield on what seemed to be a private estate, and had introduced him to the aircraft with as much pride as if he himself were the designer.

She was eight metres long overall and painted dark green. She had two-bladed main and tail rotors and tubular skid landing gear with small ground handling wheels. The fuselage was enclosed; so was the bottom half of the cabin, the top being a clear perspex bubble. The cabin seated two side by side, and there was an unusually roomy luggage compartment behind the seats. A powerful, vertically downward-pointing searchlight was mounted beneath the cabin, for use if he had to make an emergency landing. When he had first gone up in her Petros had found the engine remarkably silent, conversation in

58

normal voices being perfectly possible.

Alex had said: 'Maximum speed at sea level 170 km/h. Recommended cruising speed 145 at an altitude of five hundred metres. Ceiling, with two up, about 35 hundred. Range, more than adequate for your needs.'

Prior to tonight, Petros had had two sessions in her. The first had been a thorough three-hour lesson with Alex; the second, on another day, a practice solo flight. Alex had been waiting for him when he had landed after the second one.

'You'll do,' he had said. 'Just,' he had added.

He was glad now Alex had been so thorough – particularly in the cockpit drill, in making sure he could locate every one of the controls instantly without looking at it. Because he had no chance to look at them now. His eyes were staring continuously at the specks of light on the dark shadow above and ahead of him. His arms and legs and neck were aching. Any time now he could drop back from the MAS helicopter. He had delayed this move as long as possible – just in case there *was* somebody below who would notice and remark on two aircraft passing overhead a few seconds apart – but now he ought to postpone it no longer. He waited until the hand of the stop-watch came round to the minute mark, then throttled back. He fixed his gaze on the air-speed indicator as it rapidly dropped. When it showed 110 km/h, he stabilized his speed, then looked again at the leading helicopter. Already it was noticeably farther ahead. He waited, his eyes flicking back and forth between the stop-watch and the receding lights ahead of him. The hand of the stop-watch seemed to crawl round the dial, the MAS machine to get an awfully long way ahead. At last a minute and three quarters came up and he accelerated again up to 130 km/h. The lights of the helicopter in front of him were now just spots in the darkness. For a while all he had to do was concentrate on not letting them get any further away.

Sixty-nine minutes showed on the stop-watch. Petros's hands were clammy on the controls. His eyes flicked again to the lights six hundred metres ahead, to the air-speed indicator, and back to the stop-watch. Sixty-nine and a half minutes. Seventy. Any second now he should see the landing light. He forgot the stop-watch, forgot the other helicopter, forgot his air-speed indicator. He just stared ahead and downwards into the blackness. He was almost afraid to blink.

Seconds passed. Still there was nothing. Petros started to feel uneasy. Suppose he'd stayed too close to the other helicopter and had gone past the beacon before Mr Pelli's friend had switched on?

His eyes were smarting. He closed them tightly for a few seconds, then opened them again and turned his head slowly from left to right, leaning forward in his seat as he did so. But in no direction was there any break in the curtain of night.

Petros racked his brains. What on earth was he going to do? If he had overshot the light, every second that passed was taking him farther from it. Yet if he went back, or even if he just slowed down, within seconds he would show up on the radar screens. He could drop to tree-top height, keep his speed down to a minimum, and hope to avoid detection that way. But then what? He could retrace his tracks. But Mr Pelli's friend wouldn't expect him to be coming from the north. He would think some strange aircraft approaching and would turn off the light. Or suppose the light had failed? Or some snag had arisen and he hadn't even turned up?

Whatever had happened, Petros was going to have to do one of two things. He could dash back to the frontier — almost certainly being picked up by the radar as he did so. The border guards would be alerted. They'd be waiting for him. They had searchlights and guns. He'd need unbelievable luck to get across. And even if by some chance in a million he did make it, the whole assignment would have to be planned again from scratch.

Alternatively, he could try a blind landing. Petros licked his lips. It would be risky. He had his landing light. But that would illuminate only a small circle. And he had seven or eight metres of fusilage extending behind him. Who could guess what obstructions there might be just outside that circle of light? Again, the eyes could play funny tricks. One could easily be fooled by the appearance of what lay below. Even if he did get safely down he couldn't just leave the helicopter in the open and start to walk. On the other hand, if he stayed with it, just where might he find himself when dawn broke? And what would he do with his machine then?

Then, suddenly, almost dead in front of him, there was the light, a blessed white spot, like a star sunk to earth. Petros gave a gasp of relief, opened the throttle and sped towards the beacon. He glanced at the stop-watch and gave a shaky laugh. It was still showing less than seventy-one minutes. All his imaginings had flashed through his mind in a matter of seconds. He was almost bang on time.

Petros maintained height until he was almost directly above the beacon, then went straight down. As he neared the ground, the light, although pointing skywards and southwards, illumined enough of the surrounding area with its glow to show him that he was coming in onto level grassland.

He landed just six or seven metres short of the light, disengaged the clutch, switched off the engine, applied the rotor brake, and sat back, breathing heavily. He closed his aching eyes and rested his aching hands on his knees. He could have stayed like that for hours in the silence, but after thirty seconds he opened his eyes, leaned forward and pressed the button on the stop-watch.

Petros peered through the windscreen towards the light. It came from a portable spotlamp, about the size of a car headlight, on a metal stand. An electric cable ran from it into the darkness. As he looked towards it, the glare was momentarily blotted out by a figure passing in front of it. The figure moved closer. It stopped, raised its hands to its eyes, and apparently stared intently towards the helicopter. Petros opened the door. The figure took a step or two nearer. Petros climbed stiffly down. They stood facing each other in the dim reflected light of the spotlamp.

Petros said: 'Good evening.'

'Good evening.'

The voice was a woman's.

Petros gave a slight start. This was unexpected. He asked: 'You are Mr Pelli's friend?'

'Yes.'

'Thanks for the light. I was just getting worried in case I'd missed it somehow.'

'I switched on as soon as the other helicopter had gone.' She spoke in the pleasant, soft accent of the rural south. Petros judged her to be young. She was tall, sturdily-built, had long loose hair, and was wearing a hip-length coat, and trousers.

'Thanks for going to all this trouble for me.'

'What else would I do? We're both on the same side, aren't we?'

'Well, I'm in your hands. What do we do now?'

'Get the chopper under cover.'

'Where?'

'In a barn over there.' She pointed to her left. 'It's got doors both ends. We can hitch her up to my van, tow her in, and drive the van out the other end.'

'Fine. Lead on.'

She went back a few steps, switched off the light, picked the lamp up, and walked off into the darkness, coiling the cable as she did so. Petros followed, just able to make out her movements. The cable led to a small pick-up van, which was parked with its bonnet open. The girl reached inside the engine, presumably unclipped the cable from the battery, closed the bonnet, went to the back of the van, put the lamp and its cable inside, and brought out a length of rope. She passed it to Petros.

'Fix the hook over something on the front of the chopper. I'll bring the van round.'

Petros walked hesitantly back towards the helicopter in the dark. He could feel that the rope had a hook one end and a metal ring the other. Then the girl switched on the headlights of the van and he could see more clearly.

She backed up to the front of the helicopter and Petros fastened the rope. Then he walked beside the helicopter as the girl towed it slowly away.

Ten minutes later the helicopter had been put safely out of sight, and Petros was sitting in the passenger seat of the pick-up as it bounced along a rough lane, the girl at the wheel.

He glanced sideways at her. 'I expected a man,'

'Why?'

'I don't know. I just assumed Mr Pelli's friend would be a man.'

'Oh.'

'Mr Pelli said his friend would put me up for the night.'

'I'm taking you to my home.'

'Oh, thanks very much. Is it far?'

'No.'

'Good. By the way, I'm sorry to keep you up half the night like this. Are you able to sleep late normally on Sundays? Or do you have to work?

She didn't reply to this. After a pause, Petros tried once more. 'I don't know your name, I'm afraid. What should I call you?'

'Nothing.' Her voice was hard.

Was she always like this, he wondered, or was it simply *him*?

But then she spoke. 'Look, I don't know anything about you – who you are, why you're here, where you're going – and I don't want to. But I get the impression that you haven't been a friend of Mr Pelli very long.'

'No, I haven't.'

'And you haven't perhaps met many of his other friends?'

'You're the fourth.'

'Then I ought to explain that we don't talk more than is absolutely necessary. It's policy. The less we know about each other the better. We avoid each other socially as far as possible. We only see each other at the Meetings normally, and then we don't use names. There are only three or four of the others in this area whom I know at all, and that's only by coincidence: I've seen them at the Meetings and then happened to run across them openly somewhere else. It's always a kick when you do that – but it's one we try to avoid, all the same. It's the only safe way. Just to say that I don't work on Sundays because I'm a typist in an office, for example – I'm not, but if I *were* – could bring trouble one day.'

'I'm very sorry,' Petros said. 'I should have realized. Stupid of me.' He paused, then asked. 'Do you know Mr Pelli well?'

63

'Not so well as I'd like to.'

'You have met him, though – he does come here himself, does he? Or shouldn't I ask that either?'

'He has been here, but as far as I know not for a long time. And I have met him – whatever some people may say.'

Before he could reply to this somewhat cryptic remark she stopped the van. 'Take a look at that tree,' she said.

Until that moment they had been on the same rough track. It was bounded on each side by trees. Now Petros saw they were about to join a narrow, macadamed road or lane, which was running at right angles in front of them. The tree she'd mentioned stood alone on the other side of the road, exactly opposite the track they were now on. Petros stared at it. It was dead; and thin, bare, branches stuck out from it in all directions.

'What about it?'

'Wait. This is the wrong angle. Sorry.' She slipped the van into gear and pulled onto the road, turning left. She drove for about thirty metres, then made a three-point turn, so that the van was facing back towards the tree, its headlights again shining directly onto it. 'Now – what's it remind you of – taken with the hedge at the bottom?'

Petros looked carefully, then said: 'A stag's head – with lots of antlers.'

'Distinctive-looking, isn't it?'

'Very.'

'Get it fixed in your mind, because that's your last landmark on your way back. Turn off opposite it. I'll tell you later how to get to this road.'

'Thanks. Actually, I'm hoping I won't have to use the chopper again.'

'So I've been told. But you'd better be on the safe side.'

'Oh, quite.'

She turned the van again and drove off in the direction she'd first taken after joining the road. Petros thought it was north, though he couldn't see the stars.

'Does anybody ever go near that farm?' he asked.

'Virtually never these days. The future of this whole region is in the

64

air. They've been talking about a new town for a couple of years now. The farm can't be worked until they make up their minds.'

They travelled in silence along the narrow road for another twenty minutes. Then they joined a wider one, on which there was some traffic, mostly lorries. She said: 'On your right, Township 43/V, on your left, Township 43/S. Go to either and take the road to the other and you're bound to come along here – it's the only route. The road we've just come along leads eventually to Village 43/152 – it's signposted over there – see?'

Petros nodded.

'Remember those three places, and you can't go wrong. But don't write them down.'

'Don't worry. I know better than that.'

They carried on along the main road for a few more kilometres. Then the girl turned off onto another side road. Five minutes after that she pulled up before a wooden gate on the right. She got out, opened the gate, and drove through. They were in a largish yard. Petros could make out a rambling building on one side, and some smaller outhouses on the other. The place was clearly another farm – or had been at one time.

The girl drove up to the side of the rambling building, stopped, and switched off the engine. 'This is it,' she said. 'Come on in.'

They both got out. Petros took his case from the back. Then she led him round to the rear of the house, opened a door with a key, and went inside. Petros followed her. She switched on a light, and Petros stood blinking in the sudden brightness. It took some seconds for his eyes to grow accustomed to it. Then he got his first clear look at the girl.

Her hair was thick, blonde, and curly; her eyes dark blue. She had a pink complexion, rather shiny skin, and looked about the healthiest thing he had ever seen. She was wearing a navy blue donkey jacket over a green sweater, and rather grubby jeans. She was, he supposed, about twenty-four or five. Suddenly he felt pale and old.

He realised she was examining his face as closely as he was hers. He bowed his head gravely. 'How do you do.'

She looked embarrased for a moment, then she laughed, showing a set of strong white teeth.

He looked round the room. It was a large, old-fashioned kitchen. It had a high ceiling, crossed by oak beams, a stone floor, dotted with rush mats. A coke-burning stove was built onto one wall, there was a large scrubbed, whitewood table in the middle of the room, and several non-matching armchairs with loose covers. There were two doors, one closed, the other ajar and apparently leading to a scullery.

'Nice room,' he said.

'Make yourself comfortable.' She pointed to one of the chairs. 'I'll just go and close the gate and put the van in the garage.'

'Can I do anything?'

'No thanks. I'll only be a minute or so.'

She went out. Petros crossed the room and sank into the largest of the armchairs. It was of old leather, deep and comfortable. He stretched out his legs and looked round the room. It was extremely tidy and completely impersonal. The distempered walls were free of paintings and photographs, and nowhere was there anything that might give some hint as to the type of people who lived here.

Of course – that was it. The room had been deliberately stripped so that he should know as little as possible of his hosts. Petros stood up and went to a heavy mahogany sideboard that stood against one wall. He pulled open a drawer. It was very heavy. The first thing that struck his eyes was a framed photograph of a middle-aged couple, but the drawer was crammed with other stuff as well. Petros didn't look at any of it, but closed the drawer quietly and went back to his chair. He had no wish to pry and had wanted only to confirm his guess. He wondered if the other residents of the house were in it now, locked away in their rooms so that he should not see them.

A minute later the girl came back. She took off her coat and hung it behind the door. 'I expect you're hungry,' she said.

'A little.' He had had a meal in a cafe in the nearest town to the take-off field, but that had been three hours before.

She made her way towards the scullery.

'Can I help?' he asked.

'No thanks. Stay there.'

She made several trips to and from the scullery during the next few minutes, gradually laying the table with a loaf, a square of maragine, a block of cheese, a piece of some kind of canned meat, and a large pot of coffee. There she said: 'Come and help yourself.'

Petros went up to the table and began to eat. But the meat was tasteless, the cheese soapy, and the margarine oily; and he couldn't get through much. He'd forgotten how bad the food was here. Even prison fare was better than this south of the frontier. But surely he hadn't noticed such a great *improvement* in the food when he'd first gone south? Then he remembered that his own people had been passing through bad times lately. Partly because of him.

The coffee was good – strong and hot – and he had two cups. The girl sat opposite him and ate heartily, not talking, just giving him an occasional shy smile. He asked if he could smoke, and she fetched him a saucer to use as an ash-tray. He offered her a cigarette, but she refused.

While he was smoking his she took the dishes to the scullery and washed up. Then she came back and said: 'Would you like to turn in now?'

'Yes, I would. I'm rather tired. Could I have a wash first? I'm pretty grubby.'

'There's only the scullery sink, I'm afraid.'

When he was ready she led him upstairs. She turned on no lights and used a small pocket torch. So he could see nothing of the rest of the house. His room was on the second floor, a tiny attic with a sloping ceiling. Curtains were drawn across a small window. The room contained just a bed, an upright chair, a chest of drawers, and a washstand. A faded patchwork quilt covered the bed. Petros put his case down.

She said apologetically: 'It's not much, I'm afraid, but the bed's comfortable.

'It's fine.'

'Will you do me a favour in the morning? Don't pull your curtains back. I don't want you to know any more than you've absolutely got to about this house or its location.'

'I understand.'

'Your train in the morning leaves at 8.50 from Township S. I'll call you about seven if that's all right.' It was 2.30 now, so he wasn't going to get a lot of sleep. 'If you want anything, I'll be in the room immediately underneath. First door on the left at the bottom of the stairs.'

'I don't suppose there will be anything, but thanks, anyway.'

'I'll say good-night, then.'

'Good-night. And thanks for everything.'

She went out, closing the door. Petros undressed, switched out the light, and groped his way to the bed. He lay on his back and stared up into the darkness, wondering about the girl, the house, the other people who lived here, and Mr Pelli's other friends. There seemed to be quite an organization here. How on earth had it come about in the first place? How did Mr Pelli communicate with them? What did they do – and why? How many of them were there? What were the Meetings?

And why had he, Petros, an amateur and an outsider, been called in to take on this, of all tasks? An assignment on the success of which depended the whole future of mankind. Because it was no exaggeration to say this. The discovery of a drug which would increase the human life-span to four or five times longer than normal was, unarguably, a thing of momentous, of truly staggering magnitude.

Neither he nor Paula had believed the story at first. But Mr Pelli had soon convinced them of its truth.

Paula's attitude had seemed cautious, her reactions muted. Petros, on the other hand, had been gripped by a fierce desire. To live for hundreds and hundreds of years . . . It was a prospect of sheer wonder.

Petros had lived under sentence of death. He had measured his remaining life in hours. Living had become something infinitely precious to him, something he could not bear the thought of losing. He found himself wanting supplies of the drug as he had wanted few things in his life before. For himself and for Paula. So when Mr Pelli had finished telling them about it Petros had licked his lips and asked tentatively: 'When – when will it be available to everybody?'

'It never will be,' Mr Pelli had said.

Then, coolly and logically, he had explained about the menace that lay ahead.

'Consider: Mehler has been given everything he asked for – un-

68

limited funds, the best facilities, freedom from every distraction. The security surrounding him is as strict as he himself will allow it to be. The reason is that the Chairman and his regime are staking everything on this discovery. If they can keep it in their own hands, all the reverses of the past five years will be wiped out. But, much more than that, it could give them almost limitless power – ultimately a real chance of world dominion.'

'How do you work that out?'

'This way. Firstly, they themselves can become the permanent rulers of their own country – living on, generation after generation. They will be the Immortals – men like gods. Who would dare question the decisions made by beings of such wisdom and experience? And that would be but the first stage; for they can then offer the rulers of other countries the same opportunities – at a certain price. They could hold out a promise of virtually everlasting life and membership of the Permanent World Government. In exchange the other rulers would have to acknowledge the Chairman's supremacy and agree to make their own countries a part of his empire. Do you imagine many politicians would refuse such a bribe?'

'No, of course not – not if they had a chance of getting away with it. But I don't believe they would have. Public opinion would stop them.'

'Before public opinion can achieve anything, the phrase has to mean both opinion *and power*. Suppose one group had the means of offering this almost irresistable inducement to every person with the power to influence what is called public opinion – every newspaper editor, television chief, religious leader – and to every person in whom executive power actually resides: every senior civil servant, military commander, police commissioner, labour union official, powerful industrialist. In such a situation, that group would have virtually absolute power.'

'But – there'd be so many people to bring in!' Paula said.

'Not so very many. In a democracy the size of this one real power is concentrated in the hands of a few thousand men and women. If at any time these people came together to work for a single end, there would be practically nothing they could not bring about here. In a dictatorship authority is vested in even fewer people. The total number of Immortals throughout the world would certainly be many thousands – but not too many for each one to be transported to your National Capital for a dose of the elixir at regular intervals.' He noticed Petros's surprised look. 'Oh yes; do not suppose that the Chairman and his inner cabinet will issue supplies of the drug freely to the other Immortals. For it could then be analysed. And exclusive possession might be lost.'

'I still think the masses would rise up to get the drug themselves,' Petros said.

'For a long time the masses will not even know of its existence. Fifteen or twenty years will pass before it becomes obvious that the continuing youthfulness of the Chairman and his colleagues is not natural. By then it will be too late. All the men and women of real power, all the moulders of opinion, all those who might incite the masses to demand access to the drug, will already themselves be Immortals, with a vested interest in keeping the elixir away from the masses. And as a rule, without leaders the masses will not rise up – not if they are well-fed and well-housed.'

'But leaders would rise up *from* the masses – they always do.'

'Yes. And then the Immortals will have only to bring these popular leaders inside the circle – one by one, as they arise. Very few would decline the offer. Even the best of them would be tempted. It would be so easy for a man to convince himself that he could do more valuable work for the people from inside the group than from outside.'

'There'd still be some who'd turn it down,' Petros said doggedly.

'True. There would be the rare, genuine, and incorruptible idealists. But their very rarity would make them harmless. Disposing of such people would be no problem.'

Petros was silent for a moment before saying: 'You make it all sound very easy for them.'

'No, it will not be easy. But it can be done. For one thing, they will have ample time. They can plan with infinite care. There will be the most intensive and subtle campaigns of propaganda, conditioning the people into accepting the concept of a caste of Immortals. A new religion could even develop around them, so that to criticize them or attempt to become like them would be considered almost blasphemous.'

Mr Pelli let this sink in before continuing: 'Remember, too, that public uprising will be even a remote threat only in the western democracies. Oppressed or starving people are unlikely to have either the courage to rebel or the desire to prolong life. This factor in itself will be a fresh motive for keeping them in that condition. Finally, if, in spite of all I have said, uprisings do occur, they can be put down – provided the Immortals have within their circle all those men who control the weapons of mass destruction. A modern government does not need a vast army to control a populace; still less will it do so a generation from now.'

'Why?' Petros asked, 'are you assuming all the time that no other scientist is going to hit upon this drug independently? Surely there are others in the same line of research? If this man Mehler can make the big breakthrough, others can do the same. And then the Chairman's plans will be shattered.'

Mr Pelli shook his head. 'Mehler's discovery came about during experiments directed towards quite another end. If pressed, he himself would admit that it was pure chance – a by-product of a different line of research – an extraordinary fluke. The chances of the discovery being duplicated in the forseeable future before it is too late, are virtually non-existent.'

8

The girl brought hot water to Petros's room at seven the next morning. He shaved, washed, and dressed hurriedly, re-packed his case, then went downstairs. All the windows on the landings and stairs were curtained, so he could still see little of the house.

He halted outside the kitchen door, uncertain whether to knock or go straight in. He decided on the latter, and opened the door. The room was warm and bright. Again, the curtains were drawn; the stove was banked up, and the light was on. The table was laid for two. As he stood just inside the door, she appeared in the entrance to the scullery. He hadn't noticed when she'd brought the water, but she had a dress on this morning. A yellow one. She looked quite attractive.

She smiled when she saw him. 'Sit down.'

Petros sat down at the table, and a minute later she brought in two plates of the thick, salty maize porridge that had been part of the staple diet of the country for so many years. Petros tasted it. 'It's good,' he said. 'I was brought up on this. It brings back memories.'

She sat down opposite him and started to eat her own. Then, rather shyly, she said: 'Nice ones?'

'Some,' he said. 'The very early ones.'

Afterwards, there was more of the bread and margarine, and dark, sweet home-made jam. Petros found that this morning he could eat, and he had a good breakfast. He made rather stilted conversation during the meal, as he might with a stranger who just happened to share his table at an hotel. Then abruptly, towards the end of the meal, the girl said: 'Listen, I'll try to slip back to the farm now and again and take a look at the chopper. If I should see any sign of life there, or any indication that somebody's discovered it, I'll try to put a warning out for you.'

'That's an idea. Where?'

'Let me think.' She concentrated for a moment, then said: 'That signpost on the V to S road, pointing to Village 152. Take a look at that on your way back. If I find anything wrong I'll leave a note for you there. I'll write something on the bottom of the post – just a single word –'

'Just "Pelli".'

'All right. If you see that, have a look round for a little box or tin can somewhere in the grass near. There'll be a note in it explaining just what I've found out.'

'Well, as I said, I don't expect to come back. But if I do, that'll be a great help.'

'Of course, there's no guarantee somebody won't turn up at the farm half an hour after I leave, and then you arrive before I'm able to go back there again. I mean, if there's no note from me, you won't know you're safe. But if there is, you will know you're not.'

After breakfast he insisted on helping her wash up. Then she went to get the van out. When she came back she said: 'Look, if you don't mind, I'm going to ask you to wear a blindfold to go out, then to lie down in the back of the van until we get well away from here. I don't want anyone to see you leaving. And as I explained, I'd rather you weren't able to describe this house or say where it is. I hope you're not offended. They use truth drugs, you know. You might not be able to help talking.'

'I don't mind in the least.' But as she tied a scarf round his head, he reflected that her precautions were probably pointless. If he was caught and given a truth drug, he'd be able to tell them quite a lot already: that he'd been helped by a tall girl with fair hair and blue eyes, who drove a pick-up van and who lived in an old farmhouse, parts of the interior of which he could describe very accurately, off the V to S road. That would enable them to narrow the field considerably.

She led him outside and helped him into the back of the van. He lay flat on his back, his suitcase beside him. The girl got in the driving seat and the van moved off. About ten minutes later she said: 'All right, you can take that off now. And come in the front if you like.'

He untied the scarf and then clambered over the back of the seat and sat beside her. They were on a straight, wide road, with no buildings in sight, only level fields each side. There was a fair amount of traffic about. It was a grey morning, dry but muggy. His first real glimpse of his homeland again after five years was not a cheerful one.

'Where are we?'

'The V to S road again. The 152 road – and your signpost, of course – is about ten kilometres behind us. We'll get to Township S in about half an hour. You'll be in plenty of time for the eight fifty.'

'Is it a crowded train as a rule, do you know?'

'Yes, it's the popular one for anyone going up to the District Capital for the day – as quite a lot of people do on Sundays.'

For a while they drove in silence. Petros was feeling tense and a little jumpy, as he had done the previous few days, before leaving home. The feeling had passed once he'd taken off yesterday night, but now it was like starting his mission all over again.

Eventually he asked: 'Suppose somebody who knows you sees me in here with you when we get to town – or getting out by the station? Mightn't that be risky for you?'

'Don't worry about that.'

'But I shall. I don't want to make things unnecessarily difficult for you. Drop me off before we get to town. I'll walk the rest of the way.'

'You'd have a long walk if I did. You'd probably miss the eight fifty, and there isn't another train for two hours.' She thought for a moment. 'I'll tell you what: there's a new housing estate on the outskirts of the town, this side. I could drop you just before we get there and you could catch a bus. They're pretty frequent this time of the day, and it'd take you right into the centre.'

'That'll be ideal.'

A few minutes later she slowed down, turned right, up a narrow lane, and stopped. 'If you walk on along the main road for about seven or eight hundred metres, you'll come to the estate. You can't miss the bus stop. There are bound to be people waiting.'

Petros said: 'I don't know how to thank you.'

'Then don't try.'

74

'But I must. It's my turn to say I hope you're not offended, but Mr Pelli gave me quite a lot of money for this trip – I'm sure far more than I'll need. As we're sort of co-workers, and it's money from him to help in his work, well, I'd like you to have a little. I mean, you're out of pocket already – food and petrol. So would you take some?'

She looked at him. 'Only fools and snobs take offence when offered money – especially when it's offered like that. And the answer's yes, I could use some.'

'Good.' He took out his wallet and gave her a thin sheaf of notes. She counted them. 'That's too much.'

'Take it.'

She folded them and put them in the pocket of her coat. 'Thanks.'

'I'd better go,' he said. 'I'll never forget how you've helped me.'

'I wish you'd try. Don't get me wrong. You know what I mean.'

'Yes, of course. It's forgotten already.'

He reached into the back, picked up his case, and got out. 'Good-bye. And thanks – for nothing.'

'Good-bye. God be with you.'

He walked rapidly back to the main road and turned towards town.

He soon got a bus to the town centre and caught the eight fifty with a few minutes to spare. The journey to the District Capital took just over an hour. On arrival there he left the station, giving up his ticket at the barrier, then went round to the entrance and bought a ticket to the 45th District Capital. There was a little under an hour to wait. He went to the buffet and spent the time smoking, drinking coffee, and trying to remember as much as he could about the 45th District.

'Have you ever been there?' Alex had asked.

'No, but I've heard it's quite pleasant. Doesn't it have more sun than the rest of the country?'

'Yes, especially this low-lying area in the extreme east.' His finger had traced a circle on the map which lay open on the table. 'It's right in the lee of the eastern mountain range. It's got easily the warmest climate of any part of your country. The soil's very rich and fertile,

75

there are lots of farms – even a few vineyards. There's been hardly any industrial development. In places it's very beautiful.'

'I can't remember ever hearing about it.'

'No, they don't advertise it much. There seems to be a sort of Establishment conspiracy to try to keep it exclusive. A lot of the top brass have got villas or weekend cottages there. And it's a popular holiday centre for the not quite such top brass who can't run to permanent places there, but aren't allowed foreign travel. These people like to keep the place to themselves. So you won't find it mentioned in the guide books, or on the itinerary of the official tours.'

'Is that where Mehler lives?'

'Yes.' Alex touched the map again. 'There.'

Petros bent over. 'Village 127,' he read.

'Now that's an interesting part. Mehler's house is about five minutes' drive south of the village. It roughly marks the point where the character of the countryside begins to change. The land starts to rise towards the foothills of the mountains in the extreme east. To one side Mehler has this low-lying area, with its farms and vineyards and villas; while to the east are the uplands – rugged, uncultivated moors, heather and gorse, odd clumps of trees, outcrops of rock, little hidden valleys with fast-flowing rivers running through them. Beginning to sound like a guide-book myself, aren't I? Anyway, it's very popular with naturalists and ornithologists and horsemen – people like that.'

'So I wouldn't be unduly conspicuous there?'

'Not as long as you didn't show any undue interest in Mehler's house. Mehler spends a lot of his leisure time walking on the moors himself – always with two security guards near.'

He took a photograph from his pocket. 'This is Mehler's house, by the way.' The photograph showed a square, two-storeyed building of white stone. 'This was taken from the road,' Alex said. 'The laboratory is built on at the back. The house is on the left of the road as you leave the village. Just past it the road climbs. The house occupied by the security men is further on up the hill, the other side of the road. So they look down on Mehler's house.'

Once more he pointed to the map. 'Mehler's nearest town is Township 45/N, thirty kilometres north of the village. It's a spa. Grew up early in the nineteenth century. It's still a popular holiday resort. There are good hotels and restaurants, golf, fishing, riding, all that sort of thing. It's also the market town and natural centre for this whole area. It'd be a good idea to make it your base. You wouldn't stand out there – it's got a resident population of about fifteen thousand, I believe, apart from visitors.'

'Is there an airport there?'

'No, the nearest one is at the District Capital, eighty kilometres to the west.'

Petros nodded. 'I fancy I've heard of it. It's an international airport, isn't it – plenty of flights to other countries?'

'That's right. If things go well you and Mehler might well leave from there on your way home.'

Petros dragged himself back to the present and took a sip of coffee. It was tasteless and tepid. Just like all these miserable numbers, he told himself. Living abroad had made him appreciate place names, and he thought how pleasant it must have been here before the Reorganization, in the days of the Old Names. The present system was efficient, of course – everyone admitted that: the country divided into forty-five Districts, numbered from east to west, north to south, with the First District in the extreme north-west of the country, and the Forty-Fifth in the south-east; each District with its own capital; towns designated by the District Number followed by a single letter; villages by a three-digit number. Occasionally, to avoid the confusion of too many numbers, colourless street names were necessary. Apart from this every address in the land could be expressed in six to eight characters. Yes, it was efficient. But very dull.

The journey east to the 45th was tedious and tiring. He discovered after it started that his was a stopping train, not an express, and the trip was scheduled to take seven hours. The coaches were crowded, and the seats hard and uncomfortable. Petros spent the first part of the journey jammed between two stout old women, his suitcase across his knees. He had a passable lunch of soup, sausages, and ice-cream in the restaurant car, and afterwards managed to obtain a corner seat. He

77

dozed on and off most of the afternoon.

At about four thirty the train was making one of its frequent stops when someone in the compartment murmured: 'Check coming up.'

Petros jerked awake and stared out of the window. Half a dozen uniformed policemen were approaching the train. His heart beat faster. He told himself it was almost certainly just one of the regular routine checks. These had always occurred frequently on the railways. A number of police would board a train at one stop, check the identity cards of all the passengers, ask a few perfunctory questions, get off at the next stop, and repeat the procedure on the next train back in the other direction. This would occupy them for a full day. But it was possible this was not a routine check. They might be looking for a specific person.

Petros felt inside his jacket to make sure his identity card was easily to hand, then forced himself to close his eyes again and let his head loll forwards. The train moved off. Five, ten minutes passed. His nerves got more and more strained. Where the devil were they? Then he heard the door open, and a bored voice said: 'Cards.' There was a stirring in the compartment. Still Petros didn't open his eyes. A minute later he felt a hand shaking his shoulder. He opened his eyes and looked sleepily up.

'Card.'

'Oh.' He groped inside his jacket, drew out his identity card and held it out, being careful not to look up.

The policeman took it and opened it. 'Destination?'

'Forty-Fifth – District Capital.'

'Purpose of visit?'

'Vacation.'

'How long?'

'Two weeks.'

He kept his head turned away as the policeman looked at the card. But he could sense the eyes flicking back and forth, comparing his face with the photograph. Surely the other passengers' cards hadn't been scrutinized for as long as this? He braced himself for the order to come into the corridor. Then the card was thrust back at him. Petros took it with a steady hand, giving a little yawn. The policeman

78

turned to the man opposite. Petros put the card back in his pocket and closed his eyes. His heart was pounding and he felt sure his face was white. Half a minute later the policeman was gone and conversation among the other passengers started up again.

Petros did not really relax until the train arrived at the next station and the policemen got off. Then he felt good. The identity card supplied by Mr Pelli had passed muster. It probably didn't mean much really, but it was reassuring, and it gave him greater confidence in the rest of his documents. There were four principal ones apart from the identity card: passport, exit visa, driving licence, and ration book. They were in the name of Frederic Danton at an address in the 23rd District.

'A genuine address?' Petros had asked when Alex had brought them.

'Yes, and a genuine man.'

Petros had raised his eyebrows.

'He's about your age and looks a bit like you. He's unmarried and he lives alone. Next weekend he's going on a touring holiday for a couple of weeks. So if the 45th District police enquire about you, the 23rd District will confirm that Frederic Danton, who answers roughly to the same description as you, does live at the address on the card, is of good character, and is at present on a touring holiday. This won't stand up to any really intensive investigation, of course – no cover would – but it should see you through a routine enquiry, the sort of snap check they do often make on strangers in their Districts.'

'I see he's a garage manager.'

'That's one of the reasons for giving you his identity – that he is in a line of work you do know a little about. Oh, one word of warning. The I.D. card, the driving licence, and the ration book are identical with Danton's genuine ones, but he hasn't got a passport or – naturally – an exit visa. So if the cops should check yours they'd soon find out they were fakes. Then, of course, not many of your countrymen have got passports anyway, and the mere fact of your having one would draw attention to you a bit. So I should keep yours out of sight. Don't brandish it around.'

Alex had also supplied a wallet containing a number of other personal papers – a season ticket, membership card of a trade association, some bills, receipts, and one or two letters. 'They'll all help to add authenticity,' he'd said.

Well, the new Frederic Danton had passed the first test. Perhaps, with luck, there wouldn't be many more.

The train arrived at the District Capital just before six. The sun was shining and it was pleasantly mild. Petros booked in at the first small hotel he came to. He ate in the dining-room, then went out, walked round for a while, had a couple of drinks, returned to his hotel, and turned in straight away.

The next morning he checked out early and took a coach to Township N. He arrived at nine forty-five. He got out of the coach in the town square and looked around him. It was an attractive little place, he thought. Most of the buildings in the centre seemed to date from the late eighteenth or early nineteenth century, the time when the taking of mineral waters had first become fashionable. It was sunny and warm – warmer than he could remember it in this country before. The streets were broad and tree-lined and crowded with people in summer clothes; people mostly middle-aged or over and plainly more than moderately prosperous.

Petros's two immediate requirements were transport and accommodation; neither, he thought, should present any great problem. As far as transport was concerned he was right. He entered the first car hire office he came to and rented a car, paying three weeks rental in advance. He had to produce his driving licence as well as his identity card, and it, too, was accepted without comment. Within fifteen minutes he was driving away in a dark blue BFR $1\frac{1}{2}$ litre saloon. Then he started looking for a place to stay. Two hours later he was still looking.

He had been far too sanguine about his prospects of finding a place. It seemed as if every hotel and boarding house in the town was booked up. Even the girl in the Tourist Bureau was unable to help. It was worrying. There were no other towns of any size within eighty kilometres, so if he couldn't get fixed up here, he'd have to go out of town. There were plenty of inns and guest houses in the surrounding countryside – probably even one in Village 127 itself – but in a place like that he'd stand out. It was only here he could lose himself and yet be within easy reach of Mehler.

During lunch the answer came to him. He was staring thoughtfully out of the window of the restaurant when a car went past towing a caravan. He watched it absently for a few seconds before something clicked. He finished his lunch quickly and went back to the Tourist Bureau.

He asked the girl: 'Any caravan parks round here?'

She got on the 'phone. She drew a blank at the first attempt, but the second park she rang had one two-berth caravan vacant. The manager agreed to hold it for half-an-hour.

Petros drove straight out to the site. It was just outside town, to the east, a pleasant, secluded little park, with about twenty caravans. It had a car park, a small general shop, showers, and electricity laid to each caravan. The vacant one was at the end of a row, near the entrance. Petros took one look at it and booked it for three weeks on the spot. He moved in at once.

Once in occupation, he started to unpack his case. Everything in it – spare shirts, socks, handkerchiefs, underwear, a sweater, toiletries, a pair of field-glasses, and a compass – had been supplied by Mr Pelli, as indeed had the drab check jacket, dark grey trousers, and black leather lace-up shoes he was wearing, and the wallet, pen, comb, and lighter in his pockets.

'You dare not take anything with you that was manufactured in this country,' Mr Pelli had said. 'If the police searched you and found that most of your clothes and effects were foreign, they would be highly suspicious of you.' The only thing of his own he'd been allowed to bring was his watch, which was Swiss.

Petros put the things from his case away in the drawer, then drew the curtains, reached inside the empty case, pressed a stud, and lifted the bottom out. Beneath it was a shallow compartment about eight centimetres deep. In this were four envelopes of various sizes, a revolver, and a box of cartridges. The first three envelopes contained

81

respectively his own passport and exit visa, a complete set of false documents for Mehler, and the letter from Mehler's friend. It was the fourth envelope which Petros took out. He drew from it a thick wad of banknotes and transferred them to his wallet. The rest he put back in the envelope, which he replaced in the secret compartment. He refitted the false bottom and closed the case. He hesitated for a few seconds, then put the case under one of the bunks. No point in trying to hide it: he had to have the things handy; and if the security police ever did grow suspicious of him, they'd find it eventually wherever he hid it.

Next, Petros left the caravan and drove back to the town centre to do some shopping. He bought a good supply of food and drink, including bread, cans of meat and fruit, eggs, biscuits, cheese, jam, beer, and coffee. There seemed to be plenty of foodstuffs in the shops; in fact, during the whole of his stay in the region he was to find the restaurants and the retail shops much less affected by the shortages than the rest of the country was reported to be. As an afterthought he also purchased a strong and capacious rucksack.

He took his purchases back to the caravan, put them away, then went and had a shower. After this, he slept on his bunk for an hour. When he woke up, he made himself some coffee, then once more locked the caravan behind him and drove off in his car.

The first thing was to have a look at Mehler's house and start to plan some way of contacting him. There was time for a preliminary reconnaissance that evening. Village 127 was to the south of the town. The drive took about thirty minutes. It was a revelation to Petros, who had spent most of his life in the cold, industrialized, central regions of the country. The narrow, winding road led past vineyards and rich farm lands, large villas, and small but beautifully-maintained cottages. In the distance, but getting ever-closer, were the moors, bright with sun-yellow gorse. He marvelled that this area was so little known.

The village itself consisted of three of four shops, an inn, a garage, a school, a number of houses, and a solid old building, standing apart, that had once been a church, but which now, of course, served as a public hall.

Looking carefully about him, Petros drove slowly through the village and out the other side, travelling almost due south. He continued to pass private residences at intervals of about a hundred metres. They were of varying sizes, but most of them looked in first-class condition. Many of them had shuttered windows.

Five minutes from the village, Alex had said. Actually, eight minutes – but eight minutes of very slow motoring – passed before he saw Mehler's house. It was set in a slight hollow about twenty metres back from the road on the left-hand side. Petros drove down the slope and past it as slowly as he dared.

The number on the gate was 30. There was an attractive, well-kept garden, with a man working in it. For a second Petros wondered if it was Mehler himself. But no. This man was older, more thick-set, than the one in the photos Mr Pelli had shown him. So it was presumably the official bodyguard-chauffeur-handyman who lived there with his wife.

There was no other sign of life. At the back of the house Petros could see a long, low extension jutting out. The laboratory. At the far end of the garden was a row of pine trees, obviously planted many years previously to serve as a windbreak; and beyond these the moorlands stretched up and away into the distance. The moors where Mehler spent so much of his time.

'I'm surprised they give him so much freedom, you know,' Petros had said to Alex. 'Even with the guards following. I'd have expected them to put him under lock and key and surround him with an entire regiment.'

'I'm sure they'd have liked nothing better. But you can't expect high-power brainwork from a guy in those conditions. And he was in a position more or less to name his own terms. One of the things he demanded was a certain degree of freedom and solitude. Walking on the moors is just about his only relaxation, apart from a trip to town once or twice a week and perhaps a visit to the movies. There isn't any real way they could stop him. And he's a model in other respects – has very few visitors, doesn't get drunk or chase women – just stays at home and works. Then, of course, the authorities probably trust him — as much as they trust anybody, that is. He went to the Chairman with his discovery of his own accord. He didn't attempt to skip the country and sell to the highest bidder. All the evidence they've got points to his being loyal. They don't expect him to defect. Again, they genuinely believe the existence of the drug and their plans are secret. So they don't really anticipate any attempt to kidnap him. I reckon this security set-up's largely a matter of routine. The regime is quite ruthless and horribly efficient in some ways. But there is a tendency towards over-confidence.'

Petros nodded. 'I remember — somebody else saying as much once. He said it was their great weakness.' It had been Kauffman who'd said it, but he didn't tell Alex that.

'Don't get me wrong,' Alex said. 'The security boys aren't slack. They don't care two hoots whether their bosses trust Mehler or not. They've been ordered to protect him and let no unauthorized person contact him. They'll do this to the best of their ability. But they are being hampered by the amount of freedom they've been instructed to allow him. It's quite an important factor in your favour.'

Petros had no time to see more of Mehler's house before he had passed it and was climbing the hill. Then he was approaching another house, on the other side of the narrow road. This had to be the one occupied by the security guards. It was newer-looking than Mehler's house, and was built with its side to the road, so that its front windows faced straight down the hill towards number 30. Just inside the window of one of the upstairs rooms Petros could clearly see a man sitting behind a table. A pair of field-glasses were to his eyes and they were fixed on Petros's car. Petros drew level with the house. Towards the top of the side wall a large, metal-framed window had been made, giving a view of the moorlands to the east, behind Mehler's house.

The road ahead was clear, and when he'd got a little way farther up the hill Petros risked a quick glance over his shoulder. It needed only a second's look to tell him that from their quarters the security men had a perfect view of Mehler's house, of the road leading to it from both ways, and of the countryside in every direction. He was momentarily tempted to stop, get out, and make a really good survey of the area, but it was too risky. It was a thing that would have to be done some time, but, if he wasn't to arouse suspicion, only after careful planning. Although it would mean a long round trip, he decided he wouldn't even risk turning and passing the house again in order to get back to town.

He thought deeply during the return drive. It seemed incredible that in that quiet country house there lived a man who was to change the very nature of mankind and reshape the future of the world.

Incredible. That was the word. Then, not for the first time, came a frightful sinking sensation and the thought that perhaps he was making the most awful fool of himself. What proof, after all, did he have that Pelli was telling the truth – about anything? Who was Pelli, anyway? What was he? He'd turned up out of the blue, with the wildest story imaginable, and Petros had swallowed every word he'd said. Simply because Pelli had known the truth about Kauffman's death.

No – that wasn't quite right. There were other grounds for trusting him, besides that: Pelli had proved that he did have extensive contacts in both countries and sources that gave him knowledge of the innermost counsels of governments; he had apparently unlimited funds, could provide, and risk losing, an expensive helicopter, arrange for a call for rare blood to go out from a leading hospital at a specific time, furnish excellent forged papers, and give advance information which, so far as it went, had been completely borne out by Petros's experiences until now. He had answered every question put to him without prevarication, and to date Petros had not caught him out in a single untruth. If it was not for the very unlikeliness of the story he'd told there would not be the slightest reason to doubt him.

But all this speculation was quite pointless. Whatever the truth about Pelli, or about Mehler, Petros was stuck with the assignment.

Why? Why had he come? He asked himself the question yet again. And still he couldn't give himself a satisfactory answer.

It wasn't only that if he didn't get hold of the papers in Mehler's possession, he would never know another moment's freedom from the fear of being murdered. Though, that, of course, was a big part of it.

It wasn't only that he wanted supplies of Mehler's drug for Paula and himself, and that if he pulled off this assignment he'd stand a good chance of getting in on the ground floor when they started issuing it. Though he did want it. Badly.

It wasn't only that he wanted to receive official acknowledgement that he'd paid his debt to his adopted country, to be granted naturalization, publicly honoured, given a chance to start afresh with the slate wiped clean. Though he wanted these things, too.

Any combination of these factors might have beeen enough to make him risk it. But there was still more to his motivation. Perhaps it was the fact that Mr Pelli had wanted him, Mikael Petros, to do the job – not just because he was expendable, but because he thought Petros would be a good man for it. It was a long time since anyone had wanted him to do anything for that reason.

Perhaps, also, there had been a nagging feeling that maybe he was under some sort of moral obligation; that he had to make a decision, to take one side or another; and that the side represented by Mr Pelli, by Manson, at one time by Kauffman, was obviously a better side to be on than the one represented by the Chairman or by Marcos and the other people who had planned Kauffman's assassination.

But which was the strongest driving force? He didn't know. He just couldn't pinpoint any one motive. Hope, aspiration, fear, pride, conscience – they were all present, though in what proportions it was impossible to say.

Paula had seen the crux of it. 'He gets at you from every angle, doesn't he?' she had said. 'Whatever sort of person you are he's got a good chance of getting through to you.'

In this, Petros thought, lay the cleverness of Mr Pelli's appeal. Or did it? For, if everything Pelli had told him was, quite simply, true, cleverness didn't come into it. Just honesty. There *would* be rewards for Petros if he succeeded; if he failed – or didn't even try – he *would* suffer. And the suffering would not be of Mr Pelli's making.

Anyway, he had made his decision. He'd concluded that Pelli had told the truth. He had staked everything on it. He might have been wrong. He might have been set up. But if so it was an extraordinarily elaborate and convincing setting-up.

Herschel, for instance. It was difficult to believe that Julius Herschel wasn't genuine . . .

'This friend of Mehler's,' Petros had said, 'this bloke whose letter I'm going to deliver: who is he, exactly? How well did he know Mehler?'

'He is known now as Julius Herschel, but he adopted the surname only after arriving in this country,' Mr Pelli had said. 'Some years ago he was one of the foremost scientists in your country. But then he offended the government and was marked down for death. I arranged his escape to this country. Your government believed he was killed and his body lost; he was officially certified dead. He was at one time Mehler's closest friend, and he can tell you more about him than almost any other person; also about the papers which are going to provide your protection.'

'Do I get to meet him?'

'Yes. He is a science teacher at a State junior school the other side of town. Alex will drive us over to see him this afternoon.'

The school was a big modern building, all glass and concrete. Herschel's office, on the other hand, seemed to be tiny. But this was largely due to Herschel himself. He stood up as Mr Pelli opened the door, and Petros's first impression was that he filled all available space. He was a full head taller than Petros and must have weighed half as much again, for he bulged with fat. He had a very pink face, thick glasses, an almost bald head, and an immense double chin.

Now he was beaming broadly. 'My dear Mr Pelli, how very good to see you.' He had a deep and rather fruity voice. He extended a pudgy hand to Mr Pelli, and with the other beckoned expansively to Petros, who was standing in the doorway.

'And you, my dear chap. Come forward, if you can make it.'

Petros edged into the room and saw for the first time a very small red-haired girl standing in front of Herschel's desk. Herschel picked up a grubby and tattered exercise book off the desk and handed it to her. 'Go, child, and make room for these gentlemen. They can hardly get in with you taking up so much space.'

She gave a giggle. 'And,' Herschel said, 'be profoundly thankful that their opportune arrival has prevented my inflicting the most ghastly punishment on you for that last answer.'

She giggled again, her hand to her mouth. 'Yes, sir.'

'And stop giggling, girl,' Herschel boomed. 'Here.' He pushed a large paper bag towards her across the desk top. 'Put a toffee in your mouth instead and depart.'

She took one, said: 'Thank you, sir,' and fled, still giggling.

Herschel gave a sigh. 'One might as well order a duck to stop quacking.'

Mr Pelli introduced Petros to Herschel, then left. Herschel said: 'Sit down.'

Petros sat on an upright chair across the desk from him. Herschel prodded at the paper bag. 'Have a toffee.'

'No thanks.'

'Wise, very wise, not to get hooked. I'm trying to give them up.' He took one, unwrapped it, popped it in his mouth, and chewed it vigorously, eyeing Petros in an appraising manner. He said: 'So you're the guy who's going to bring Thomas out.'

'I'm going to try.'

'What can I do to help?'

'Tell me anything that might be useful about Thomas Mehler. What sort of man is he?'

Herschel thought for a moment. Then: 'Nice,' he said. 'Modest. Quiet. Rather shy. Idealistic. Straight. And when I knew him, disappointed.'

'Disappointed? Why was that?'

'As a scientist he'd never come up to early expectations. He took a brilliant first – something ridiculous like ninety-eight per cent overall, I believe. Then old Berrog took him under his wing. Led everyone to expect great things of him. But – well, they just didn't happen.'

'Could his wife's death have had anything to do with that?'

Herschel scratched his nose. 'Don't think so. That came later. Oh, it shattered him for a while. He was driving, you see. Christine was asleep in the passenger seat. She was killed outright. He was hardly scratched. He was completely exonerated, but he still blamed himself. He never drove after that. But I think by the time that happened he'd already turned out to be not quite such a good biochemist as everybody had expected. The accident just finished things off. Afterwards he definitely settled for being second best.'

Petros looked surprised. 'I'd hardly say the elixir could be the work of a man who'd settled for being second best.'

'Wouldn't you? I would.'

'But how could he have made a discovery of this magnitude – '

'Luck.'

'Yes, so Mr Pelli said, but surely there must have been a little more to it than that.'

'Well, I only know what Mr Pelli tells me, but what he says makes perfect sense. I just can't believe that Thomas deliberately set out to find an immortality drug. For one thing, I don't think he would have believed such a thing was possible. I certainly wouldn't have. But he *has* made the discovery. So I have to assume he hit on it by chance. Know any science?'

'Hardly any.'

'Well, chance discoveries can happen. Not often, but sometimes. Penicillin is the best-known example. My guess is that Thomas was working on some more or less routine experiments, noticed an unusual reaction, and followed it up from there. Don't get me wrong. You need ability just to do these things. I'm not suggesting Thomas is incompetent – far from it. Merely that it was chance set him off in the first place—and has led to the Chairman being within an ace of getting his sordid little fingers on something that'll make him the most powerful man in the world.'

'What I can't understand is why Mehler went to him in the first place.'

'Who else could he have gone to? He needed the freedom and the facilities to carry on his research. He would have gone to the top man in whichever country he'd been living. I'd have done the same. He must have realized, too, that production and distribution of the drug will have to be in the hands of the politicians. He *needed* the government.'

'But *that* government? They're utterly corrupt! Didn't he realize that?'

'No, of course not. Did you, when you lived there? Did I? When I knew him Thomas was a normally patriotic man. But he was certainly no fanatic. And he positively didn't have any particular love for the present regime. On the other hand, I don't think he thought, either, that they were worse than any other government. *I* didn't at one time.'

'You think he believes they'll be willing to give the secret of the elixir away to the whole world?'

'Well, I'm only guessing, of course. But Thomas isn't simple. He must have thought about the political implications of his discovery, and it must have occurred to him that there can hardly be a politician alive in any country who wouldn't *like* to gain personal control of the drug. He's probably prepared for all sorts of pressure – for them to appeal to his patriotism, attempt to bribe him, and so on. But I daresay he imagines that as long as he stands firm and insists on publishing, they'll just have to give in. I mean, all his demands have been met so far: he's been given a country house, a private laboratory, assistants, ample funds, a considerable amount of personal freedom. He must think he's got them in the palm of his hand. He's just naive enough not to realize that once he's finished his experiments, has written them all up, and produced an adequate amount of the drug, they won't need him any more and can just quietly put him out of the way.'

'That's where your letter's going to come in.'

'Ah yes.' Herschel opened a drawer in his desk and took out a bulky sealed envelope, which he slid across the desk to Petros.

'This spells everything out, does it?' Petros asked. 'The government's plans for the drug and world dictatorship, and that he himself will be in great danger once he's completed his work?'

Herschel nodded. 'In words of one syllable.'

'Do you think he'll believe it?'

'I think he'll more or less have to. He knows I wouldn't lie to him.'

'But he could believe you're mistaken.'

'He could. But I've been as persuasive as I know how. And the mere fact that we know about the elixir will in itself shake his faith in the government's reliability, I should think – plus learning that I'm still alive years after they certified me dead.'

'You think he'll accept that you *are* still alive? He couldn't think this letter is a forgery?'

'No.' Herschel shook his head decisively. 'There are things in it only I *could* have written. Incidentally, it occurs to me that you may need some way of proving yourself to him quickly – before he actually reads the letter. Well, say you come from Julius – don't mention the name Herschel, it won't mean anything to him – and tell him I want to know if he remembers a Sunday in Rome with Gina and her sister Carla. That'll shake him. Nobody in the world knows about that except the two of us.'

'Except Gina and Carla, I suppose.'

Herschel shook his head. 'More than that I'm not saying. Now – what else do you want to know?'

'I want to know about these secret papers Mehler has got that can be used to bring pressure on the government.'

'Ah yes.' Herschel had nodded slowly, unwrapped another toffee, and put it in his mouth. 'The Berrog papers. That's quite a story.'

9

The only possible way to contact Mehler would be to try to pass him a message during one of his regular trips to town. At least, that was the only way Petros could think of. For he couldn't call, telephone, or post Mehler a letter without the authorities knowing. Nor, without the knowledge of the guards, could he get close to him when he was out on the moors. So that left just the one chance.

Fortunately, as Petros knew from Mr Pelli, Mehler stuck to a fairly rigid routine. He always went into town at least once a week. And his usual time was Wednesday afternoon.

Which was going to leave just long enough for Petros's preparations.

On Tuesday morning Petros was up at five. He packed his rucksack with field-glasses, compass, and map, some bread, cheese, and a bottle of beer, and by five thirty was on the road again to Village 127.

Just short of the village he stopped and consulted the map.

The road on which Mehler's house stood went almost due south from the village. It marked the approximate fringe of the fertile lowland area, and to the east the moorland rose gradually in undulating folds. It continued to rise until it reached a crest, beyond which the ground fell sharply in a narrow, north-south ravine; along this ran a river. Beyond, the land rose again in further moorland to the foothills of the mountains in the extreme east.

Due east from the village ran another road. This climbed steeply at first, then levelled off and swung south, starting to skirt the top of the ravine. It was this road that Petros now took. It was narrow from the beginning and after it turned south became little more than a track. The surface was very rough. Up here the road was cut into the moorland, and just beyond the highest point west of the ravine – the crest that ran above and parallel with it – there was a sharp bend, and for a few metres the track ran not more than a pace from a precipitous drop to the bottom of the gorge. Nothing but a rickety-looking wooden railing marked the outside of the track. Petros stopped the car and got out.

He put his hand on the railing and shook it easily. He stared down at the muddy waters of the river. At this point it seemed to be running more slowly than further downstream, so was presumably deeper just here. He stood for a few moments, then got back in the car and drove on. To his right a steep bank reached to about shoulder height, preventing him seeing any of the moor from inside the car. To his left the ground still fell steeply away, though not so dangerously now. There weren't any buildings on this road, and he saw no other person.

The road had become too narrow for more than a single vehicle. But there were passing places cut into the bank, and into one of these he eventually pulled. It would be too bad if two cars met just here and found the passing place blocked; but the possibility seemed extremely remote. Petros picked up his rucksack, got out, locked the car, and scrambled up the bank.

There was a fine view from here. The moorland fell gently away from him in three directions. The road on which Mehler's house stood lay a long way ahead of him, to the west. He looked at the map. Mehler's house, he calculated, was slightly to the south-west, the village north-west. Petros put his map away, swung his rucksack onto his back, and started walking.

It was a lovely morning, with the faintest of breezes. The turf was springy under his feet. Once or twice Petros found himself beginning to feel almost light-hearted. He made a wide detour, and the sun had risen considerably in the sky before he topped a rise and looked down on the road he had driven along the previous evening. He could see the trees screening Mehler's house, the security men's house a little farther up the hill, and, in the other direction, a good stretch of the road leading from the village. There were three other houses on this

93

section of road, the nearest three or four hundred metres from Mehler's.

Petros didn't stop walking, because it was almost certain that even now someone had glasses on him. He looked at his watch. It was a little after 7 a.m. He started to climb higher up the slope. Soon he came to a point at which the land flattened and then dipped. He walked along the level stretch a little way, then stepped down into the hollow beyond, out of sight of the house. Here he stopped, got down on his stomach, and wriggled back until he could pick out the road once more. He couldn't see the security men's house from here, so they wouldn't be able to see him either. He hoped that he'd looked to them like a hiker, who had just happened to be passing along that stretch of the moors, and who had now vanished over the crest of the hill.

He took out his field-glasses, laid them on the turf beside him, and lit a cigarette. Now it was just a matter of waiting and keeping an eye on the road.

During the next hour five vehicles passed along the road: two private cars; a lorry; a milk van, which stopped at several of the houses, the milkman leaving cartons just inside the front gates; and one of the familiar little bright blue Post Office vans. The last came from the direction of the village, and made deliveries at most of the houses in Petros's view, including Mehler's and the security men's, before disappearing over the brow of the hill.

It was eight o'clock before Petros saw what he'd been looking for. A figure emerged from the rear of Mehler's house, went through the back door of the garage, and a minute later drove a car slowly out of the front and down the short drive to the road. Petros studied it intently through his glasses. It was a large grey BFR limousine, several years old, but beautifully maintained; a typical government issue car. Petros could just make out the licence number, which he carefully memorized.

The driver got out to open the gates, then drove the car onto the road and turned right in the direction of the village.

Petros wriggled backwards down the slope, stood up, and walked on. He'd found out all he wanted to know.

To park near enough to Mehler's to be able to watch him leave the following afternoon, and then to trail him all the way to town would plainly be far too dangerous – especially as the security men had most probably made a note of the licence number of the hire car as having been driven along Mehler's road the previous evening. But fortunately there was only one direct route from Village 127 to Township N. And now that Petros could identify Mehler's car, all he had to do was park somewhere just off the main road on the outskirts of the town, wait for the limousine to come along, and follow it for the last two or three kilometres only. There would be lots of other traffic about and, if he was careful to keep a couple of other vehicles between Mehler's car and himself, it was unlikely the guards would spot him. Then, as soon as Mehler got out, he would follow him on foot and hope sometime during the afternoon to get close enough to pass him a note.

Put like that, it sounded quite easy.

Petros spent the rest of the morning exploring the moors within an hour or so's walking distance of Mehler's house. It was a fascinating piece of country, full of little hidden valleys, busy meandering streams, and unexpected clumps of trees, forming miniature dense woods. There were also occasional great tors, the tops of which gave magnificent views. Petros took regular compass readings, marked his map, and made notes.

He saw a number of people as the morning wore on – two or three anglers, a couple of girl hikers, who passed quite close and gave him a wave, a pair of horsemen in the distance, and a family party of parents and three children picnicking in a hollow near one of the tors. He was pleased to see them all, because every person on the moor made his own presence less noticeable.

At mid-morning he ate his bread and cheese and drank his beer, then slept for half an hour before continuing.

Towards lunchtime he gradually made his way eastward and eventually arrived back at the narrow track on which he'd parked. He walked along it and reached his car at 12.45. He turned it with diffi-

culty and drove down to the village, again seeing nobody on the track, and from there back to Township N. He had lunch in the same restaurant as the previous day and afterwards returned to the caravan, stopping on the way to buy some writing paper and envelopes.

Then he settled down to draft a letter to Mehler. This turned out to be a longer job than he had anticipated. He tried at first to write an innocent-seeming note of three or four lines, so that if he was caught passing it, they wouldn't have too much against him. But he found it impossible to do this and at the same time make the note both urgent and convincing. So at last he threw caution to the winds. It would be just as easy to pass a fairly long letter as a short one; and if he should be caught trying to pass it to Mehler, it would probably mean the end of everything, anyway – however innocuous he made the letter seem. So he might as well make sure that if Mehler ever *did* read it he was left in no doubt as to its meaning.

Even then Petros had some difficulty in getting it just right, and by the time he'd made a fair copy the afternoon was nearly over. He read through what he'd written.

Dear Dr Mehler,

Your life is in danger. The Chairman plans to have you killed after your work on the elixir is completed, and to keep its secret in the hands of his own circle. I have a letter for you which will confirm this. It is from your friend Julius, whom you thought was dead. In fact, the Chairman tried to have him killed, but he got out of the country in time and is now well and happy, living abroad under a different name and doing useful work. He has told me to ask you if you remember a Sunday in Rome with Gina and her sister Carla. I do not know the significance of this, but he says that you will.

I believe I can help you to escape, and so ensure that your discovery is used for the benefit of all men. Go walking on the moor the day you receive this, and I will see that you get Julius's letter. Take a magazine with you. Thirty to forty minutes walk east south-east of your house there is a small circular copse on the crest of a hill. Just beyond it there is a narrow strip of flat turf, and then the

ground falls away to a small valley. At the edge of the flat turf there is a large boulder. Sit down on or near the boulder, with your back to the copse, looking down into the valley, and pretend to be reading. Provided your guards are not within earshot I will speak to you and tell you where to find Julius's letter. If for any reason you cannot go at this time, go either of the two following days.

Mention this to nobody at all. You may or may not know that your mail is normally opened and read by the authorities before being delivered, hence this unorthodox method of delivery. Please burn this letter.

It wasn't perfect, but it would do. Petros left it unsigned, folded it, and put it in an envelope. He sealed the envelope, wrote 'DR MEHLER. CONFIDENTIAL' on it, and placed it in his coat pocket ready for the next day.

Would it do the trick? Would the mere mention of Gina and Carla convince Mehler that the writer really did come from Julius and so could be trusted? Or would it have been wise to have referred to the Berrog papers as well? Herschel believed himself to be the only person to whom Mehler had mentioned them. If, then, Mehler were suddenly to learn that Petros also knew about them, it might just tip the scales in convincing him that Petros really had been in touch with Julius.

But on reflection he decided it would not have been good policy to speak about them at this stage. To do so might make Mehler suspect that to obtain them simply to have a lever to use against the government was the main purpose of the whole exercise. And then he might doubt that Petros was really interested in *his* safety at all.

Besides, if Mehler had had any wish to see pressure brought on his government by means of the Berrog papers, he would surely have done something about it himself by now.

They were, after all, potential dynamite . . .

'Do you remember the so-called "mystery epidemic" that ravaged

Europe ten years ago?' Herschel had asked.

'Yes, of course.'

'More than fourteen thousand people died.'

'I know. It was a terrible thing.' Petros was puzzled, but he didn't show it. This had to be relevant.

'It was a previously unknown infection,' Herschel said. 'The medics couldn't do a thing. It was believed to have started in our country – probably in the north-west, in District Eleven or Twelve. That's where the first deaths occurred.'

'That was never proved, though, was it? They could never track down the actual source or the cause?'

'That was the official story. However, a few people do know the truth – among them Thomas Mehler.'

Petros felt a quickening of interest.

'The mystery epidemic,' said Herschel, 'was the direct result of the action of our government, and the explicit instructions of the Chairman. It was an experiment in biological warfare research which went wrong.'

Petros let out a long, low, almost silent whistle.

'Have you ever heard of Conrad Berrog?' Herschel asked.

'Yes, of course. He was probably the greatest scientist we've produced this century – one of the greatest in the world. He died about seven or eight years ago. Don't ask me about his work, though. I just know he won the Nobel Prize – and practically everything else going.'

'Well, Conrad Berrog was a member of the committee set up to advise the government on all matters pertaining to biological and chemical warfare. A team at an official research laboratory succeeded in isolating and cultivating a previously unknown and lethal strain of virus. They also produced a vaccine which they believed would be effective against it. It had been tested successfully on animals. But they needed a controlled test on a large sample of human subjects. They applied to the government for permission to conduct such an experiment. The application was referred to the committee – which decided that the test could proceed. Only Berrog dissented. He sent in his own report, maintaining that the experiment was far

98

too dangerous. His report was ignored.'

'They must have been crazy!'

'Well, Berrog was an old man by then, and it was thought by many that his intellectual powers had failed, that he was becoming over-cautious. But he persevered. He wrote a long memorandum to the government, repeating his warnings. That received a mere formal acknowledgment. Next he wrote a personal letter to the Chairman. The Chairman's secretary replied, saying he had been instructed to inform Berrog that it had been decided the experiment should proceed, as it was essential to go into large-scale production of the vaccine with all speed. Berrog could do no more. A village of about five hundred people in the Eleventh District was chosen. Its population was inoculated and then exposed to the virus.' He paused. 'Three-quarters of the people in that village died. Quarantine precautions were inadequate, and the rest is a matter of record. Now, naturally, it hadn't been intended that so many should die, so it – '

Petros interrupted. 'What do you mean – *so many*?'

'Well, it was inevitable that some people of the village would be killed. That was expected. The dosages of the vaccine administered to the different subjects were deliberately varied in relation to body weight, in order to ascertain the safest and most effective strength. The truth, of course, was hushed up. Only a very few people knew the facts, and it was to the advantage of all of them to keep the secret. You can well imagine the effect it would have on the position of the government if, even today, it would be proved that against the advice of their most eminent scientist they deliberately approved and encouraged an experiment that resulted in the deaths of fourteen thousand people. Most of those men are still in power. And the ultimate decision, as the letter to Berrog proves, was the Chairman's own.'

His use of the present tense was not lost on Petros. '*Proves*? It's still in existence?'

'Yes. Thomas Mehler's got it.'

'The Berrog papers,' Petros breathed.

'One of them.'

'There are more?'

'Oh yes. Thomas has got Berrog's own account of the whole affair

99

in Berrog's own hand, copies of the researchers' original application for permission to conduct the experiment, of the committee's recommendation to the government that permission be granted, Berrog's own minority report, his memorandum to the government, and the personal letter he wrote to the Chairman.'

'But how on earth did he get them?'

'From Berrog himself. Mehler had been his pupil many years before, and was by way of being his protégé. So he sent them to Mehler just before he died.'

'Why? Did he expect Mehler to use them to show the government up?'

'No, there's no evidence Berrog opposed the experiment on moral grounds. He simply considered it foolhardy. He foresaw it could get out of hand. But he didn't object to the fact of a *few* people being killed.'

'You're saying he was no better than them.'

'He was, in effect, *one* of them. Until a few years previously he'd been the government's chief scientific adviser. He was absolutely loyal. If he hadn't been, he would never have been able to retain those papers. No, Berrog didn't want the government exposed.'

'Then why send them to Mehler?'

'I don't know. I suspect that he merely wanted a record of the truth to remain in existence – a natural wish in a scientist. I imagine, to say the least, that he wasn't very pleased when the authorities rejected his advice. And of course, when he was proved to have been right, he'd be quite determined the facts shouldn't be lost for ever. Thomas was a fellow scientist, who would be able to understand the papers, and whom he knew he could trust.'

'Do you think Mehler would be prepared to use them against the government?'

'He'd be a fool not to.'

'But he's never attempted to take advantage of them so far.'

'It's probably never occurred to him. Remember, he's always been loyal himself. Many of the men named in Berrog's papers are respected colleagues, even friends, of his. He wouldn't *want* to see them exposed. He'd ask himself what good it would do. Then again, he's never *needed* to bring pressure against the government. He's been given everything he wants without that. And in order to use the papers for that purpose safely, he'd have had to get out of the country first – which is plainly something else he's never had any desire to do.'

'These papers could be verified as genuine?'

'Oh yes. There are samples of Berrog's handwriting all over the world. And whatever his faults, it would be acknowledged as inconceivable that he would lie about such a matter.'

Later, Petros had spoken to Mr Pelli about the papers.

'You say that if I get hold of them, and the Chairman knows they will be published if anything happens to me, I shall be safe?'

'Yes. If you wish, you can hand them to me, and I will store them in a safe place, arrange for them to be released to the press if you should come to harm, and ensure that the Chairman is personally told the facts.'

Petros looked puzzled. 'But if you want to bring the regime down, won't you want to publish the papers immediately?'

'No. Because they will be more effective as a threat than an actual weapon. If the facts became known in your country, they might cause a revolution. Your people have not forgotten the tragedy of that epidemic. Over two thousand of their children died in it.'

'But isn't revolution what you want – what Manson wants?'

'No I do not wish to be responsible for the loss of life which would be entailed. My desire is for the regime to collapse of its own accord, without any popular uprising taking place. I have told you how close it is to this. The hope of the immortality drug is the one thing holding it together at present. Should that be taken away the recriminations would be likely to split the government irreparably. The Chairman would have nothing more to offer. There are, however, other reasons for holding back the papers. Censorship in your country is strict. Even though the papers were published in the outside world, news of them might not penetrate to sufficient numbers of your people. If it did, they might not believe what they heard – there would be no proof the papers even existed. Thirdly, the people might be too frightened to rebel: they have been oppressed for many years. Or, finally, a rebellion might arise and yet be crushed. These are imponderables. I am not prepared to release the papers only for them to fail to have the desired effect. Equally, however, the Chairman will not be willing to risk what might be the outcome if they *were* released. This is why I say that once he has been informed of the position, you will be safe from any possible act of revenge.'

'Suppose Mehler isn't willing to let me have the papers? Suppose he wants to keep them for his own protection?'

'You may tell him he will be welcome to keep them – if he still so wishes after he has spoken to me.'

'But you told me I could have them.'

'You can: Mehler will relinquish them after I have spoken to him.'

'You can't be sure –' Petros began, but Mr Pelli interrupted.

'Do not concern yourself with these questions. Simply bring Mehler and the Berrog papers to me and you need have no fear of the Chairman thereafter. Trust me.'

Petros was in position by one o'clock on the Wednesday afternoon. He parked in a street leading off the right of the main road into Township N from the south, about two kilometres from the town centre. By looking to his left he could see all traffic approaching on the main road from the direction of Village 127. He had his field-glasses at the ready, and with them he could pick out the licence number of each large grey car which approached while it was still some distance away. There were several other vehicles parked near him, so he did not feel unduly conspicuous.

Just sixty-five minutes and six cigarettes after he'd parked he at last saw Mehler's car approaching. He dropped his glasses onto the seat, started the engine, pulled forward to the road junction, and waited for the limousine to pass. When it did so, he saw there were four men in it. He let two other cars pass, then moved forward into the traffic stream.

Five minutes later the limousine turned into a car park in the centre of the town. Petros followed, drove across to the far side from where the limousine had stopped, found a gap, switched off his engine, and looked cautiously back out of his rear window.

A man had alighted from the front passenger seat and was opening the back right-hand door. As Petros watched, another figure emerged through it, and Petros got his first real glimpse of Thomas Mehler.

A second man got out of the rear of the car, slamming the door after him.

Mehler walked briskly away. The two other men stood together until he'd got about twelve or fifteen paces ahead, then set off after him. The chauffeur remained in the driving seat.

Petros got hurriedly out, locked his car, and followed the three men.

Once out of the car park Mehler slowed down. He strolled along the crowded pavements, his hands in his pockets, frequently stopping to look in shop windows. The security men remained about the same distance behind.

Petros had no plans. For the time being he could think of nothing to do except make up the end of the short procession – and bide his time.

He spent a frustrating hour. Mehler's first stop was at a tobacconist's. The guards peered in through the door after him, then waited outside. Petros interested himself in a shop window full of women's hats. Mehler came out, walked on, then turned in through another door. This time, one guard followed him in.

Petros hurried forward and saw that the place they had entered was a barber's shop. He hesitated for a moment before walking on past it, glancing in through the window as he did so. He just had time to catch a glimpse of Mehler, one of four men sitting waiting. The first guard was presumably one of the others, but Petros couldn't pick him out without pausing and peering in. He thought rapidly. Should he go in? It might be a good opportunity – perhaps actually to sit down next to Mehler. It was tempting. Then he decided against it. To do so would mean sitting for perhaps ten or fifteen minutes within touching distance of the guard, a man who would automatically study closely – and remember – the face of everybody who came near his charge. If, after all, it then proved impossible to pass the letter – and the odds would be against it – he would have to approach Mehler again later on. And then the guard might well start to get suspicious. No – he couldn't risk being seen near Mehler more than once.

The second guard meanwhile had strolled on twenty-five or thirty paces, and was standing in the doorway of an empty shop, taking out his cigarettes. Petros crossed the road to an open-air café, sat down at a table from where he could watch the door of the barber's, and ordered a glass of the local red wine.

It was twenty minutes before Mehler reappeared, followed by his inevitable shadow. The guard was joined by his colleague, and again the procession set off.

Mehler's next call was a bookshop. This time the second guard went in after Mehler while the first one remained outside.

Petros himself approached the shop. It was quite a large one. He opened the door and went in.

He found Mehler – naturally enough – in the science section, flicking through the pages of a large volume. Petros looked for the guard, and spotted him by a case of war fiction paperbacks. For the moment, he had taken his eyes off Mehler.

His eyes scanning the shelves, Petros shuffled round until he was facing Mehler over the top of a low, double-sided bookcase. Mehler seemed engrossed by the book he'd picked up. Petros groped for one himself, opened it at random, bent his head over it, and looked across the bookcase out of the tops of his eyes.

Except in the photographs Mr Pelli had shown him, it was the first time he'd seen Mehler close up, and he studied him intently. It took an effort to believe that this was the man who had made the greatest discovery in the history of science.

For although Mehler was not a little man – he was in fact almost exactly the same height and build as Petros himself – the small regular features, the mild brown eyes, and the dark thinning hair made him look utterly insignificant.

Petros threw another glance towards the guard. He, too, seemed taken up by the book he was reading. Petros slid a hand to his inside pocket and fingered the envelope nestling there. So easy to withdraw it and thrust it quickly over the top of the bookcase onto the open volume in Mehler's hands. The work of one second. But suppose Mehler said something, asked him what he was up to, got suspicious and called the guard? Or suppose the guard looked up anyway at the crucial moment and saw him?

Petros took his hand from his pocket empty. He couldn't risk it. The letter had to be passed in such a way that Mehler would not find it until later. The only chance at this time was to slip it into his pocket . . .

Petros pushed his book back into its place and edged round the end of the bookcase. He was now the same side as Mehler. He took one sideways step nearer, and another. One more and he'd be in touching distance. Petros again raised his hand to his pocket. Then:

'Excuse me.'

It was a woman. A large middle-aged woman. She pushed herself in between Mehler and him, peering at the shelves through thick spectacles. Petros was forced to take a step to his left, leaving Mehler and the woman standing close together. Petros swore under his breath. It would be pointless to move round to Mehler's other side, because then he'd be between Mehler and the guard. And he certainly wasn't going to try passing the letter with the guard behind him.

A minute later Mehler wandered round to another section of the shop. Petros followed slowly. But the opportunity had been lost. Although Mehler stayed in the shop a further half-hour there were no more chances to pass the letter.

Mehler bought three books, charged them to his account, gave them to the guard to carry – the first time he'd as much as acknowledged the man's existence – and left the shop.

He walked for about another ten minutes before pausing outside a men's outfitters. He looked in the window for a few moments, then went inside. This time both guards followed him in. Petros gave them sixty seconds and entered the shop himself.

On the right Mehler was examining a rack of casual lightweight jackets and jerkin-type garments. A bored-looking assistant was watching him. On the left the guards, obviously killing time, were idly fingering the contents of revolving tie stands. Several other customers were dotted about the shop.

As Petros watched, Mehler took off the jacket of the somewhat shabby grey suit he was wearing and threw it carelessly onto a nearby counter. It landed lining outwards, the inside pocket clearly showing, a wallet projecting a couple of centimetres from it.

Petros licked his lips, took a deep breath, and walked as casually as he could over to the counter. The assistant glanced up, then came across to him, raising his eyebrows. Petros asked to see some socks. The assistant went behind the counter, pulled out a couple of drawers from the cabinet behind, put them on the counter, and returned to Mehler. Petros started to rummage through the socks in the drawer, standing sideways to the counter so that he could see both Mehler and the guards. For what seemed like minutes he waited, his heart in his mouth, his gaze darting round the shop.

Then at last everything came right.

One guard picked out a tie and turned away to see it in the light. The other looked over his shoulder. At the same moment Mehler held up a blue cotton jerkin with a zip front and said: 'I'll try this on.' The assistant took it and started to help him on with it. No one else in the shop was looking towards Petros.

Like lightning he drew the envelope from his pocket, leaned forward, and tried to thrust it into the pocket of Mehler's coat.

But it wouldn't go in. He couldn't get it past the wallet. He pushed harder, then, frantically, harder still.

The jacket slid off the counter and onto the floor, one of its buttons striking the polished linoleum with a click that seemed to reverberate round the shop.

Mehler turned, the assistant glanced over his shoulder, the guards looked up sharply. But the letter was already back in Petros's own pocket.

Somehow Petros managed to bend down, pick up Mehler's coat, and replace it on the counter. He looked at Mehler. 'Sorry,' he said. Rarely had one word been so difficult to get out.

'That's all right.' Mehler turned away and looked at himself in the mirror.

With a tremendous effort, Petros refrained from glancing at the guards. He picked up the first pair of socks that came to hand, and said to the assistant: 'I'll take these.'

It needed all the willpower he possessed to stand there, sensing the guards' eyes boring into his back, while the assistant put the socks into a paper bag, took his money, and fetched his change. The slow walk to the door and into the street was even worse.

Outside he lit a cigarette with a shaking hand. His heart was pounding. So near. If only he'd been able to conceal the letter up his sleeve when Mehler's coat had fallen. Picking the coat up would have been an ideal opportunity to slip the letter into the pocket.

But perhaps it was as well he hadn't tried it. He might have fumbled it. And that could have made things very awkward.

Never again. That was going to be his first and last attempt to pass a message directly to Mehler. He'd have to think of some other plan or call the whole thing off.

He went home to the caravan.

10

The loathsome snake-like figures pranced round the bed. Thomas Mehler lay, his body rigid, his teeth gritted in terror, sweat gushing, from every pore, his eyes fixed on the creatures, pressing himself back against the headboard. He was whimpering like a child. 'Go away. Go away. Go away.' Over and over he repeated the words, like an imbecile. But they didn't go away. Instead, they started to close in on him. He shut his eyes again, but that was worse, because they were still there. Now they were changing. They were turning into animals. Ordinary animals – mice, guinea pigs, cats, dogs. But all deformed in some way. Like the ones he'd experimented on. They wanted revenge. On him. That's what they'd come for. 'No, no, I had to do it,' he gasped at them. 'It had to be tested. Don't you see?'

Then he drew in his breath in a lung-rending gasp of unadulterated horror. Because the faces were changing again. Only the faces. The hideous deformed bodies were the same. But the faces were becoming human. And female.

'Oh, please God, no.'

For every creature had the face of his wife. His wife who'd died eight years ago.

Mehler gave a strangled scream and passed into blessed unconsciousness.

Later – an hour, a week, a year later – he again became aware of his surroundings. He lay quite still, his eyes closed, and tried to discover if he was better. He decided he felt normal, and cautiously opened his eyes. There was nothing there. He moved his arms gingerly. He tried to sit up, but he couldn't make it. So he lay where he was, stared at the

108

ceiling, and shuddered at the memory.

Then, automatically, because he'd been trained most of his life to seek an answer to every problem, he set his mind again to this one.

It was the second time it had happened. Each time the pattern had been the same: waking at night with a dry throat, a headache, and a raging fever; lying, unable to move, his body dripping with sweat. Then the convulsions, the rigid limbs and set jaw. After this the things. But no – he wouldn't think about them: hallucinations – nothing more; finally the coma. Only this time everything had been worse. And, yes – he looked at his watch – the coma had lasted longer. He thought he knew the cause: the water that had been used to dilute the drug had not been sterile. He'd been careless, or one of the lab assistants had. At least, the symptoms all fitted.

But what was he to do now? He ought, if he were sensible, to see his doctor. But that would mean hospital, and he wouldn't be able to carry on with the tests. They wouldn't let him. And he had to carry on; if he stopped now, it would put him back months . . . when he was so near the end, so close to being able to publish. It wasn't, he was sure, that there was anything basically wrong with the drug. It was just this one lot. And they'd ask so many questions. They'd want to know what he'd injected himself with. And he wouldn't be able to tell them.

Suppose the trouble wasn't what he thought? He wasn't a physician. It could conceivably be nothing more than a virus infection. He might never have another attack. On the other hand, whatever it was, it might get worse. And it could kill him.

But he had to risk it. He could do nothing else. He had to carry on with the injections – with a fresh batch of the drug. If there were no further attacks, all well and good, but if he was taken ill again, then he would have to see a doctor, and go into hospital.

Though, if he told the doctor the truth, it would probably be a mental hospital.

11

Was this the time to ring the emergency telephone number?

'Memorize it,' Alex had said. 'If you find yourself in a really tight spot you can ring it; any time, day or night. Just say you're a friend of Mr Pelli, and help of some sort will be forthcoming.'

So Petros had memorized it. But he couldn't bring himself to use it. Because he couldn't honestly say that he was yet in a really tight spot. There was no immediate danger. It was just a matter of getting a message to Mehler. He couldn't deliver it personally. But it wouldn't be fair to try to get other friends of Mr Pelli to do it for him. He'd just have to work something out for himself.

Again he put his mind to the problem. The guards would know if anyone tried to speak to Mehler either face to face or on the telephone. And they would be instantly suspicious of any written communications he received; except these which arrived through the mail in the normal way, of course: such letters wouldn't concern them – because they would have already been passed by the censors before delivery. So if a letter once got past the censors Mehler would, presumably, be able to read it privately without the guards knowing anything about it. But all such letters were delivered to Mehler *by the postman*. If only, Petros thought, he could get the postman to deliver *his* letter – yet without it having to go through the sorting process, so being spotted by the censors.

For some minutes wild schemes floated through Petros's mind. Knock-out the postman, steal his van and uniform, and deliver the letter himself . . . Buy an ordinary van, paint it to look like a Post Office van, hire a uniform from a theatrical costumier . . . Bribe the postman –

He paused: that was better, but still too risky. The postman had to deliver the letter innocently. Could it just be slipped into his bag without his knowledge? That was better still. But nearly as dangerous: he daren't be caught tampering with the mails.

No, the letter had to be given to the postman casually. When did the average person have occasion to hand a letter direct to the postman?

The germ of an idea started to take shape.

The following morning Petros drove out to Village 127 again. He parked outside the inn, locked the car, and started walking. He went out along the road on which Mehler's house stood, looking closely at every building as he passed. When he reached the last one before number 30 he turned and went back to the village.

In the main street he hesitated for a few seconds, then entered the inn. There was a small bar on the left and a dining-room on the right. Petros went into the bar, sat down at a table, ordered a lager, and considered.

Between the village and Mehler's house there were altogether nine other buildings: two large villas, set well back from the road, surrounded by high walls, and showing signs of life; a working farm; three small cottages in poor repair and all occupied, probably by farmworkers; and three modernized cottages, with well-kept gardens, garages, and telephones. In the garden of one of these cottages children had been playing, but neither of the other two had shown any signs of occupation.

The barman brought his drink.

Petros said: 'Very attractive part of the country, this.'

'I think so. But perhaps I'm prejudiced.'

'You lived here long?'

'Nearly all my life.'

'You must know pretty well all that goes on round here.'

'Oh, I wouldn't go as far as that.'

'Tell me – does any property ever become available?'

'Very rarely. And it's always snapped up pretty quickly when it does.'

'Actually, I noticed a couple of cottages a few minutes ago that didn't seem to be occupied – on the road out to the south.'

'Which would those be?'

'One was number twenty-seven.'

'Oh, that's Dr Loren's place. He's a consultant at a big hospital in the north. He only uses it for holidays and weekends.'

'So most of the time it's empty?'

'Dr Loren comes and goes at odd times. Being a doctor, I suppose he has to take breaks whenever he can. He hasn't been down lately. Turn up any day now, I expect.'

Petros said: 'The other was twenty-four.'

'On the right-hand side? High hedge? Red paintwork?'

'That's the one.'

'Belongs to a couple by the name of Cranz. He's a top brass government official. They don't come down very often.'

'Cranz?' Petros furrowed his brows. 'I used to know a fellow called Isaac Cranz. Wouldn't be him, I suppose?'

'No, no. Let me see now what's the gentleman's first name? Begins with V, I think. Viktor. That's it.'

Petros drank up his lager. 'Oh well, it was just a thought. What sort of lunch do you do here?'

'Pretty fair, I think.'

'Then I think I'll go and grab a bite.'

He left the bar and entered the dining-room. He had a lunch of cold ham and salad, and afterwards drove out of the village to have a closer look at the Cranz cottage. It lay between two bends in the road and so was not overlooked by any other house. There were two gates: a small one at the bottom of a path leading to the front door; and double ones at the side opening onto a concrete drive running round behind the cottage. Neither was locked. Petros opened the small gate and walked up the path. Then he went round to the back. Here there was a garage, the doors locked. The whole place was secluded and quite private. He returned to the road, closed the gate behind him, and drove back to Township N.

He stopped at the first stationer's shop and bought several packs of different-sized envelopes, a pencil, two cheap ball pens, one blue and one black, and a rubber.

He went back to the caravan and clearly, but lightly and in pencil, addressed one of the smaller envelopes to F. Danton, care of the caravan park. Then, just in case it was opened, he wrote a short, innocuous note – 'Hope you're enjoying your vacation, and look forward to seeing you soon' – signed it with an illegible scribble, and put it in the addressed envelope. He didn't seal the envelope, just tucked in the flap.

Then he took out his own letter to Mehler and destroyed both the envelope and the final page. The latter he re-wrote so as to explain that the letter had by-passed the censors. Next, he took five envelopes of different sizes, but all larger than the one he had addressed to himself, and addressed each of them to Mr Viktor Cranz, at 24/127/45. He varied the appearance of them as far as he could, using his own pen and each of the ball pens he'd bought, and writing in block capitals and several different styles of handwriting. He couldn't be bothered to write bogus letters to put in each one, so he merely inserted blank sheets of paper and sealed the envelopes.

There was then nothing further he could do that day. He went out for a meal, posted the self-addressed envelope, went back, and turned in early.

First thing the following morning he went to the camp office and collected the letter he had mailed to himself the previous evening. He took it back to the caravan, destroyed the note inside, and carefully erased his own name and address from the envelope. Then he addressed it in ink to Dr Thomas Mehler, at 30/127/45. He took his own letter to Mehler and put it in this envelope. He was tempted, momentarily, to enclose Herschel's letter for Mehler as well, and rewrite his own letter to this effect. But he decided it would be too much of a risk. If, by some fluke, the letter went astray, his only real hope of persuading Mehler to come with him would have vanished. He sealed the envelope and put it in the secret compartment of his suitcase.

When he went out later he took with him the five envelopes

113

addressed to Cranz and posted them in five different boxes. Having done this, he drove to the District Capital. He spent his first hour there shopping. His purchases included a dressing-gown, a pair of bedroom slippers, a vacuum flask, and a small alarm clock, as well as bread rolls, cigarettes, and cans of beer.

His shopping completed, he took the opportunity to go to the airport and spend half-an-hour studying timetables and tariffs. He had lunch in the airport restaurant, then drove directly to Village 127, cutting out Township N. He passed the afternoon and early evening exploring the moors again.

He returned to town about 8 p.m. had a meal in a café, went back to the caravan park, bought a carton of milk in the shop, and was in bed by 9.30. Before turning out the light, he set his new alarm clock for 5.30. The next day was one on which whatever happened he could not afford to oversleep.

When Petros dressed the next morning, he put his clothes on over his pyjamas. He washed, but deliberately did not shave. There was a long day ahead of him, so he had a couple of boiled eggs with his rolls and coffee. He made plenty of coffee and filled his new flask with what was left over. This he packed, together with several cans of beer, some rolls, cheese, and a packet of biscuits, into the rucksack. He took his gun from the bottom of the case, loaded it, and put it in his jacket pocket, together with a dozen cartridges. In his inside jacket pocket he put his own letter for Mehler – already in the envelope with the cancelled stamp – and the one for Mehler from Herschel. Next, he put his new dressing-gown and slippers, together with the carton of milk, into a carrier bag. He carried rucksack and carrier to the car and locked them in the boot. He returned to the caravan, collected his cigarettes, and locked up. Then yet again he took the road to Village 127.

It was another glorious morning. He arrived at the village just after 6.30. There was nobody about. He drove straight through the centre and out to the Cranz's cottage. He stopped outside, walked up to the front door, and, just to be certain the cottage was still unoccupied, knocked loudly several times. All was silence.

He went back to the road, looked round carefully, then quickly opened the double gates and drove his car in and round to the back, parking it outside the garage. He returned to the road, made quite sure the car could not be seen, closed the gates, and hurried back to his car. He opened the boot. Then he took off his jacket, sweater, trousers, shoes and socks, and put on the dressing-gown and slippers. He transferred his letter for Mehler to the pocket of the dressing-gown, picked up the carton of milk, and went round to the side of the house, from where he could see a short stretch of the road in the direction of the village.

Half-an-hour elapsed. Several times he had to dodge back out of sight when cars passed. Then he saw the milk van approaching. He hid again, and when it had disappeared went down the path and put his carton of milk on the ground just inside the front gate.

Once more he returned to his position and waited. Everything now depended on the postman not knowing Cranz by sight. It was surely unlikely: the Cranzes' spent only infrequent periods at the cottage. If Cranz was in the habit of rising as early as this when on holiday, it was improbable that he often went into the garden at this time of day. The postman might conceivably have clapped eyes on him once or twice, but it was long odds against him remembering the appearance of one householder among the hundreds of addresses at which he must call. Of course, he told himself, all would not be lost even if the postman *did* know Cranz; as he might well assume Petros was a house guest. All the same, he'd probably think that for a guest Petros was behaving rather oddly. And anything, however slight, that made the the postman curious would be dangerous.

Minutes dragged by. Petros's heart was beating fast. He kept looking at his watch. Then once more he heard a vehicle approaching. He stared towards the village, ready to get out of sight again if it should prove another false alarm. He saw a flash of blue. This was it.

Petros ruffled his hair, took a deep breath, and started to stroll down the path. He reached the gate two or three seconds after the post van drew up outside it and, as the postman got out, was just bending down to pick up the carton of milk. He straightened up and leaned over the gate as the postman came towards him.

Petros spoke cheerily. 'Good morning. Something for us?'

'Yes, sir. Quite a number.' He held out a handful of familiar-looking envelopes.

Petros took them. 'Thank you.' He half turned away, tucked the carton of milk under his arm, and started to flick casually through the letters. He shot a sideways glance at the postman. The man had turned round and was crossing back in front of his van. In a flash Petros drew his letter for Mehler out of his pocket and turned back to the gate. He called out: 'I say.' The postman looked back. 'There's a mistake here,' Petros said. 'This isn't for us.' He glanced at it. 'Dr Mehler. Number thirty.'

The postman came back, a puzzled expression on his face. Petros handed him the letter. He stared at it. 'Well, I'll be – How did that get among yours?'

'Easy enough for a small envelope like that to get hidden among the larger ones, I should imagine.'

'There were five addressed to you, sir, weren't there? Did I give you them all?'

'Yes.' Petros held out the letters fanwise for him to see.

The postman shook his head. 'Careless of me. I'm sorry, sir.'

'That's all right. Better make sure Dr – er – Mehler gets it now, though. It might be important.'

'Oh, don't worry. He'll be getting it in a couple of minutes.' He peered at the envelope. 'It's been delayed one day already, I see. Funny. I've noticed before his often are.' He went back to his van, carrying the letter.

Petros walked slowly back up the path, making as if to open one of the letters in his hand. It had worked! He'd forgotten about the post-mark showing the letter was a day late. But it hadn't mattered. It had even helped in convincing the postman that the letter was genuine. It was the censors, of course, who held up Mehler's letters.

The post van disappeared. Petros hastily looked through the letters again to make sure that there were no genuine ones for Cranz among them. But no. They were the five he had posted the previous day. He went round behind the cottage again, threw them into the boot of his car, took off the dressing-gown and slippers, put them in the boot as well, and dressed again. He stowed the carton of milk in the rucksack, and a minute later was driving away from Cranz's cottage back towards the village.

He wondered again if his plan had been over-elaborate. But he could still think of no other way he could have worked things. Given that the only method of getting a message to Mehler without the guards knowing was to have it delivered as regular mail by the postman, then the only way to avoid having such a letter read by the censors was to give it to the postman after the mail had left the post office. And the only relatively safe way to induce the postman to deliver a letter that had not gone through the mail in the normal way was to convince him that it *had* gone through the normal channels, and that by error he had delivered it to the wrong address. The five 'letters' to Cranz, all in larger envelopes, had made reasonable the belief that Mehler's letter had been hidden among them all the time. The only strictly unnecessary touches had been the dressing-gown, slippers, and milk. And Petros was conscious of the element of absurdity in the charade. But he felt that psychologically they had been powerful aids. Had he merely stood by the gate in his ordinary clothes, it was conceivable that the postman might have doubted his identity, suspected an attempt to steal the mail, and insisted on pushing it through the letter box. But Petros had been sure that if a tousle-headed, unshaven man in pyjamas and dressing-gown were seen picking up a carton of milk outside a house in the early morning, it would never occur to anyone that that man was anything but a member of the household. And given that strong preconception, who would suspect that Mehler's letter wasn't genuine?

Petros drove back through the village and took the now familiar track to the moors. He parked in the same place as on Tuesday, got his rucksack from the boot, hung his field-glasses round his neck, and set off. He had a long walk ahead of him.

He arrived at the copse, hot and tired, at 9.30. He made his way into the middle and put his things down. He was in a cool glade about twenty metres across, with a surface of moss and dead leaves. The branches of the circle of trees that surrounded it met in places overhead, and the light was dim. There was no sound but the wind in the trees. It was very peaceful. It was also ideal for his purpose. The copse was set on high ground, which rolled down in three directions, giving him a superb panoramic view. He could stand in half-darkness just inside the circle of trees and sweep the moor with his binoculars. From one direction only could he be approached without his knowledge: along the bottom of the valley which ran behind him, and up the steep slope, the top of which was about five or six metres away from the near edge of the copse.

But Petros was not afraid of surreptitious approach. If his letter didn't work – if Mehler handed it straight to his guards – they wouldn't bother with stealth. There would be no point. A quick call to HQ, the despatch of some troops by helicopter, and he'd be cordoned off in minutes. His only chance, the second he saw or heard any sign of danger, would be to go straight down the slope into the valley and then along it under cover of the trees at the bottom. If he could, by some miracle, get back to his car, he might – just might – get away. But it would mean the assignment ending in ignominious failure. And he'd still be a long way from getting out of the country.

Through the field-glasses he stared in the direction of the hollow in which Mehler's house stood. He could just make out the tops of what he thought must be the trees screening it. There was no sign of movement anywhere on the moor. He turned round, went back across the glade and out the other side of the copse. He crossed the narrow strip of level ground to where a large boulder stood, knelt down by the side of it, picked up a small pointed stone, and dug a little hollow in the earth at the base. He took out the envelope containing Herschel's letter, pushed it into the hollow, and covered it over with earth. Then he went back to the copse. He knew he ought to keep a constant lookout from now on. But he had to have a rest first. Mentally and physically the morning had already been a hard one.

He sat down on the soft floor of the glade with his back against a tree, opened his rucksack, poured himself a cup of coffee, and lit a cigarette. How long before something happened? Had the letter been opened yet? Was Mehler an early riser, or did he work into the night and sleep late? Suppose he was sick and didn't read his mail today – or either of the next two days? Suppose the censors put some secret mark on letters they passed, and the housekeeper or her husband noticed that this was missing from Petros's envelope? Suppose Mehler opened it in the presence of one of them and was unable to conceal his reactions? So many things could go wrong. Well, there was nothing to be done about it. The dice had been thrown. He was in the lap of the gods.

Petros stopped his train of thought and considered that phrase. He repeated it to himself. And wondered.

The course of events five years ago had led him later to the almost inescapable conclusion that there were real grounds for a belief in something which might be called Fate or Destiny. It had been so remarkable how, through it all, good had come out of bad. He had committed murder. Then, to save his life, he had let himself be sent to kill again. And as a result, the Chairman's regime had been discredited and weakened; Manson had come to power; and he had met Paula again – purely by coincidence it had seemed to him at the time.

Now it seemed as if the pattern was strangely repeating itself – only in reverse. Another unknown visitor had called on him, given him a warning, and sent him on a mission – back to his own country; not this time to take life, but to save it. The whole thing really did seem to be somehow purposed.

He couldn't help the nagging idea that he actually was in the lap of the gods.

Or the lap of God.

The thought of being a puppet in the control of some dark and mysterious power of which he knew nothing was rather frightening. But he couldn't do anything about it.

Or could he? Perhaps he couldn't help being under the control of this Power – perhaps no man could. But did It – or Him – have to be unknown? Could he possibly learn something about It? Kauffman had talked as if he had done so. He had spoken almost as though God was a friend. Apparently the girl at the farm believed in Him, too. Or was 'God be with you' just a saying like 'Good luck'? This was possible. But Petros doubted it. He couldn't remember ever having heard the phrase used in this country before. No, it was more likely that she'd used the words literally – that she did believe.

Odd that the only two people he'd met who did should be such differing types. A middle-aged intellectual and a young country girl. At one time he would have been scornful of people who held such views. But he hadn't felt scornful of Alexis Kauffman. Nor did he feel scornful of the girl. Anyway, logically, how could he? Didn't his own vaguely formed deterministic ideas necessarily imply the existence of Something to do the determining?

He remembered again – and as always it gave him a twinge of embarrassment to recall it – how, during a moment of crisis in the Kauffman affair, he had found himself – quite involuntarily – praying. And what he had asked for in the prayer had come about. Later, in prison, he had started thinking for the first time about the whole concept of Providence. Furtively, he'd even tried to pray again – this time logically and in cold blood.

But it hadn't worked: he hadn't heard any Voice or felt any Presence. He'd gone to the prison library and begun to read the Bible, concealing it while he read inside a big encyclopaedia. But the stories – about things like magic and giants and dead bodies coming to life – seemed so obviously fairy tales that he'd given up in bewilderment.

That had been the extent of his religious experience. Nevertheless, he had been unable to throw off the idea that his life was somehow ordered. Nor had he been able to get out of his mind the fact that the thing he'd asked for in that first desperate prayer had – against all the odds – happened. Nothing but luck, he'd often told himself. But yet – luck or not – it had worked. Might it work again? It wouldn't do any harm to have one more try. And no one would ever know.

Feeling rather silly, he closed his eyes and mumbled a few hesitant words. Nothing really ambitious. Just that he'd get back home again.

Home. Paula. She'd be in class now. He tried to remember her timetable. He thought it would be Senior Italian at this time. Italy. Rome. Gina. Carla. Had Mehler read the letter yet?

He went to reach for his cigarettes, and then realized he was already smoking – had been all the time he'd been praying. That didn't seem quite right. Would it invalidate the whole thing?

What utter rubbish! He must be going out of his mind.

Petros jumped quickly to his feet, went to the edge of the copse, and swept the moor with his field-glasses. It was an action he was to perform countless times during the hours that followed.

The day seemed never-ending. The sun rose in the sky, casting a chequered pattern of shade and sunlight onto the floor of the glade. Time and again, Petros moved across it to gaze out across the expanse of moorland. Unconsciously, he developed a routine: a long look towards Mehler's house; a slow pan over the entire stretch of country within his range of vision; a sweep of the sky; then a change of position, first to the north and then to the south sides of the copse for the same procedure; finally, a few steps outside the copse to the boulder, and a look into and along the valley. He'd repeat this course of action three or four times, before pausing for refreshment. He found that he needed to be continually eating and drinking. He got through half the cheese, several of the rolls, most of the biscuits, all the coffee, the milk, and two cans of beer. In between, he smoked continually. He knew that it was nervous reaction – the result of a desire to be doing *something*; and rather than let the tension get on top of him, he pandered to it.

He kept a count of the people he saw: there were over thirty in all, mostly on foot, but a few on horseback, in twos, threes, and fours, and one party of six or eight children with an adult. But none of them came near the copse. And none of them came from the direction of Mehler's house.

As the day wore on Petros found that he was spending more and more time gazing down towards that distant row of trees. His mind became obsessed with thoughts of what might be going on in the house beyond it; and eventually the one question filled his mind: what – in heaven's name, what – would he do if nothing happened, if he stayed here until dark, did the same again the next day, and the day after that, and there was no response of any kind at all? He tried to tell himself to meet that problem when it arose, but he couldn't help constantly reverting to it.

The day dragged by. The sun dropped inevitably towards the horizon. Petros's legs ached and his eyes ached. In spite of all the liquid he'd taken in, his mouth and throat were dry. He was sated with tobacco, but went on smoking. He longed for a bath and bed. He seemed to have been for ever in the copse.

Afternoon turned into evening. He'd stay till seven, not one second longer. Six-thirty came, and Petros stood, the glasses clapped to his eyes, gazing fixedly towards Mehler's house. He'd abandoned his routine: if the security men were going to come after him they'd have come by now.

A movement. A flicker or a shadow against the background – the far distant background. Petros blinked and looked again. A figure, a moving creature of some kind. A human being. On foot. Petros licked his lips. It was a man. He was coming straight from Mehler's house, up towards the copse. He disappeared into a dip. Perhaps just another hiker who had happened to pass near Mehler's house. He had probably turned away by now and wouldn't reappear.

But no – there he was again, still coming straight towards the copse. Minutes passed. The foreshortening effect of the field-glasses made it seem that the man was constantly coming forward without getting any closer. Petros lowered the glasses. Immediately he noticed two specks some distance behind the first. He raised his glasses again and focussed on them, but could not pick out any details. Alternately with and without the binoculars, he continued to watch the three figures. The pair were certainly following the same course as the first man, but not getting any nearer to him. Nor were they making any attempt at concealment. Petros drew a deep breath. It had to be Mehler and his guards.

Soon the man was close enough for Petros to make out his appearance. There was no doubt: it *was* Mehler. Herschel's letter had worked.

When he was about four hundred metres from Petros, Mehler veered away to his left. Then he carried on and passed the copse about a hundred paces north of it, moving out of Petros's sight. Petros drew well back into dark shadow, moved across to the north of the copse

122

again, and peered through the trees. Mehler had gone right up to the crest of the hill and was standing sideways-on to the copse, his hands in his pockets, staring down into the valley.

Where were the guards? Petros crawled back to his original position. He saw them toiling up the slope, still about one hundred metres away from Mehler. As he watched, they stopped and one sat down on the turf. It suddenly occurred to Petros that if Mehler now turned to his right and walked along the crest of the hill to where the boulder lay, he'd pass out of sight of the guards. Then they might well cut across at an angle, coming right up to, perhaps even passing through, the copse, so as to get him quickly in view again. Mehler, of course, did not know that his contact was *in* the copse. But he would almost certainly guess. Would he realize the danger?

At that moment there came a shout from Mehler's direction. The two men started up the slope again. For an instant they seemed to be coming towards the copse, and Petros stopped breathing. Then he realized they were making straight for Mehler. He wriggled hurriedly back to the north side.

Mehler was standing in the same place as before. But now he had a pipe in his mouth. In a few moments the guards had joined him. Mehler spoke to them. One took a small object from his pocket and handed it to him. Mehler took it, fiddled with it, bent his head, and raised his hands towards it. Then a small cloud of smoke appeared. Petros nearly laughed aloud. Mehler had called them up to ask for a light.

Mehler tossed back the box of matches, then started to stroll along the crest of the hill towards the copse. The two men stayed where they were. They would presumably wait there until Mehler had put the usual distance between himself and them. That would be all right. Mehler would still be only sixty or seventy metres from them when he reached the boulder. The manoeuvre had been cleverly calculated virtually to guarantee they wouldn't come near the copse.

Mehler was walking slowly. He stopped once more and stared out over the valley, as though thinking deeply. Then he moved slowly on, closer and closer to the boulder. Petros noted that he had on the blue garment he'd been trying on in the shop. Under it he was wearing a grey roll-necked sweater. He wore grey trousers and black leather shoes. He again passed out of Petros's sight, and again Petros moved silently on hands and knees round further to his right, to the point from which he could see the boulder. By the time he'd reached this point Mehler was standing by the boulder. His back was to Petros. If he guessed where Petros was concealed, he displayed no sign of it. Petros felt a sudden tinge of admiration. In spite of Herschel's message, Mehler could not be absolutely certain that this whole thing was not a ruse leading up to a kidnap attempt.

It was important now not to startle him: the guards weren't too far off to notice if he showed any marked alarm.

Petros drew a deep breath, then spoke in a low voice. 'Thank you for coming, Dr Mehler. May I suggest that you turn to your right slightly, so that the guards won't be able to see your face?'

Mehler didn't move, didn't so much as flick a muscle. Petros opened his mouth to repeat his advice. But then Mehler slowly did as Petros had said. His face was very pale. He didn't look like a man who spent hours walking on the moors. But that might have been just nervousness.

'That's better,' Petros said. 'Now we can talk. But don't look towards me.'

'Who the hell are you?' There was the slightest of tremors in his voice.

'That doesn't matter now. We haven't got a lot of time. Did you bring a magazine with you?'

'Yes.'

'Then sit down on the ground, lean against the boulder, and pretend to read it.' Mehler did this. 'Now feel down by the side of the boulder with your left hand,' Petros ordered. 'The earth is loose. Dig into it and you'll find Julius's letter. Read it now. But keep it inside your magazine all the while. Take your time.'

Petros watched closely as Mehler carried out these instructions. His face as his eyes criss-crossed the paper was quite expressionless. Petros left him to it and crawled away to have another look at the guards. He saw that they were in the same place, one standing, one sitting, apparently quite unconcerned. He wriggled back.

Mehler came to the end of the letter, leaned his head against the boulder, and closed his eyes.

Petros let a few seconds pass, then asked: 'Well?'

'Yes. Julius wrote this all right.'

'Do you believe it?'

'I have to.'

'Does he explain everything you need to know at this stage?'

'Except how this man Pelli is involved.'

'I don't suppose he knows that. I don't, exactly.'

'Yet you both trust him?'

'I do. Julius — well, you've read the letter.'

'You'd have to say that though, wouldn't you. You're a professional spy. You'd hardly say you don't trust your controller.'

'I'm not a professional spy. And he's not my controller.'

'Just do this sort of thing for a hobby, do you?'

'Something like that. Listen, we're wasting time. Are you willing to let me get you out of the country?'

'You mean now — this moment?'

'Of course not! But soon — in a few days.'

'Oh. I see. Why should I trust myself to an amateur?'

'Because there's no professional around. Julius trusts Pelli. And Pelli trusts me.'

'I think the thing's impossible. Do you know about the security set-up here?'

'Yes.'

'And you still reckon I'd have a chance?'

'A damn sight better chance than if you stay here.'

Mehler was silent.

Petros said: 'Well?'

'I'll have to think about it.'

'All right. But not for too long. Twenty-four hours.'

'Very well.'

'Can you come up here again tomorrow at the same time?'

'No, I want to talk to you properly — face to face. I'll have a lot of questions to ask. I couldn't sit here that long. They'd think it odd. Besides, I don't often go to the same part of the moors twice in one

125

week. If I came up here two days running it would look suspicious. And if you were spotted it would be obvious we'd been plotting something. You'd better come to the house.'

Petros thought he'd misheard. 'What did you say?'

'I said come to the house.'

'You're not serious?'

'Of course I am. Just let me explain, will you? I've got an old friend due to visit me tomorrow. From my old university. His name is Anton Spenz. He's just been appointed associate professor of microbiology at the 45th University – in Township R, forty kilometres west of the District Capital. None of the guards here have ever seen him. The visit's been cleared with the authorities. And he's got first-class security rating, so we'd be allowed to talk privately. You take his place.'

'I don't understand.'

Mehler sighed. 'Ring him up this evening. Say you're my assistant or secretary or something – he doesn't know anything about the set-up here. Tell him I'm ill, if you like. Only don't make it out to be too serious, in case he rings back to enquire after me. Say I've got 'flu, and I'll be in touch with him in a few days. I can't do it myself. I'm pretty sure my 'phone's tapped.'

Petros didn't say anything for a moment. His mind was working fast. It could be a trap. But then he told himself that if Mehler wanted to trap him he had only to dodge behind the boulder at this second and yell for the guards.

So he said: 'Suppose I can't get through to him for any reason?'

'Well then, he'll turn up here as arranged, won't he? Obviously, in that case you don't come. I'll have to see you up here on Monday, after all, and hope for the best.' Mehler spoke irritably.

'OK, OK. If it works, what time shall I come?'

'The train he was going to catch gets in to Township N about 2.30. He said he'd be with me around three.'

'Right. I'll get a taxi from the station myself.'

'I'll write down Spenz's number for you.' Mehler wrote in the margin on a page of the magazine, tore it off, and inserted it in the envelope which had contained Herschel's letter. He pushed the enve-

126

lope down under the boulder. 'Is there anything else?' he asked.

'One thing. When you went into town last Wednesday there were two guards with you. Any likelihood I'll see them tomorrow?'

'No. They don't normally come to the house. You'll just see Shenkar the chauffeur and his wife, who live with me. Why?'

'I'll tell you later.' Shenkar hadn't seen him on the Wednesday, he was sure of that.

'Then I'll be getting back.' Mehler knocked out his pipe, put it in his pocket, and stood up, folding Herschel's letter inside his magazine as he did so.

'Don't let anyone see that,' Petros said.

'I'm not a complete fool.'

He strolled casually away. Petros stayed where he was for five minutes, then got to his feet and went to the other side of the copse. Mehler and the guards were already tiny figures, almost lost against the vast expanse of rolling land.

Petros collected the envelope, gathered up his rucksack and binoculars, and started on the long walk back to his car.

He had to make four attempts that evening to get hold of Anton Spenz. To the first two calls there was no reply, and the third time a woman answered and said the professor was out. But at 10.30 Petros at last spoke to him.

Spenz seemed to accept what Petros said. He expressed no undue surprise or curiosity, simply passed on his best wishes to Mehler and said he'd look forward to hearing from him.

Petros rang off and breathed a sigh of relief. If only he could be sure everything else Mehler had suggested would go as smoothly.

12

In the morning the whole of the previous day was to Petros like a dream. His plan had worked perfectly. But, in retrospect, it all seemed just too bizarre to be true.

On top of his own weird exploits, there had been the strangeness of Mehler's attitude – his complete lack of surprise at anything he had heard. He had expressed no delight at having learnt that Julius was still alive, no shock at being told of the Chairman's plans for him and his discovery; at the suggestion that he himself should defect he had exhibited neither fear, excitement, nor horror. At some moments he had been irascible; at others had seemed almost bored. Yet he had himself worked out the details of Petros's visit to his house, and had appeared quite keen to do so. It was very odd.

At about 11 a.m. Petros took a bus to the railway station and spent some minutes studying timetables. There was a train to the District Capital at 11.45, and he caught it. It arrived at 12.35. He had lunch near the station, then went back and bought a ticket to Township N. The through-train from the 44th District came in at 1.30. It left again for Township N ten minutes later with Petros on it.

An unnecessarily involved procedure, perhaps, but there was no point in taking chances. Spenz had been going to arrive by train in Township N at 2.30. So that was what Petros was going to do. It wouldn't do any harm. And in this sort of work the fewer lies one spoke or acted the better.

The train arrived on time. Petros left the station and took a taxi, telling the driver to go to Village 127, house 30. They drew up outside Mehler's house just after three. His heart in his mouth, Petros got out, paid the fare, then turned to see Mehler, smiling broadly, standing by the front gate.

'Anton! Good to see you.'

Petros conjured up a smile of his own. 'Hullo, Thomas.'

They shook hands and started up the path to the house. A man — presumably Shenkar — was working in the garden.

'Well, how are you?' Mehler said.

'I'm very fit. And you?'

'Oh, fine.'

They went into the house. A gaunt, middle-aged woman was standing quietly in the hall.

Mehler said: 'I read your paper in the *Journal* last month.'

'Oh – er, did you? Good.'

'Bit above my head, I'm afraid. But I enjoyed that dig at old Mendorp's theory.'

'Yes, I thought you might like that,' Petros said. 'You're not the first to have mentioned it by a long way. It seems to have been the one paragraph that everybody noticed.'

Mehler laughed. 'Come into my study.'

The study was a pleasant, conventional room, book-lined, with a large desk, deep leather armchairs, and a thick carpet. Mehler closed the door behind him. He said: 'Well done.'

Petros didn't reply, just held out a small piece of paper. In preparation he had written on it: *Could this room be bugged?*

Mehler looked at it and shook his head. 'No. I've checked it carefully. You see, there had to be a place where I could talk privately to government people about my work. Because neither the Shenkars, nor any of the security men, know exactly what it is I'm working on. So not only isn't it bugged, it's virtually soundproof.'

He went across to the desk, struck a match and set fire to the piece of paper. He dropped it into an ash-tray and crumbled it to pieces with the end of a pencil. 'Sorry about that greeting. It's what I would have said to Spenz if he'd come. I thought I should be as authentic as possible.'

'I hope *I* sounded authentic,' Petros said. 'I was ad-libbing desperately.'

'You did all right. Sit down.'

Petros did so. Mehler sat opposite him. He said: 'I suppose you *are* the guy who was in the copse yesterday. The voice sounds the same.'

'Of course,' Petros said slowly, 'I was forgetting. You didn't see my face.'

'Not yesterday. But' – he stared – 'I have seen you somewhere before.'

'Last Wednesday afternoon. In the outfitters. I accidentally pushed your coat off the counter.'

Mehler's face cleared. 'That's it. But what –'

'I'll explain.'

He did so, then said: 'Incidentally, there was no trouble with Spenz last night. He sent you his best. Hopes to hear from you soon.'

'He'll be disappointed.'

'Does that mean you'll come?'

'I'll have a go. Provided you can give me satisfactory answers in the next hour or so.'

Petros wasn't surprised. He'd expected this reply ever since he'd first spoken to Mehler. Nor was there any feeling of elation: the thought of the job that now lay ahead stopped that. So it was with a curious lack of emotion that he said: 'Good. What do you want to know first?'

'What about money? I wouldn't be able to take much cash with me. I haven't got a lot of call for it these days. If I wanted to draw some it would mean a special trip to the bank. The guards would wonder why. They might smell a rat. So I'd be practically penniless. Would this Pelli guy see me all right?'

'You can depend on it. He told me to tell you he can supply all your needs.'

'I'm just expected to trust, is that it?'

'That's it. Like Julius did.'

Quietly, Mehler said: 'Well, he does say in the letter he's never regretted it. So I suppose I've got no choice. How would we get clear of the guards? You know two go everywhere with me? And radio in to their HQ every few minutes? Pre-arranged signals at pre-determined times.'

'Yes, I know – at irregular intervals. And they've only got to press an alarm button to set off a virtually unstoppable homing signal. I know all about it. So there's no thought of just putting them out of action and making a dash for it. Because I'd have to kill them both simultaneously if I wasn't to give one of them a chance to activate his alarm. And even if I somehow managed to do that, it would only be a matter of minutes before their colleagues knew something was wrong – when they didn't receive the scheduled signal. And I know they've got a chopper behind that house up the road and they'd come hunting for you in it.'

Mehler looked impressed. 'Then what's the answer?'

'Well, I haven't worked out all the details yet, but basically it's to prevent them knowing you've escaped until it's too late for them to do anything about it. Tell me: when you're out on the moors do the guards keep you in sight every second of the time?'

'Well, no. It wouldn't really be possible unless they came very close, and I won't have that. I mean, there are all sorts of sudden dips in the terrain, clumps of trees, and so on, so they're bound to lose sight of me now and again.'

'For how long a period at most?'

'Oh, I don't know. Not long. Thirty seconds, say. Perhaps very occasionally three-quarters of a minute. But of course they always know exactly *where* I am. And I could never move more than a few metres in any direction without coming into their view again. Why do you ask?'

'I'll tell you what I've got in mind,' said Petros.

Mehler rubbed his chin. 'It might work,' he said. 'Everything'll need to go just right.'

'That applies to any plan. If you can think of anything better, then let's have it.'

'No, I can't. I've been trying since yesterday. If you're willing to take the risk, I am.'

'You realize you'll have to drive a car a short distance. Will you mind that?'

Mehler shrugged. 'If I've got to, I've got to.'

'Good. I'll let you have all the details about where and when later.

131

We'll have to have another meeting before the actual break.'

Mehler nodded. 'Next: assuming all this works, how do we then get out of the country?'

'We should have a couple of hours before the hunt for you starts up. In which case we could leave quite openly – by air or land. I've got passports and exit visas for both of us. And in an emergency – well, your guards aren't the only ones to have a helicopter standing by.'

Mehler raised his eyebrows. 'You've got one? Where? Near here?'

'No. A good distance away – in the 43rd.'

'Pity. We might have made a dash straight for the border from here – before they'd even discovered I'd done a bunk.'

'A pity you don't live nearer the only section of the frontier I was able to cross in it undetected. To have tried to fly it all the way from there to here would have been suicidal. Besides, as I said, I only want to use it in an emergency. Getting across the frontier in a chopper wouldn't be any picnic.'

'So when you said about going by air, you primarily meant scheduled commercial flight?'

'Yes.'

'You couldn't book in advance, though – we couldn't be sure of keeping to a timetable – so how do you know we'd get seats?'

'There are half-a-dozen free countries within a few hours' flying time from here. Initially we can make for any one of them. We'll get on the first flight that has vacancies – whichever one of them it's bound for.'

'You could afford the fare for two to any of them – and out again?'

'Just about.'

Mehler took his pipe from his pocket, slowly filled it from a tobacco jar on the desk, and lit it. Then he said: 'When do you want to make the attempt?'

'As soon as possible. What's the earliest you could manage it?'

Mehler considered. 'Wednesday, possibly.'

'Not before?"

'No. I've got a lot of preparations to make – and masses of personal and scientific papers to destroy, without anybody knowing. It'll take all of three days.'

'Very well. We'll say Wednesday afternoon, then, provisionally. Will you need to take much with you in the way of work notes?'

'No. Most of it's in my head. I can reduce everything I need to a few sheets of foolscap.'

'And can you burn the rest of your notes? You mustn't leave anything behind that another scientist could use to duplicate your work.'

'It's highly unlikely that anybody could, but I suppose it's advisable to be on the safe side.'

'What about the elixir itself?'

'There isn't a lot of it yet. The first batches were all faulty in various ways and had to be destroyed. I've pinpointed the last of the troubles now, but I can carry all the sound stuff in my pocket.'

'That's good. Now something else. Professor Berrog's papers.'

Mehler drew his breath in sharply. 'What do you know about those?'

'I know that he left them to you, and that they prove the Chairman was personally responsible for the mystery epidemic ten years ago.'

Mehler was silent.

'That's true, isn't it?'

'It's true. What about it?'

'We've got to take them with us.'

'Why?'

'Insurance – for one of us.'

'I don't follow.'

Quickly, Petros explained Mr Pelli's plan. When he'd finished, Mehler said thoughtfully: 'Yes, I see. Clever. It hadn't occurred to me before that I had the means of blackmailing the Chairman to hand. I suppose because I never imagined I'd want to. But what do you mean – insurance for *one* of us?'

'For you – if you want it. But Mr Pelli has some plan for safeguarding you without need of the papers. He thinks that if you're satisfied with his arrangements, you might be prepared to hand the papers over to me for *my* protection instead.'

'Don't bank on that.'

'Look, it's agreed that you get first chance. The important thing is that we don't leave without them.'

'I haven't got them here.'

'Where are they?'

'In a safe place. I don't yet feel disposed to tell you exactly where.'

'Can you get hold of them?'

'Not if you want to make the break on Wednesday. They're some distance away, and I just won't have the time.'

Petros gnawed at his lip. This was an unexpected hitch. He said: 'Tell me at least if they're in this District.'

'No – the 44th. Couldn't we pick them up on the way? It wouldn't take long. And there's a big international airport at the 44th District Capital, too – just as many flights go from it as the 45th, and the fares shouldn't be that much different. We could leave from there just as easily.'

Petros shook his head. 'The hunt might be up for you by the time we got that far. Every second might be precious. I'm not going to risk it. Suppose we put the escape back a day – to Thursday? Could you get them then?'

Mehler thought. 'Just about, I should think. I'd have to apply for permission to leave the District – and make up some story why. The guards would come with me. But there's no reason for them to know *what* it is I'm collecting. They'll see that they're documents of some kind, and they'll report what I've done. But I'll be out of the country before the authorities can ask me about them officially. Or I'll be recaptured – and finished anyway.'

'Right, then. Make the arrangements. Now – if I were really Spenz, would it be normal for us to go for a walk on the moors?'

'Yes, I should think so. Do you want to go?'

'I want us to have a look at a few landmarks together. I'd hate either of us to go to the wrong place on Thursday. But there's just one thing: you said you don't often go to the same part of the moors twice in one week – that the guards might have got suspicious if you'd gone up to the copse again today. What will they think about your going to the same spot now and again next Thursday?'

'That's all right. There are two teams of six guards doing a week's duty each in turn. They change over on Monday mornings. So there'll be a different team on duty next Thursday. Only the Shenkars are on all the time.'

'So the ones who'll follow us now might be the same ones who were in town with you last Wednesday?'

'They might be. It'll be two from the same team of six. I can't say which ones. But they won't see you close up. I'll just ring up, tell them I'm going out, and they'll fall in some distance behind us.'

'OK,' said Petros, 'let's give them a bit of exercise.'

They went out through the back gate onto the moors and walked east for five or ten minutes. Then they came to one of the many footpaths that criss-crossed the moors. Here they turned north and strolled on slowly. It wouldn't have been obvious to the guards, but Petros was leading the way, and with a definite end in view. Eventually the path began to fall, and they passed along the bottom of a small hollow. They now increased their pace a little, so that the distance between them and the guards was lengthened. At the end of the hollow, on the right, was a towering outcrop of rock, which overhung the path in places. The path skirted the base of it, then turned sharp right. Petros and Mehler rounded the corner and for the first time were out of the guards' view. Petros took a quick glance at his watch, then pointed to the rock. 'There – see?'

Mehler looked. In the base of the rock there was a narrow cleft, about half as high again as a man, receding into the darkness.

'It goes back about three or four metres,' Petros said.

A few steps farther on, the ground became overgrown with bracken, and the path divided. The right-hand arm of the fork carried straight on due east and ascended quite steeply. The other turned sharply left and continued north along level ground.

Petros took the right-hand path, then pointed to the left-hand one over his shoulder. 'You know where that leads?'

'Yes. It comes to that narrow road which climbs up from the village. It continues on the other side and eventually runs into a lane which takes you out onto the main road to Township N – the far side of the village from here.'

'And just where the lane joins the main road there's a lay-by.'

'I know.'

All this time they had been climbing the path, until now they were level with the top of the rock. Petros looked at his watch again. He said: 'Have a look and see what the guards are doing.'

Mehler glanced back. 'They've seen us. They're leaving the path – cutting across behind the rock.'

'That's what I thought they'd do. If they'd followed exactly the same path as us, right round the rock, they'd have lost sight of us again – and they'd have had to walk quite a bit further.'

'If the ones next Thursday do the same, we won't need the cleft.'

'I know. But we can't be sure they will.'

'How long were we out of their sight today?'

'Thirty-five to forty seconds. It should be enough. Now, correct me if I'm wrong, but if we carry on up in this direction we'll eventually come to that same narrow road you mentioned just now. Is that right?'

'Yes, but much higher up, of course, after it's turned south. It's not much more than a track by then. And this path won't take you all the way to it. It peters out shortly.'

'Then we've gone far enough, I think. We might as well make our way back.'

They returned to Mehler's house by a direct route. On the way Petros said: 'We'll have to meet again before the actual break to go over the arrangements and check that no snags have cropped up. As there'll be different guards from yesterday on duty, I suggest the copse again.'

'Very well.'

'When?'

'Tuesday? About five?'

'OK.'

After that they didn't talk much till they were nearly back at the house. Then Mehler said: 'What now?'

'There's nothing else. I can leave now.'

'You'd better not go yet. You're an old friend, remember? You've come a long way to see me. You should stay for another hour at least.'

So they went into the house and back to the study. Mehler poured

136

some drinks, and they sat silently for some minutes. Now that the practical arrangements had been made there seemed to be nothing to say.

At last, rather diffidently, Petros said: 'Is it in order to congratulate you on your discovery? It's a fantastic thing. Unbelievable, really.'

Mehler gave a shrug. 'Lots of things that would have been thought unbelievable a few years ago don't cause a raised eyebrow now. If anyone had told your grandfather that you would be able to look at a glass screen on a little box in your own living-room and watch human beings walking on the moon, he'd have probably backed away from him in alarm.'

'Oh, I know. But your elixir is a greater advance than things like space flight or television.'

'Don't call it an elixir. It sounds too much like magic – something out of a fairy tale. Life Extension Therapy – LET – I call it.'

'Call it what you like, it *is* magic. I mean, anything that makes it possible for someone like me to live to perhaps three hundred and fifty years old – '

'Hang on,' Mehler said. 'I'm not promising anything like that yet. All LET will do is slow down the ageing process by a factor somewhere between four and five.'

Petros looked puzzled. 'Well, then, surely if you multiply the average human life-span – '

Mehler interrupted. 'You're forgetting that you've already used up about half your life expectancy. I made the same mistake when I made my first calculations. But you've got to remember that your ageing process is already far advanced. My drug won't do anything about that. It's not a rejuvenator. It will just arrest ageing. How old are you?'

'Thirty-nine.'

'Then let's say you've got a normal life-expectancy of about another thirty-five years. If you started on the therapy tomorrow you could multiply that by four or five. If we're optimistic and say five, that makes one hundred and seventy-five years to be added to your present age. So stay healthy and avoid accidents and you could statistically expect to live to about the age of 215.'

'I see.' Ridiculously, Petros felt a pang of disappointment. He said:

'I feel you've just robbed me of about a hundred and thirty years of life. Still, I'll settle for 215.'

'Oh, don't do that,' Mehler said unexpectedly.

'What do you mean?'

'Well, those figures are based on the drug as it is now, and on my present state of knowledge of it. It's virtually untested, relatively crude, and the most effective dosages haven't been precisely formulated. I should say it's quite probable that refinements and improvements will take place which will significantly increase the factor of five. Then again, you can assume that within fifty years virtually all major diseases will become curable. And there'll be great advances all round in medicine and the biological sciences generally. There's no saying what could happen. You could live for ever, my friend.'

Petros stared. 'Are you serious?'

'Quite serious. I've made the vital breakthrough – proved that the human life-span can be substantially extended. Others will carry on from here. There won't be any stopping us now.'

Petros shook his head. 'One just can't take it in.'

'I know. Mind you, although I'm satisfied with it in my own mind, none of the experiments I've been able to undertake could demonstrate conclusively that the drug is one hundred per cent safe. The scientific and medical establishments will no doubt want years of large-scale clinical tests before they're convinced. So don't expect to see it on the market at once.'

'What do you mean by "years"? How long before it's available to the general public?'

'Your guess is as good as mine. Even when it's passed all the tests, the governments of the world are going to have to make the most intensive preparations before they unleash it on their peoples. Because obviously it's going to turn the whole social system in every country upside down.'

'Yes, I suppose it will cause quite a few changes.'

'A few? Do you realize that, with a very few exceptions, people will have to choose between having the drug and having children? A combination of the present birthrate with an eventual almost zero deathrate would clearly be quite out of the question. Now, once this principle is generally accepted, I imagine there will be an almost complete embargo on births – because plainly a first priority will be the reduction of the world's population to a more manageable level. It will be allowed to fall gradually, as older people die off – which, of course, they will do, even with the benefit of LET: if a man of ninety has got a life expectancy of, say, two years, and you multiply that by five, he's going to die in 10 years, anyway. On top of that, younger people are going to continue to be killed off in accidents and natural disasters. When the population is down to a satisfactory level, a few chosen couples, specially qualified mentally and physically, will be licensed to have children, in order to make up the wastage and keep the population stable. So there'll be only a tiny fraction of the infants in the world that there are today. No need for things like maternity hospitals or, eventually, schools. All the schoolteachers will be out of work. All the factories geared to making children's things – babyfood, toys, clothes – will have to switch to other products or shut up shop. Later, ninety per cent of the colleges and universities will either have to close down or become centres of pure research. With no old people and virtually no children around, the medical profession will have to be completely reorganized.'

It was almost as if Mehler had ceased to be conscious of Petros's presence. Clearly he had given a lot of thought to the implications of his discovery – without ever having had much chance to talk about it. Now he was making the most of the opportunity.

He continued: 'So, within a comparatively short time the world population will be overwhelmingly composed of fully mature, widely experienced men and women, all having what we today would call "young" bodies. They will continue for many years in that state – perhaps indefinitely. They will be the most highly-educated and highly-skilled people who have ever lived – because they will be able to go on learning, mastering their subjects, their professions, with minds and bodies at peak power, for perhaps hundreds of years. But – after working for what we now call a full lifetime people are going to have a perfect right to retire and enjoy leisure – possibly centuries of it. There are going to have to be facilities to keep them occupied – to teach tennis, say, or the violin, or mountaineering, to centenarians. Then, after a hundred-year retirement some people may want to take up new careers. So in the distant future colleges of a quite different kind from the present ones are going to have to be opened. Again, take marriage: are people – who will not be allowed to raise families, remember – going to be willing to take each other for life – knowing that that life need theoretically have no end? Somehow, I doubt it.'

Mehler smiled. 'Sorry – I seem to have wandered rather from your question. What I'm trying to say is that eventually, for all practical purposes, my drug will mean the virtual abolition of death. Which is going to be a pretty traumatic experience for mankind. Homo sapiens is going to have to be very gradually prepared for it. So it may be – oh, a decade, perhaps more, before the world is ready for LET. Though I've no doubt there'll be a small number of specially selected, valuable people – great brains nearing old age, for example – who will be given it much sooner than that, as soon as the authorities are satisfied the drug is safe.'

It was on the tip of Petros's tongue to ask if he and Paula could be among the specially selected few. But he restrained himself. The time wasn't ripe yet.

Mehler said: 'Of course, according to Julius – and to you – all this depends on your getting me out of the country safely. So you'd better not fail.'

Shortly after this Mrs Shenkar brought in tea and cakes. Petros and Mehler made conversation a little longer. Then Petros took his leave. He was driven by Shenkar to the railway station in Township N, took the train to the District Capital, got off, and returned to Township N by the next one back. He got home to the caravan just before nine.

One of the first things Petros did the following morning was to count his money. Then he consulted some notes he'd made at the airport the previous Friday, and put aside enough for two first-class daytime tickets to the furthest of the destinations which it might be necessary for him and Mehler to make for, and for two more tickets from there back home. It left him rather short. But he had to be on the safe side, and with care he thought he should just manage. He found himself, nevertheless, somewhat regretting his generosity to the girl at the farm.

Petros left the caravan at 10.30, walked to the town centre, and took an express coach to the District Capital. He didn't want his face to get too well-known around the railway station.

At the District Capital he started a tour of used car lots. He drew several blanks before he eventually found the sort of car he was looking for. It was a large, battered, and very old estate car, extremely dirty, with the seats gaping open, one headlamp cracked, and the tyres practically bald. He bought it – paying less then he'd allowed in his budgeting, and so was slightly in pocket.

Next he went to a motor cycle showroom and picked up a second-hand scooter in fairly good condition. For this he had to pay a little over the odds, which offset what he'd gained on the first deal.

He had the scooter loaded into the back of the estate car, ate a quick lunch, and afterwards went to the cheapest men's outfitters he could find and bought some more things to wear. Then he drove the estate car slowly and carefully back to Township N, took it to a public car park a few minutes drive from the caravan park, and left it there.

Except for the meeting with Mehler the following afternoon, there was now nothing to be done until Thursday. He could relax. Or, at least, try to.

Petros was in place in the centre of the copse in plenty of time on the Tuesday afternoon. Mehler arrived promptly. He walked up from his house by a more circuitous route than on the previous Saturday, so that there was no possibility of the guards going near the copse, and he did not this time need to use the ruse of asking for a light. Petros watched him stroll along the crest to the boulder and sit down in the same place as before, then whispered: 'I'm here. Everything all right?'

'I think so.'

'Got the Berrog papers?'

'Not yet. I'm going tomorrow.'

'So it'll be OK to make the break on Thursday?'

'I should be just about ready.'

'Good, what's the earliest you can leave the house?'

'Say 2.30.'

'Right. Now don't forget you've got to wear the same clothes as last Saturday: that blue jerkin affair you bought last week — it stands out well — the grey polo-necked sweater, grey trousers, and black shoes.'

'I know.'

'And something else I forgot to mention: obviously, you must wear a hat — any sort, but preferably one you can pull down to cover the back of your head and neck.'

'Understood.'

'Now I'm going to go over everything again. This will be the last chance to clear up any queries.'

13

Among Petros's own purchases at the District Capital had been a grey polo-necked sweater like Mehler's, and on the Thursday morning he donned it under his jacket. He tucked his revolver in his belt, and put some spare ammunition in his left-hand trouser pocket. He put all the remainder of his money in one hip pocket, and in the other his credentials. His right-hand trouser pocket he reserved for the key to the estate car. In the left-hand side pocket of his jacket he placed his compass, and in the inside pocket the credentials for Mehler.

These were in the name of Hugo Stohlmek, with an address in the Eighth District.

'A real man with a real address?' Petros had asked Alex.

'A fictional man. The address is the largest apartment block in the Eighth – one of the biggest in the country.'

'Surely that's a bit of a risk, isn't it? The police would only have to check to find out no such person lives there.'

'It wouldn't be quite that easy. There's a legal loophole which says that only the District, town or village, street, and number in street, have to be on ID cards, driving licences, and so on. Apartment numbers aren't necessary. So everybody who lives in that block – and there are more than four thousand of them – has exactly the same address on his or her ID card. Stohlmek is a common name in that part of the country, and there are sure to be several dozen Stohlmeks living in the block. If the police were to check, the only immediate information they'd be likely to get would be that no one called *Hugo* Stohlmek is an apartment *holder* – although I suppose it's even possible that there is one. It would take time to prove that the man who fits this card doesn't live there at all. Of course, they could find out the truth eventually; but if they take their enquiry that far it implies a fairly intensive investigation. And, as I said about your own papers, no cover we could devise would get him through that. These papers are just meant to get him past a routine check.'

Petros completed his preparations by putting on a cap and a pair of dark glasses, also purchased the previous day. He locked the caravan behind him and put the key in the right-hand pocket of the jacket.

He drove the hired saloon to the car park where he'd left the estate car and pulled up next to it. With considerable difficulty, he got the scooter out of the estate car and hoisted it half into the boot of the saloon. The other end rested on the open lid of the boot. He lashed it in place, then drove off in the direction of Village 127.

A couple of kilometres before he reached the village he pulled onto a lay-by near a narrow lane leading off the main road to the left. He turned the car round before getting out. He unlashed the scooter and lowered it to the ground, locked the saloon, and put the key in his right-hand jacket pocket, along with the key of the caravan.

Then, in a somewhat wobbly fashion at first, he rode the scooter back to the car park in Township N. Here, he reloaded the scooter into the estate car and yet again took the road to Village 127. He passed the saloon, still safely parked in the lay-by, went straight on into the centre of the village, and took the narrow road up to the moor.

The worn old engine had difficulty in making the steep first section; and after the road levelled off and swung south there were even worse problems. The surface was rough and loose, the vehicle large, heavy, and unwieldy, with sloppy steering, inefficient brakes, and nearly treadless tyres. When he came to the sharp bend, with just the frail wooden railings between him and the steep drop to the river below, he held his breath. But he got round safely, and then faced the trickiest part of the whole procedure. He pulled into the first passing place, and with infinite caution made what seemed to be about an eighteen-point turn. Then he opened the door, leaned out, and started reversing up the track. Now, in addition to all the previous difficulties, and the added handicaps both of going backwards and being on the 'wrong' side of the car, he had to contend with an even narrower track. At times his wheels were only centimetres from the edge, and

144

although the drop here was not so precipitous, it was still steep enough for him to be sweating freely when he eventually pulled into another passing place and stopped.

He got out, unloaded the scooter for the last time, locked the estate car, put the key back in his right-hand trouser pocket, and rode the scooter back down the track to the village.

He had an early lunch at the inn, then, stopping only to buy a box of matches and a packet of sweets in brightly-coloured wrappings at the village shop, rode back up to a point a little below the sharp bend with the wooden railings. He dismounted, lowered the scooter into the ditch, and covered it over with bracken. Then he walked up the track, past the estate car, still parked where he'd left it, and on about another forty metres. Here he clambered up the bank, took out his map and compass and studied them for a few moments, made a mental note of his exact position, climbed down the steep far side, and started walking.

As he went, he left a trail; not one that would be obvious to anyone else, but one he was confident he couldn't miss – matches, sweet papers, and half-smoked cigarettes.

Westward he went. Towards the overhanging rock with the cleft in the base.

The rock threw a black shadow like an enormous ink stain onto the short, coarse grass. The only sound was the distant song of a bird. The sun blazed down, but standing in the cleft of the rock, Petros could not feel its heat.

His jacket was over his arm, the dark glasses in the breast pocket. He threw down the fourth cigarette he had lit from the stub of a previous one and wiped his sweaty palms on the side of his trousers. He licked his lips, unwrapped a sweet, and put it in his mouth, crunching it vigorously. He glanced at his watch. Any time now.

He came forward out of the cleft, walked to the corner of the great rock, and peered round it, along the path through the hollow where Mehler would come. The glare of the sun hit him like an exploding flashbulb. He blinked several times, put his dark glasses on again, and had another look. Nothing. He drew back. He ran his fingers through his hair. He kept his eyes on the second hand of his watch as it made a complete circuit of the dial. Then he stepped forward and looked round the corner of the rock again. Still nothing.

Then he stiffened and stared. A moving figure. He waited. Yes — it was Mehler.

Petros dodged back behind the rock, holding his breath. He waited, staring at the corner of the rock, tensed for action.

Mehler came round it. He was dressed as on the Thursday, with the addition of a brown felt hat, the brim down all round. He saw Petros and came hurrying towards him, tearing off his blue jacket. He thrust it into Petros's hands and hissed: 'They're about a hundred metres behind.' His face was very pale.

Petros handed Mehler his own tweed coat. 'Your papers are in the inside pocket. Car and caravan keys in the right-hand one.'

'What's your name and address? There might be a routine check — they'd want to know who hired the car.'

'My name is Danton. There's a receipt from the hire people in the glove pocket, with my full name and address.'

'Right.' Mehler started to struggle into Petros's coat.

'Leave that till I'm gone. Hat — quick!' He tore off his cap. Mehler took it and handed Petros his hat. Petros rammed it onto his head. 'See you at the caravan,' he whispered, and turned away.

Mehler hissed: 'The glasses!'

Petros jerked them off, pushed them into Mehler's hand, then turned and ran off along the path pulling the hat down at the back as he did so. He had to make up the distance Mehler would have covered if he hadn't stopped. He took one glance behind and saw Mehler disappearing into the cleft.

Petros took the right-hand fork and continued upwards. Just before he got level with the top of the rock he slowed to a walk. He didn't know whether the guards could see him yet and he didn't dare look back. Would it work? Would they be fooled? If not, he'd know within minutes — seconds, probably.

Every muscle in his body tense, sweat on his face, and breathing heavily, Petros ambled on, waiting any moment for the sound of running footsteps approaching, for angry shouts. He slid his hand to his belt and fingered the butt of his revolver under his sweater. But no footsteps, no shouts, came.

He wasn't even sure they were behind him. They may have spotted the real Mehler and be after him now. The tension grew unbearable, the urge to look back just once irresistible. At last he could stand it no longer. He had to know.

He bent down and pretended to fix his shoelace. Keeping his head well down, he cast a lightning glance over his shoulder.

They were there! About seventy metres behind now, apparently quite unconcerned. Petros straightened up and walked on, fighting to keep down his elation. He didn't know whether they'd crossed behind the rock, or followed Mehler round the base. But it didn't matter. He'd fooled them! Now he had to keep it up. Mehler would be well along the left-hand path, down to the main road, by this time. But he wouldn't have reached the car yet. For the time being, all Petros had to do was keep walking – and not look back.

From the rock to the crest was a longer walk and a steeper climb than he'd realized when going the other way. In places, too, he had to go downhill, and in others make detours, to avoid a clump of trees or a steep-sided gully. So it took more time – and energy – than he had anticipated. But he didn't flag. Along rocky ridges he walked, through little glens, with the ground soft and marshy under foot, across high plateaux, where the turf was short and springy, always making towards the same point, following his own trail of sweet papers, matches, and cigarette ends. By the time the crest at long last came in sight his legs were aching numbly and his lungs were straining.

It suddenly occurred to him that there was no reason why he couldn't take a rest: the guards wouldn't come any closer – the real Mehler often stopped – and he ought, anyway, to get his breath and summon up his strength before the next, vital moves.

A stunted tree stood a little way ahead. Petros approached it and sank down onto the ground the far side of it from the guards. He leant up against it, making sure they could still see one shoulder and his leg sticking out. They mustn't think Mehler had vanished. Yet.

He decided to risk one more glance back. It would be as well to know how far away they were. He turned and peered round the tree trunk.

They weren't quite so close to him as they had been — probably eighty metres away. They were in the act of sitting down themselves. They were both big men, and had their coats off. He couldn't see their faces, but he was sure they were red and sweating. Did Mehler often take such energetic walks as this? They must hate his guts if he did. Well, though Petros was tired himself, they were certainly equally so. That was something.

Feeling surprisingly calm now, Petros closed his eyes and leaned his head back against the tree. For the hundredth time he mentally rehearsed what he had to do: walk casually up to the crest; stand on the very top for a few seconds, as though admiring the view of the mountains in the east. Then suddenly throw himself down the far side, and run like the devil to the estate car. Reach it, with luck, before the guards had hauled themselves up to the top of the crest. But make sure they clearly saw 'Mehler' running to the car and getting in. Then —

'Excuse me.'

Petros opened his eyes with a start.

A man was standing by him. A short, stocky man of about forty-five, with grizzled red hair and a rather cross expression. Petros got hurriedly to his feet. He stared stupidly, speechlessly at the man, his mind not working properly.

'I saw you apparently making towards the track,' the man said. 'So I assume you're going down to the village. Would you do me a favour?'

The guards wouldn't allow this. No one was permitted to approach Mehler. Any second they'd be rushing forward to investigate.

'No, I'm sorry.' Resisting the strongest impulse yet to look back, Petros started hurriedly forward again. Perhaps if he got away from the man quickly, the guards would relax again.

But the man started trotting alongside him. 'It won't take a

148

moment,' he said. 'I only want you to make a 'phone call for me.'

'I'm sorry, I can't. I'm in a terrible hurry.' For some reason it just didn't occur to him to say he wasn't going to the village.

'Well, I must say, you didn't seem to be. You were sitting down. And it *is* important. You see, my wife's expecting us home at five, but the children's damn dog has run off and they won't leave without it. Of course, I can't leave them up here alone – '

'Look, will you shut up and clear off.' Petros snapped the words, not even looking at the man. The guards would be running. They couldn't be more than seconds away by now.

'Well, really!' Angrily the man grabbed him by the shoulder and pulled. Petros wasn't prepared for this and was very nearly swung round. In a second he would have been looking straight towards the guards. But he tore himself free and managed to keep facing ahead.

Then three things happened almost simultaneously.

The red-haired man darted round in front of Petros and barked into his face: 'I'm not used to being spoken to like that.'

From behind – not more than fifty metres behind, Petros judged – came a shout: 'Hold it, you. Get away from him.'

And Petros punched the man on the jaw as hard as he could and started to run.

For a few seconds there was silence behind him. Then the same voice shouted again. 'It's all right, Doctor. We've got him.'

Petros kept on running.

The voice came again. 'Dr Mehler! Wait, sir, please. We've got to question this man.'

Then, when Petros still didn't stop, a second voice, hoarse and startled, shouted: 'Get after him! He's doing a bunk.'

Then there was silence again, and he knew they were saving their breath to chase. There were perhaps two or two-fifty metres to the crest. Uphill all the way. Rough, tussocky turf. He'd had a short start. His lead might be sixty or seventy metres. Not more.

Petros crashed on, straining every sinew in his body. His eyes were fixed on the point of the crest from which he'd started out. It seemed to get no nearer. He still didn't know how close the pursuit was. He was going to have to run to the car, get in, and start it. So he just had

149

to have a good lead when he went over the top. Ten or fifteen metres wouldn't do. But his lungs were bursting and his head pounding. He couldn't go any faster.

It was the last few paces that nearly finished him. It was much the steepest section of the whole route, and he took it on all fours. With a desperate effort, he dragged himself to the top and fell flat. Now at last he was able to take one more – and final – look back.

With a huge relief, he saw the guards were still forty metres below him; even though he'd had to slow down to take the final section while they continued at full speed. They'd gained hardly anything during the chase. And now *they* would have to slow down. He was still in with a chance.

Petros rolled and slithered down the far bank onto the track. He landed in a heap on the rough surface, scrambled to his feet, and started the last mad dash down the track towards the estate car.

He fell up against the side gasping for breath and fumbling in his pocket for the key. He got it out and jabbed at the lock. It wouldn't go in.

He nearly panicked as he heard the first of the guards stumbling down onto the track behind him. But at the same second the key went in. He tore the door open and tumbled into the car.

The heat struck him like a solid wall. He thrust the gear lever into neutral and released the handbrake. The car started to run forward. He glanced in the mirror. The guards were charging down the track, the leading one not more than thirty metres behind.

Petros turned on the ignition, stood on the clutch, pushed the gear into second, and lifted his foot again. But the engine didn't fire. The car jerked and nearly stopped.

Horror swept over him. He'd bungled it. If he'd been content to let the car coast, he'd have thrown the men off. He cast another terrified glance at the mirror. Now the first guard was only twenty metres away.

Petros had already stamped on the clutch again and the car, its gears disengaged, was picking up speed. But too slowly. The men were still gaining. He'd have to risk it once more.

He closed his eyes and again lifted his foot.

With a roar and a cloud of exhaust fumes the old engine sprang into life. The car shot forward. The guards, half-hidden by the smoke, still ran, but every second now they fell further back.

The car bounced and skidded down the track, Petros gripping the steering wheel like a limpet. He came to a slight curve, slowed, and took it carefully. Now for the first time he was out of guards' vision. He accelerated down the short straight leading to the sharp bend with the wooden railings. Just before he got to it he braked. The car slithered to a halt. Petros wound down both front windows, pushed the gear lever into neutral, opened the door, and took his foot off the brake. The car started to trundle forward, gathering speed. Petros held the wheel straight as the car coasted towards the corner. Then, at the very last second, he threw himself sideways out of the door. He fell sprawling onto the track, but was on his feet again as the car smashed through the railings and toppled over the edge.

For three seconds he watched it hurtling down the precipitous hill-side. Then, tearing his eyes away, he spun round and clambered up the bank on the left of the track, his fingers clawing into the turf. He hauled himself to the top, rolled away from the edge, and lay listening, praying he'd got the timing right – that the guards weren't too far behind to see the last part of the car's fall.

Then he heard running footsteps, startled exclamations, a moment's complete silence – and a distant splash. Petros froze, not daring even to pray for what he wanted to hear next.

A voice called: 'Come on!'

'We could break our necks going down there!'

'We're finished anyway, if we've lost him. There might be a chance to save him. We've got to try. Come on!'

There was a scrambling noise, an oath, then silence. Petros wriggled to the edge and peered over. In the river far below, the upturned wheels of the estate car were just sinking beneath the water. The two men were stumbling down towards it. As he watched, one fell and rolled. The other sat down and slid feet first, trying to control himself by grasping at clumps of turf.

Petros slithered back down to the track. Keeping well to the left, he ran to where he'd hidden the scooter. He dragged it out, pulled off Mehler's coat and hat, pushed them both into the ditch, jumped on the scooter, and rode sedately off down the hill.

It seemed too good to be true. But, in spite of the intervention of the red-haired man, everything had apparently turned out as he'd prayed it would. The guards were convinced they had seen Mehler run to a car, get in it, and drive off. They had seen the car plunge into a river. But they hadn't seen that the car was empty. They'd assumed Mehler was in it.

So for the time being there would be no manhunt, no watches kept at airports or at border checkpoints. Even when the police got divers down to the car and discovered that the body was missing, they might easily assume it had been swept away by the water. Only when Mehler's body failed to appear downstream would it be suspected that he hadn't, after all, perished.

By which time, with a bit of luck, Mehler and he would be out of the country.

Always provided Mehler had made it to the caravan in safety.

He must have got as far as the lay-by satisfactorily, at least, for the hire car had gone when Petros rode past. But how would he have got on for the rest of the drive, some of if through heavy traffic, after so many years away from the wheel?

This question nagged at Petros during all the ride back to Township N, and he stared round with anxious eyes when he rode into the car park at the caravan site.

The car was there, undamaged and properly parked. Petros breathed a sigh of relief, pulled up next to it, jumped off the scooter, and ran to the caravan.

Mehler had the only key. Petros rapped on the door with his knuckles.

There was no reply. He knocked again, louder. Still there was nothing. In a sudden panic, he rattled the handle.

The door opened in his hand.

Petros burst in. Then he stopped dead, a stab of fear piercing the pit of his stomach.

Mehler was lying on his side in Petros's bunk. His mouth was open. His face was grey and glistened with sweat. His eyes were closed. He showed not a flicker of life.

For perhaps ten seconds Petros stood staring helplessly, his brain not working. Then he gathered his wits and ran to the bunk, shouting

Mehler's name. But there was no response. He took Mehler by the shoulder and shook him. Nothing happened. He grabbed for Mehler's wrist. There was the faintest of pulses.

Petros shouted again. 'Mehler! Wake up!'

Then he slapped the pale face two or three times. The skin felt cold and clammy. Still Mehler didn't stir. Petros fetched some water and splashed it over his face, shouting his name all the time. But nothing had any effect. Mehler was unconscious.

Petros had just decided to fetch some whisky or cognac and try that, when he noticed a piece of paper with some writing on it lying on the floor by the bunk. He snatched it up. The words were scrawled in big, childish letters.

MY DISCOVERY – TESTED ON MYSELF – FAULTY – MAKES ME ILL – SEE THINGS – PASS OUT – FEEL ATTACK COMING – HOURS – SORRY – HAVEN'T GOT . . .

There were a few more words, but they were indecipherable. Petros screwed the paper into a ball, sank into a chair, and buried his head in his hands. Of all the evil luck! It wasn't fair. After all his efforts, all his planning, it just wasn't fair.

He simply could not think what to do. 'Hours'. What did that mean? Two? Three? Twelve? Suppose Mehler did not come round at all? He might not, without treatment. Yet to get medical help for him was impossible. Any doctor would almost certainly send him to hospital.

Petros racked his brains desperately. He couldn't possibly afford to wait in the hope that Mehler came to. So he had to get him out of the country as he was. But how? He would certainly never be allowed to take an unconscious man across the border by road – let alone on to an airliner.

That left only the helicopter. He could get Mehler on board that. Then make a dash for the frontier – and hope for the best. It was a terrifying prospect. If he started immediately it would be dark by the time he got to the farm. There was no radar or radio in the helicopter; and when he tried to cross the border he'd almost certainly be under fire. But it was the only way.

Petros looked at his watch. It was three-quarters of an hour since the estate car had gone into the river. They might have got divers down to it already. He had to get moving straight away.

The car and caravan keys which Mehler had had were lying on the table. Petros picked them up, ran to the car, drove it to the nearest garage, filled up with petrol and had his oil, battery, radiator, and tyres checked. He paid with some of the plane ticket money. He wouldn't be needing that now. He drove back to the caravan park and took the car right up to the door of the caravan.

Now there was the danger that somebody would see him lifting out what would look like a body, and would think it suspicious enough to call the police; but this was a chance he had to take. Only from the caravan next to his and the two opposite them could he be observed. He had seen little of the tenants of any of these, but he knew that the one next to his was occupied by a middle-aged couple, the one dead opposite by a family party with several young children, and the one next to that by two girls. Fortunately, at this moment all these people seemed to be out.

Petros hurried back inside the caravan. Mehler was still unconscious. Petros crammed all his own things haphazardly into his suitcase and rucksack, took them outside, and put them in the boot of the car. He went back into the caravan and took from the clothes cupboard the last of the purchases he had made the previous day – a black blazer. This had been meant for Mehler. But there was no time now for clothes switching. So he left his own coat on Mehler, put the blazer on himself, and transferred the gun from his belt, and some things from his overloaded trouser pockets, to the pockets of the blazer.

He was hungry and his throat was dry, so he grabbed a handful of biscuits and washed them down with water. Heaven knew when he'd get a chance to eat or drink again.

He made a quick but thorough search of the caravan to check that nothing was left, and was then ready to go. He wrapped Mehler in a blanket off the bunk, hoisted him onto his shoulder, and carried him out of the door and down the steps.

'Oh dear, what *is* the matter?'

It was a woman's voice. Petros turned slowly round. The middle-aged lady from next-door was not out after all; she was standing in the open doorway of her caravan.

Petros said: 'My friend's been taken ill – food poisoning, I think. I'm taking him to a doctor. I wonder – could you open the car door, please?'

'Why, yes, of course.' She came bustling across, uttering expressions of concern.

'It's locked. You'll have to lean through the driver's door and open it from the inside.' She did so. Petros turned round, bent at the knees, and with the woman's help, lowered Mehler onto the back seat. 'Thank you. Could you just keep an eye on him for a moment, please? I must get another blanket.'

As he turned and ran back up the steps of the caravan, he saw the woman lean through the car door and bend over Mehler. Good: at least she'd know now that he wasn't dead. He picked up the cap and dark glasses from the floor where Mehler had let them fall, snatched up another blanket, and was finally ready to leave. He was stealing both blankets, but the extra week's rent he'd paid would more than cover the cost. He cast a last quick glance round and went out, slamming the door after him. The woman turned an anxious face towards him.

'He really looks awfully ill. I hope he'll be all right.'

'So do I.' He put the second blanket over Mehler and shut the door. 'Thank you for your help.' He jumped into the driving seat, raised a hand in acknowledgement to the woman, and drove out of the caravan park for the last time.

The traffic was heavy at this time of day and through the town he had to stop frequently. At every set of traffic lights and every hold-up he was apprehensive that someone in a nearby bus or car, or a foot policeman, might spot Mehler lying like a corpse in the back. Round every corner he expected to see a road block ahead. Once out of town and on the freeway he breathed more easily. He was able to keep his foot hard down, and he made good time. The kilometres flashed by. Mehler lay silent and motionless, but whenever Petros put his arm over the back of the seat and groped for the wrist, he felt a flickering pulse.

Three endless hours passed, and Petros realized he was getting low

155

on petrol. He pulled onto the verge, sat Mehler up, leaned him against the side, and put the cap and dark glasses on him. He drove on to the next filling station and when the attendant came stood up against the rear side window, chatting to him as he filled the tank, and blocking his view of the interior of the car as far as possible. The man didn't seem to notice anything amiss.

Petros drove on. It grew dark. He was out of the 45th now and half way across the 44th. With every kilometre that passed his fear of being stopped receded further. His worries now were Mehler's condition and the prospect of the actual flight. He tried not to anticipate this and forced himself to think instead about success: home, Paula, the immortality drug, naturalization, the wiping out of his past, a new job, freedom from fear of the Chairman's revenge –

The Berrog papers! He'd forgotten about them.

Inexplicably, crazily, the trauma and confusion of Mehler's illness had driven them right from his mind. Had Mehler got hold of them? Were they on him now?

Petros had to know. He drew into the side, stopped, switched on the interior light, leaned over the back of the seat, and started hurriedly to search Mehler's pockets. His fingers encountered a thick wad of paper in the inside pocket, and excitedly he pulled it out. Then he swore and threw it down. It was his own map, which he'd left there. He went rapidly through the rest of the pockets: the false credentials, out of their envelope, a pen, notecase, pipe, tobacco and matches, a handkerchief, some small change – and a small phial of pinkish liquid. The elixir.

Petros held the phial up and stared wonderingly at it for a few seconds; but at this moment the Berrog papers were even more important to him, and he put it back. There was nothing else in the pockets. Then he felt something stiff under Mehler's sweater. He pulled the sweater up and revealed a manilla folder tucked into the waistband of Mehler's trousers. Petros gave a gasp of relief and drew it out. He opened it. A moment later he gave a groan of despair. The folder contained nothing but four or five sheets of plain foolscap paper, each covered with writing and figures in black ballpoint, all in the same hand. They were Mehler's own notes.

The Berrog papers weren't on him.

Perhaps they were somewhere in the car. Petros started a frantic hunt – in the glove pockets, under the front seats and down inside the rear one, on the parcel shelf, even under the carpet. But it was unavailing.

Petros straightened up. With a hand that shook slightly he took out a cigarette and lit it. He sat for minutes, engulfed by a terrible wave of despair and defeat. Then he somehow managed to pull himself together and think.

Only Mehler knew where the Berrog papers were. Mehler was unconscious. Without treatment, he might die. If he died, the papers would be lost to Petros for ever. Mehler had to be brought round. That meant a doctor.

There was only one hope. To ring the emergency number.

It would probably put him back hours. There was no guarantee that Mr Pelli's friends would be able to get hold of a 'safe' doctor. Or even that a doctor would do any good. But it was his only chance. And, luckily, the number *was* on the 44th exchange.

Petros drove on to the next filling station. He parked away from the pumps, in shadow, ran to the public telephone, and dialled. The ringing tone buzzed only twice. Then a man's voice said: 'Hullo.'

Petros pushed a coin into the slot. 'Is that – is that Mr Pelli's friend?' 'Yes.'

'He gave me your number. He said I could ring you if I needed help.'

'What help do you need?'

'I'm trying to get a man out of the country – on Mr Pelli's behalf. The guy's been taken ill – he's in a coma. He needs a doctor. But I can't go to one because the police are after us – or will be soon. Can you – do anything?' He knew talking so openly on the 'phone was a fearful risk. He just had no choice.

'Where are you?' the man asked.

'On Freeway 9. In the middle of the 44th – about thirty kilometres from the District Capital.'

'Wait a moment.' The line went dead. Petros waited, gnawing at his lip, his left hand twisting and squeezing the telephone wire. The

157

voice came back. 'Drive straight to the 44th District Capital. Go to the goods entrance at the rear of the City Hotel in 7th Street. Someone will be waiting for you there. Got that?'

'Yes.'

'What sort of car are you driving?'

'A BFR one and half litre saloon – dark blue.'

'Right. You will be contacted. Good-bye.'

There was a click. Petros stood, the receiver still to his ear, stunned with relief. He could hardly believe the conversation had taken place. It had been so quick, so easy, the response so immediate.

He rang off and ran back to the car.

It was eleven o'clock when he got to the District Capital, but already the city seemed dead, with few cars on the roads and fewer pedestrians. 7th Street was away from the centre of the city, in an ill-lit, seedy-looking area towards the railway station. Petros had no difficulty finding it. Streets in all the District Capitals were numbered on the same plan. He drove slowly along, looking for the City Hotel.

Soon he saw it – a grim-looking, nineteenth century building on the right of the street, standing on a corner next to a school. Petros drove past the front of it, turned right along the side of the hotel, and right again to get round to the back. The street behind was narrow and unlit. On the left was a tall, modern building, probably an office block. The rear of the hotel was in darkness, except for a dim light seeping through a small fanlight over what, when he got close enough to see, turned out to be double doors. Petros pulled up outside them. He turned off his engine and lights, and waited.

For quarter of a minute nothing happened. Then a chink of light showed between the doors, widened, narrowed again, and the figure of a small man darted up to the car. Petros wound down the window. The man bent down to Petros's level and spoke in a low voice.

'On Mr Pelli's work?'

'Yes.'

'Where's the patient?'

'In the back.'

'Let's get him inside.'

Together they half-carried, half-dragged Mehler across the narrow pavement and in through the double doors.

'Hang on to him for a second,' the little man said, and while Petros supported Mehler, he closed and locked the doors, pocketing the key.

From where they were standing, four stone steps with an iron handrail led up to a dimly-lit, bare, stone-floored corridor. They carried Mehler up the steps and walked a short way along the corridor to some sliding doors on the left. The little man said: 'Stop here. We'll take the service lift.' He pressed a button, and Petros heard the lift descending. The door opened automatically. They carried Mehler in and propped him up in the corner. The little man pressed a button marked '2', and the lift started upwards.

There was a light inside, and Petros got his first close look at the little man. He was about fifty, with closely-cropped black hair and dark, darting, birdlike eyes. He was dressed in a navy blue uniform with silver buttons.

'You're the porter here, are you?' Petros asked.

'Night porter. Boris is the name.' He was looking concernedly at Mehler. 'What's wrong with him?'

'I don't know. Poisoning of some sort, I think.'

The lift stopped. The porter pulled back the doors and peered out. 'All clear,' he said.

They lifted Mehler out. Straight ahead of them was another corridor, quite short, with linoleum on the floor and papered walls. They carried Mehler along it and at the end turned right. Now they were in a much longer corridor, with a carpeted floor. Doors led off both sides, lights showing under some of them.

The corridor seemed endless, Mehler to increase in weight with every step. But finally Boris stopped outside a door on the left, which bore the number 277. The porter didn't knock, just turned the knob, and they went in. Petros looked around. They were in a sitting-room, dingily equipped with old-fashioned dark wood furniture.

Then his eyes lighted on the man who was standing in front of the big open fireplace, and he gave an involuntary gasp.

It was the physician.

14

Petros gaped at the physician. '*You*! What are you doing here?'

'Explanations later.' He came across the room and took Mehler's weight from Petros. 'Bring him into the bedroom,' he said to Boris.

They took Mehler through a door in the right-hand wall and closed it after them. Petros half staggered to an armchair and fell into it. A blessed sense of relief swept over him. Tremendous problems still confronted him; but the immediate one had been lifted from him. For the moment, responsibility for Mehler was no longer his. It might become so again; but for a little while, at least, he could relax.

A few seconds later the door to the adjoining room opened again and the porter came back. He closed it behind him and walked quietly, almost on tip-toe, to Petros's chair. He spoke softly.

'He says he isn't to be disturbed whatever happens. He's going to do what he can for your friend, but it might take some time and he can't promise anything.'

Petros nodded mutely.

'He suggested you might want something to eat.'

'I could do with something.' In twelve hours he'd had only a few biscuits, but he hadn't realized until now just how hungry he was.

'I'll see what I can do.'

'Thanks very much.'

Boris went out, and Petros closed his eyes. The chair was hard and the springs were sticking up, but it felt wonderful. The questions and worries that should have been filling his mind seemed suddenly unimportant. All he wanted was rest.

He stayed like that, his mind blank, for some five minutes, then opened his eyes with a start as Boris came back into the room. He was carrying a tray. He came across and put it down on a small table near

Petros's chair. It contained a plate of sandwiches, a pot of coffee, and a cup. Petros sat up. 'Thanks a lot.'

'I can't stop. If you want me, there's a telephone over there. I'll be near the switchboard all night.'

Petros said: 'I'm very grateful – for everything.'

'No need to be. We're both on the same side, aren't we?'

He went out, and Petros fell to on the sandwiches. They were filled with some kind of highly-flavoured spread. But they tasted good to Petros, and so did the coffee.

He finished the sandwiches, poured himself a second cup of coffee, and lit a cigarette. He felt relaxed and content. Crazy, really because his situation was no less perilous now than it had been half an hour ago. It was just that the mere presence of a familiar face, and that of a man whom, from the first, he had sensed he could rely on and whom he could consult, made it seem so.

Petros glanced at his watch. It was past midnight. He stubbed out his cigarette, kicked off his shoes, sank down into the chair, and went immediately to sleep.

He awoke with a jerk and looked round the room in alarm. But nothing had changed. He rubbed his eyes, and ran his fingers through his hair. He felt cold and stiff. He glanced at his watch and gave a slight start. Two-thirty: he'd been asleep for two and a half hours. And the physician must have been in the other room with Mehler for three. He felt a pang of anxiety. Pointlessly, he looked at the bedroom door. Then he heard a faint sound beyond it. He stiffened.

The door slowly opened and Mehler walked through.

Petros leapt to his feet with an exclamation of amazement. Mehler's face was still pale, but his step was steady and he was smiling. 'Hullo, chum,' he said. 'Seems I gave you a bit of bother.'

Petros stammered: 'How – how do you feel?'

'Better, thanks. Much better.

'I thought you were a goner.'

'I did for a while, too, before I passed out.'

The physician followed Mehler through the door. He looked pale and desperately tired. Petros stared at him anxiously. 'Are you all right?'

'I shall be.'

'What on earth are you doing here?'

'He sent me.'

'Mr Pelli? When?'

'A few days ago.'

'But why? He couldn't have known Mehler was going to be ill.'

'There were others here who needed help – who could not call on any local doctor.'

'Oh, I see. And have you finished this other work?'

'Nearly.'

'So what are your plans now? Are you coming with us?'

'That depends on what your moves are going to be.'

'Frankly, I don't know yet. I want to talk it over with both of you.'

'I don't think I can help. This is your assignment. So the decisions must be yours. I don't want to influence you.'

It was a bit of a blow to have full responsibility thrust so suddenly back onto him, but Petros didn't attempt to argue. He turned to Mehler. 'How much do you know about the general position?'

'Well, the doctor and I had quite a chat after I came round. He's explained a lot of things.'

'Then perhaps you can guess what I want to know first: where are the Berrog papers?'

'Oh, I'm terribly sorry I wasn't able to bring them. I was just too ill to go for them yesterday. I didn't think I'd even be able to make the break today. This morning I was better and I decided to try it, after all. By then, of course, there was no time to get them. I'm afraid I've let you down.'

'Never mind about that now. Just tell me where they are.'

'In my sister's house – Township 44/D, about fifty kilometres from here; 148 South-East Avenue is the address. They're in a trunk with a lot of other old documents – scientific papers, letters, diaries, and so on. I didn't want the bother of dragging it to the 45th when I moved two years ago, so I asked Elsa if I could store it in her attic.'

Petros sat down slowly. He said: 'The authorities will know by now that you've defected. The first thing they'll have done is put a watch on her house.'

'Could I 'phone her — ask her to meet me somewhere with the Berrog papers?'

'They'll have tapped her telephone.'

'Well, *I* don't have to go. You go. I'll give you a note for her.'

'Thanks, but I don't want to be picked up, either.'

'You wouldn't be. Listen: Martin — my brother-in-law — is a dentist. They live over his surgery. Patients are trooping in and out of the house all day long. If the cops are watching the place they'll probably ask for your ID card, but if that's in order you'll be all right. They couldn't possibly run extensive checks on everyone who calls.'

'But the others would all be registered patients. I'm not. That would make me suspect from the start.'

'Not necessarily. If you're challenged just say you're on holiday in the area. That would tie up with the address on your card. Tell them you've got a raging toothache and you want some emergency treatment.'

Petros hesitated. Then: 'All right. I'll do it. But you'd better let me have your new ID card before I leave.'

Mehler looked surprised. 'Why?'

'Because the name on my card is Frederic Danton. The cops will soon tie that name in with your disappearance. For a start, when they recover the estate car they'll find Frederic Danton is the registered owner of it. It won't take them long to clear the real Danton and realize there's a false one as well. They're bound to take the name of everyone who calls at your brother-in-law's place. And if they find the name Frederic Danton among them, your sister's going to be in trouble.'

Mehler said: 'Silly of me. I should have seen it. But listen — won't she be in equally bad trouble when they find that one of the visitors had false papers — was a man who doesn't officially exist?'

'I don't think they will find that out. As you yourself said, the police are not going to run extensive checks on everyone who calls there. They won't give each name to the Ministry of Internal Affairs to find out if that person really does exist. Even if they check the apartment block it will be some time before they can be sure no Hugo Stohlmek lives there.'

He explained briefly what Alex had told him when first showing him Mehler's credentials, then continued: 'So my guess is that they'll just check the names with their own records and once they find that nobody called Hugo Stohlmek has a criminal record, or history of subversive activities, or known connection with you, then they won't bother any more about him. But even if I'm wrong and by some chance they do find out he doesn't exist – well, there'd be no evidence he had anything at all to do with you; so your sister and her husband would still be in the clear. All that the cops could prove would be that a man carrying a false ID card had called at the house. And neither of them could be held responsible for that.'

Mehler nodded. 'OK, then. You'd better take the driving licence, too.'

Petros said: 'This means we won't be able to cross the frontier until tomorrow night.'

'Why not? Do we have to go at night? I take it we'll be going by helicopter: wouldn't that be easier in daylight?'

'Maybe. But we'd also be a sitting target for the border guards.'

'What sort of armament have they got?'

'Machine gun emplacements at intervals of five hundred metres. The foot patrols carry rifles.'

'No anti-aircraft guns?'

'No. The guards aren't there to stop aircraft. There are missiles for that. And anyway, *they're* designed to destroy attacking aircraft approaching the country.'

'There we are, then.' Mehler spoke excitedly. 'I'll risk machine guns five hundred metres apart, rather than try to get over in the dark.'

'You may have a point. It'll be hairy either way, but I'm willing to go by daylight if you are. How long will it take me to get to your sister's place? About an hour?'

'I should think so.'

'And what time does your brother-in-law start surgery?'

'Nine, I believe.'

'Then I'll leave here at eight. You'll stay here, of course — out of sight. With luck, I could be back by ten thirty. We'll set out for the farm where the helicopter's hidden straight away. We should get there by late afternoon.' He turned to the physician. 'Right, we've made our plans. Now what about you?'

'I'll come with you, if I may. I'll go now and finish my other work, then come back in the morning and stay with our friend here while you go for the papers.'

A minute later he left. After he'd gone, Mehler tentatively mentioned food. Petros rang Boris and asked if some could be brought up. While they were waiting he quickly told Mehler the events of the previous day. Boris arrived with another tray of coffee and sandwiches, and while Mehler ate and drank, Petros went downstairs, and Boris let him out of the goods entrance to fetch his suitcase from the car — he'd want a shave and a clean shirt in the morning. He brought the case inside. Then Boris suggested he moved the car.

'There's no parking out there, officially,' he said, 'only unloading. Besides, some deliveries are made very early and you might obstruct the vans. And we don't want to draw attention to your car.' He directed Petros to an open space a couple of hundred metres away where long-term parking was allowed. 'You can come in by the front entrance afterwards,' he added. 'I'll take your case through to the lobby and you can pick it up there.

Petros did as suggested.

When he got back he asked Boris to call them at 7.15 and to take up some coffee and rolls at 7.30. Then he went back up to Room 277, locked the door, and went into the bedroom. It contained two single beds. Mehler was lying on one in his shirt and trousers, smoking his pipe and staring at the ceiling.

He pointed to Petros's jacket, which was lying on the other bed. 'You'd better have that back. I've emptied the pockets, except for the Stohlmek papers.'

'Thanks.' Petros took off the blazer, emptied the pockets, and threw it across to Mehler. Then he had a wash at the basin, kicked off his shoes, slipped his gun under the pillow, and lay down on the second bed, covering himself with the eiderdown. Suddenly he felt

165

wide awake, so got out his cigarettes and lit one.

Mehler said: 'What are our chances?'

'I don't know.'

'I must admit I'm frightened.'

'You *want* to get away now, do you? When I first spoke to you up on the moors last Saturday, you didn't seem all that interested.'

'I know. I thought I was going to die. I'd just had my third attack – the worst of all. I knew the next would probably kill me – and I was expecting it any minute. My only chance was to see a doctor immediately. Then I got your note, and, later in the day, met you, and read Julius's letter. If I went to a doctor, I'd be sent to hospital, lose the opportunity of going with you – and eventually be murdered by the government. But it was going to be several days before we could make the break, and I thought I'd probably have a fatal attack before then. There seemed no way out. It was grim knowing I was going to give man real life for the first time in his existence – and yet die myself in the process. Then, when the attack still hadn't come by the time you arrived on the Sunday afternoon, I thought that perhaps I was going to be all right after all, and I was able to take a little more interest. Monday and Tuesday I was all right, too. Then, yesterday . . .' Mehler tailed off.

'But you feel all right now, do you?'

'Yes, pretty good.'

'What exactly did he do for you?'

'I've no idea. I just came to with him standing over me. Then we talked. He seems to be completely in this Pelli man's confidence. He added a lot to Julius's letter – about the Chairman's plans, and why it was essential he didn't get control of LET. And about a lot of other things as well.'

'Did you never realize before what sort of men you were planning to give your secret to?'

'Not really. Oh, I knew they were no saints. I knew they were schemers. I knew they were power-hungry. But what politicians aren't?'

'But even after you read Berrog's papers and learned the truth about that germ warfare experiment?'

'I've never blamed the government for that. They took the majority advice of the committee.'

'But they were quite prepared for people to die in that village.'

'So he told me just now. I must admit that I didn't realize that from reading Berrog's papers. I thought it was just that they hadn't appreciated the danger. Perhaps I blinded myself to the truth. Actually, when you come to think of it, it's pretty obvious that there would have to be deaths. But frankly, I've never given it a lot of thought. I never attached much importance to the papers. I read them when they first came to me, and then put them away. Their strategic value didn't occur to me. I certainly wouldn't have left them with Elsa if it had. Anyway, I never imagined myself wanting to pressurize the government.'

'And you never suspected what they would want to do with your discovery? Or that your own life would be in danger?'

'I suppose subconsciously I must have known something was wrong. In a way, I've felt vaguely uneasy for quite a time now – even though I had everything I wanted. I told myself that it was the constant surveillance which was getting me down; but there was more to it than that. When you contacted me and gave me Julius's letter, nothing that he said or you told me surprised me. It was as though I'd known it all along. And incidentally, I'd like to thank you for all you've done.'

This was too good an opportunity for Petros to miss. 'My motives are largely selfish,' he said. 'I want something in return. You said it might be a decade before the drug is available to the general public.'

'Yes, possibly longer.'

'Except for a few, specially selected people?'

'That's right. I'm thinking of ageing scientists, statesmen – people like that.'

'Well, what I wanted to ask was, if I get you back safely, can my wife and I be among those few? We're neither of us particularly valuable, or great brains, but if the world at large does get the benefit of your drug, I suppose I'll be able to claim at least a small part of the credit. I don't want to use up another ten or fifteen years of my life-expectancy before I start taking it.'

'Well, of course you won't have to wait. Naturally, I'll arrange immediate supplies for my friends, and for all the people involved in getting me out – plus their immediate families.'

'Thanks very much. I appreciate it.'

'You'll probably have to promise to keep quiet about it, if we don't want to cause trouble. Because, as I said, the only other people getting it so soon will be those who really need it, and they'll all be from the older age groups. Of course, it'll be years before those who are young now will need it. Apart from those chosen for experimental purposes, kids will be allowed to grow naturally to adulthood before being issued with it.'

'What do you mean "experimental purposes"?'

'Well, for example, it would be fascinating to retard the growth of some children for a long period: imagine human beings with thirty-five or forty years of life behind them, but with the bodies and brain sizes of children of ten. What sort of people would they be? Again, there are eventually going to be an awful lot of women around with frustrated maternal instincts. Well, assuming it does become possible to increase the factor by which ageing is slowed above five, why not have a sort of pool of more or less permanent babies? Any woman who wanted one could have one to look after for a couple of years. I think that in time the average woman is going to get tired of a baby that hardly grows at all, and will be prepared to hand it back to somebody else to care for. That's the sort of thing I meant.'

'It's fascinating,' Petros said. 'So was everything you told me on Sunday. I hadn't begun to realize all the implications of this drug.'

'I didn't myself for a long time. Anyway, I've said enough now. Shall I put the light out?'

The morning was raw and grey and there was a fine drizzle in the air when at five minutes to nine the next day, Petros turned into South-East Avenue in Township D. It was a quiet residential road for professional people, long and straight, and flanked by detached three-storey houses. He drove along to the first side turning, pulled into it, and parked. Then he got out and started walking. By now, the police just might be looking for his car.

He had quite a long walk before he reached number 148. His mouth was dry and his heart beating fast. Several cars were parked near the house. He drew close enough to read the brass plate on the gate post. 'M. VANDAR. DENTAL SURGEON'. Then he noticed that in one of the cars, a large black saloon, two men were sitting. Petros's step faltered for a second, then he took a deep breath and forced himself to walk on. He reached the gate and put his hand out to open it. Then: 'Hold it.'

Petros stopped and turned. The door of the black car had opened and one of the men was getting out. He strolled along the pavement, a thin man of medium height, with short fair hair, and wearing a navy blue suit.

Petros allowed himself to look a little annoyed. 'You talking to me?'

'What's your business in this house?'

'What the devil's that got to do with you?'

'Security Police.' He held a warrant card under Petros's nose for a second.

Petros immediately adopted a conciliatory attitude. 'Oh, I'm sorry, sir.'

'Well?'

'I – I want to see the dentist.'

'Got an appointment?'

'No. I – '

'ID card.' The man held out his hand.

Petros fumbled in his pocket, produced the Shenkar card, and handed it over. The man opened it and his eyebrows went up. 'What are you doing so far from home?'

'I'm on my vacation.'

'Staying where?'

'On my way to the 43rd by coach. But this damned toothache came on during the night. So I stopped off to try to see a dentist. Chap in a café suggested Mr Vandar. Said he'd sometimes see patients who weren't registered with him. I thought my best chance would probably be just to turn up here.'

'Where's your luggage?'

'At the bus station.'

'Let's see the receipt.'

Petros produced this, thanking his lucky stars for the hunch that had led him to drop his suitcase off there on his way through the town centre. The man glanced at it, then handed it back, eyeing him keenly. 'You frightened of something, Stohlmek?'

Petros gave a weak smile. 'Well, yes. Dentists. You know. Always have been. Silly, really, I know.'

'Very well.' The policeman handed back the identity card, turned, and returned to his car without another word.

His features set firmly, Petros opened the gate and walked up the path on legs that felt made of rubber.

There was a notice on the door, saying 'Ring and Enter. Petros put his hand on the bell, in case the police could see him from the car, but he didn't press it. Then he turned the knob, opened the door, and went quietly in. Immediately facing him on the left was a door marked 'Private'. It was evidently at the bottom of a flight of stairs, though it hid these from view. To the right of the stairs was a short passage running towards the back of the house. At the far end of this was another door, bearing the word 'Surgery'. On his immediate right was a third door. The plaque on this read 'Waiting Room'. Anyone in there might have seen him coming up the path. But that couldn't be helped now.

Petros tiptoed to the door at the foot of the stairs. A bell-push was set into it. He looked to the right, along the passage. A wooden partition had been built up outside the bannister, completely dividing the ground floor from the rest of the house.

Petros stood uncertainly for a moment. Then he gave a start as there came a muffled but high-pitched whining sound from the end of the passage. He had a moment of panic before relaxing fractionally. It was a dentist's drill. And it meant that probably no one would be leaving either surgery or waiting room for several minutes.

Quickly, Petros jabbed at the bell-push. He heard the bell ring, far away at the top of the house. At that moment the drill stopped and there was complete silence. He stood, every muscle tensed. If Martin had heard the bell, if he came into the hall and asked what Petros wanted . . . . There'd be a patient in the surgery, probably a nurse. They'd be able to hear every word. He wouldn't be able to explain . . .

The drill started up again. There was no sound from above. Petros risked another stab at the bell-push.

Then he heard footsteps on the stairs, coming down slowly. The door opened.

A small, dumpy woman of about forty-five, with a pink, round, frightened face, whispered: 'Yes?'

Quietly, Petros said: 'Mrs Elsa Vandar?'

She nodded, her eyes big.

'I've got a message from your brother Thomas.'

She stared as though frozen, not reacting at all. He was about to repeat the words, when her hand went to her mouth, and he knew she understood.

'Can I come in?' he asked urgently.

'You – you know where Thomas is?'

'Yes.'

She licked her lips. 'Then you'd better tell the police. They're looking for him. You must have seen them outside.'

'I've got a letter from him.' He drew a sealed envelope from his pocket and held it out to her. She took it with a hand that shook slightly, tore it open, and started scanning the letter.

'Let me in, please,' he said. 'It's dangerous here.'

She made up her mind quickly. 'Very well.' She stood to one side. 'Go on up.'

He went past her, up the stairs. He heard her close the door quietly and start to follow him. He reached the top, turned, and waited for her. He noticed she was breathing heavily when she got to the landing.

She said: 'We'd better go into the kitchen. The sitting-room overlooks the street. The police in the car might see us, and I daren't draw the curtains.'

She led the way into a bright, modern kitchen, and said: 'Sit down.' She pulled out an upright chair from against the table. Petros sat down. He watched her face as she stood, reading the letter, her lips moving silently. At last, she lowered it and looked straight at him. 'Where is Thomas?'

'I don't think I ought to tell you that – for your own safety.'

'Is he safe?'

'At the moment.'

'Who are you?'

'I've been hired to get him out of the country.'

'Why?'

'His life is in danger here, Mrs Vandar. He's made a very important scientific discovery – '

'I know.'

'You know what it is?'

'No. Just that it's going to be of great benefit to mankind.' The words sounded unnatural to her, and Petros guessed she was quoting her brother verbatim.

'It won't be if the government have their way. They're determined to keep it in their own hands. Thomas is equally determined it's going to be given to the world. The government will kill him to prevent this. That's why he's got to get out.'

Mechanically, she pulled another chair out from the table and sank onto it. Her face had paled. She said: 'I'm sorry about just now – telling you to go to the police. I thought you might be one of them – that it was a trap to make me admit I knew where he was. They came last night – questioned us for hours. They're stopping everyone who comes to the house.'

'Thomas explains in the letter why I've come?'

'You want some papers out of the trunk he left here.'

'You've still got it?'

She nodded. 'It's in the attic.'

'And the papers haven't been disturbed? The police didn't go through it?'

'No. I don't suppose they knew about it.'

'Then can I look for the papers he wants?'

'I'll take you up.'

172

She led him up to the top floor, to a small lumber-room at the back of the house. She pointed to an old, battered, brass-bound cabin trunk in the corner. 'That's it.'

Petros dragged it to the centre of the room and opened it. It was full of notebooks, diaries, bundles of letters, folders, large, bulging envelopes, a lever-arch file, and several cardboard wallets. There must have been hundreds of papers His heart sank. Unless he was lucky, this could take an hour.

'Do you know what these papers look like?' she asked.

'I think so. The trouble is he couldn't remember if they were in an envelope, or a folder, or what.'

He started going through the trunk. Elsa said: 'Do you mind if I leave you to it? I want to write a letter for you to take to Thomas.'

'Go ahead.'

She went out and he heard her going down the stairs. He waited ten seconds, then sidled along the passage and half way down the top flight of stairs himself. From here he could see the first floor landing and the top of the stairs leading to the ground floor. She might not have believed him – might have been stringing him along to get a chance to call the police.

It was all right. She neither went down the stairs, nor did he hear her on the 'phone. He worried for a moment, in case she was signalling from the front room window; but after five minutes had passed with nothing happening he decided she was trustworthy and went back to the lumber-room.

It took him nearly half an hour to find the papers. They were folded together in a large manilla envelope. Among them were carbon copies of several letters, apparently sent by Berrog to various departments and officials; of Berrog's original report to the government; half a dozen lined sheets, clipped together and covered with small, neat handwriting in black ink, every sheet initialled 'CB' and the last one signed 'Conrad Berrog' – clearly Berrog's account of the whole affair; and a short, typewritten letter, on heavy paper, with an embossed heading 'From the Office of the Chairman', and addressed to Berrog. There was no time to read it. Petros stuffed the papers back in the envelope and put the envelope in his pocket. He closed the trunk, pushed it back into the corner, and went downstairs. Elsa was waiting for him on the landing, an envelope in her hand.

'Did you find what you wanted?'

He nodded.

'Will you give this to Thomas, please?'

'If I'm arrested the police will find it. Sure you want to take the risk?'

'Quite sure, thank you. I didn't put his name on it anyway. And it's very guarded.'

'As you wish.' He took the envelope from her and put it in his pocket with the other one. He said: 'That letter I gave you from him – you ought to destroy it.'

She hesitated, then said quietly: 'It'll probably be the last I'll ever get from him.'

'It could be very dangerous.'

She gave a sad sigh. 'All right. If you say so.'

'Good. Now – I told the police outside I was coming to see your husband for treatment. Will you tell him that if they check later, to say he did see a Hugo Stohlmek this morning – that I wasn't a registered patient, but a visitor to the area?'

She hesitated. 'That would be awkward. He has to keep records of everybody he treats, and the dental work he does on them. If they *are* suspicious of you, they're sure to ask to see your NP form and record card.'

'I see.' Petros thought hard.

Elsa said: 'If you like, he could actually give you some treatment – fill a tooth or something. Then he could make out a form and record card – which would confirm your story.'

He shook his head. 'Hugo Stohlmek's only a pseudonym. At the moment the police have got nothing on either of you. All they could prove was that I called at the house and left again. But if your husband actually enters false details in his records – which I would guess is an offence, even if it's done innocently – and they later discover Hugo Stohlmek doesn't exist, it'll give them just the excuse they need to question you both. No, in view of what you say, I think the best story will be that he couldn't fit me in – that I waited half an hour, but then got fed up and decided to try someone else. That's what *I'll* tell them if they stop me. Can you get your husband to confirm that I did try to see him?'

'Better still, I can get Sonia, his receptionist, to confirm it.'

'You can trust her?'

'Yes.'

'Right. That's settled.'

'Do you think you will get past the police outside? Could they have found out by now that you're using a false name?'

'I don't think they'll have had time. All they might have done is check their own records. And that'll give them a negative result. So they'll have no *more* reason for suspecting me than when I came in here. Anyway, I'll soon find out. I must go now. Sorry if I frightened you. Don't give up hope of seeing Thomas again. This government may not last much longer. The country could be free again soon. What he's doing might help make it so. He'll be able to come home when it happens.'

'I'll try to believe you're right. Thank you for helping him. You must be a very brave man.'

'I'm far from that, Mrs Vandar,' he said awkwardly. 'Now – will you come to the bottom of the stairs with me, please, and see if the hall is empty?'

She went down in front of him, opened the door at the bottom, looked around outside, and beckoned him. He ran lightly down the stairs, whispered 'Good-bye,' and went quickly through the hall and out of the front door.

He took a deep breath and started down the path. He tried to compose his features into an expression of irritation or impatience, but felt sure that he looked only frightened. Which wasn't surprising.

He reached the gate. The black car hadn't moved. The same two men were in it. He didn't look at them, but opened the gate, went out onto the pavement, closed the gate after him, and walked briskly off. There was no challenge.

After a hundred metres he stopped and lit a cigarette. He was shaking all over and longed to sit down. He couldn't quite believe he'd got away with it.

Unless – Unless they had already discovered he was using false papers, and were letting him go, hoping he'd lead them to Mehler. He looked over his shoulder. But there was no sign of a tail. He hurried on to where he'd parked the car, frequently glancing behind him. He had another good look round before he got in, and then drove at random through back streets for ten minutes before being satisfied that he was in the clear.

What a risk he'd taken! Or had he? For, after all, the police knew nothing about the Berrog papers. So they could not have anticipated that Mehler would send an emissary to Elsa. Only that he might seek shelter there himself. Therefore they would have no real reason for suspecting a casual caller. Perhaps he had over-stressed the danger of the visit.

He collected his case and started back. His chief worry now, one which had been growing on him all the morning, was the car. If the police had unearthed 'Frederic Danton's' connection with the affair, it was possible they had also discovered he'd hired this car. In which case, every cop in the country would be watching out for it by now. But there was nothing he could do. If he abandoned it and hired another, he would have to use the Stohlmek credentials. Then he'd have to leave the car at the farm after taking off in the helicopter. Eventually the police would connect it with Mehler's defection and discover it had been hired by a man called Hugo Stohlmek – who had also called at the Vandar's. Which would put Martin and Elsa in it up to their necks. It would help to get some false number plates; but he didn't know how to set about that. Perhaps, provided he got back to the 43rd, one of the others would be able to suggest something. But it was going to be a nerve-racking return trip.

He made it. At 11.25 he was hurrying along the corridor to Room 277 of the City Hotel. He tried the door. It was locked. He tapped lightly on the panel. Mehler's voice, close up on the other side, said: 'Who is it?'

'Me.'

There was the sound of a key turning. The door opened.

Petros pushed through.

'I've got them. And a letter from your sister.' He held both the envelopes triumphantly out to Mehler.

But there was no answering pleasure in Mehler's eyes, no exclamation of relief or congratulation. He took the envelopes heedlessly. His face was grim – drawn and frightened. Petros stopped short, a cold hand gripping at his heart.

'What's the matter?'

'It's the doctor. He's ill. In a coma. I think he's dying.'

15

The physician was lying on his back on the bed Petros had occupied. His skin was grey, and his breathing hardly discernible. Petros gazed down on him. It was like a nightmarish repeat of the previous day. There was nothing he could do. He returned to the sitting-room. Mehler was slumped in a chair. Petros said accusingly: 'It's the same as you had.'

Mehler shook his head helplessly. 'His symptoms were much the same – fever, hallucinations, then unconsciousness. But it can't be the same really. My trouble wasn't infectious.'

'How do you know? You aren't a medic.'

'My trouble was caused by the use of unsterilized water to dilute the drug. My symptoms fitted that exactly.'

'Maybe they did. But you can't tell me that it's coincidence when he goes down in exactly the same way as you just after spending hours in the same room as you.'

'I know it seems incredible. But it wasn't quite the same. He had pain, as well. I never had that.'

Petros sat down and lit a cigarette. 'Tell me exactly what happened.'

'After you left we sat down and talked for about forty-five minutes. Then I noticed he wasn't well. He was obviously feverish. He asked me to get him a drink. Gradually he got worse. Then he started having hallucinations.'

'What sort of hallucinations?'

'He thought there was somebody else in the room. He kept talking to them.'

'Saying what?'

'Oh, I don't know. One time he seemed to think someone had let him down – deserted him. Apart from that, I couldn't make much sense of it.'

'Did you suffer from hallucinations?'

'Yes. But his seemed more real – and less horrible. Then he got this pain – which was never part of my attacks. It was in his side – under the ribs. It seemed very bad. I was relieved when he eventually passed out. I got him onto the bed. Then I looked round for that case he had last night. I thought there'd be some medicine – drugs, or something – in it, that he'd used on me. But he must have taken it with him.

'What course does this trouble usually take?'

'I've told you his isn't the same as mine. My first attack only lasted just under an hour. He's already been ill for nearly three. He's worse that I was. He's been suffering real pain. I can't see him pulling through.' There was a slight tremor in his voice. He got up quickly, crossed the room, and looked out of the window.

Petros drew deeply on his cigarette. He said: 'We can't risk calling another doctor. As you said about yourself, it would mean hospital. And he's almost certainly a wanted man. He probably entered the country illegally. He's been working for Mr Pelli – whose organization is trying to bring down the government. Anything would be better than letting them get their hands on him.'

'Well, we can't take him with us. So we've got two choices. Either we wait – until he recovers or dies. Or we leave him. It's your decision.'

'You know the position as well as I do. The cops have almost certainly picked up our trail by now. I'm surprised they haven't got here already. If we wait any longer we'll probably throw away everything we've achieved so far.'

'So you say leave him?'

'I'm just pointing out the facts. But my job is to get you out of the country. That's the assignment Mr Pelli gave me. He'd want me to put that first. And he's got lots of friends in this country – perhaps even another doctor among them.'

'Unlikely. If there was a doctor among them, why would he' – he nodded towards the bedroom – 'have had to come?'

'There might be a reason. Anyway, I expect Boris would know if

179

there was another one in the organization.'

'Boris has gone off duty. He came up to say good-bye just after you left. He won't be back till midnight.'

'Well, there is a 'phone number I can use in an emergency. I rang it yesterday and was told to bring you here.'

'A 'phone number?' Mehler stared. 'Then what the devil are you waiting for? Get on to it.'

'All right.' Petros stood up. 'But I'm not going to abandon him. If Mr Pelli's friends can take care of him, all well and good – we'll leave him with them.'

'And if they can't – remembering what you said just now about what your job was?'

'We'll meet that problem when it arises.'

Petros went to the telephone and lifted the receiver.

'Put it down, please.'

They both wheeled towards the voice. The physician was standing in the bedroom doorway. He looked ghastly, his face without colour and ravaged with pain. One hand was pressed against his side.

Petros was conscious of Mehler giving an exclamation of sheer astonishment. He gathered his wits and took a step towards the doorway. 'You shouldn't be on your feet. Come and sit down.'

'No.' The physician raised a hand and Petros stopped dead. 'There's no time. I'm coming with you.' He took a step forward, and a wave of agony crossed his features. He rested his hand on the back of a chair and stood swaying slightly. Slowly, as though it were a conscious movement that had to be thought about and planned in advance, he turned his head to look at Mehler. 'Telephone down and ask them to get my bill ready immediately.' In spite of his appearance, his voice was strong. There was, moreover, a new note of authority in it. Suddenly, he sounded like Mr Pelli. Deliberately, he swung his head back towards Petros. 'The car I am using is in the street next to the hotel. It's light grey. Here's the key – the number's on the fob. Bring the car to the front of the hotel. Then come back in, pay the account, and wait for us in the lobby.'

'Right.' Petros took the car key from him. 'I'll have to fetch my things from the other car. It'll take a few minutes.'

'No matter. I shall not be able to hurry.

Petros stood in the lobby, glancing anxiously around. The receptionist was engaged with two guests. Apart from them, the place was
deserted. He threw another look up at the lift indicator, trying to will
the physician and Mehler to come now, while there were no people
about. Half a dozen or more might arrive at any moment. The lift
was on the first floor. It moved – upwards. It stopped at the second
floor. Then it began to descend – agonizingly slowly. Petros gazed at
the swing doors to the street, then at the three people by the reception
desk, still in conversation.

The lift arrived. The door slid back and the physician stepped out.
Mehler was a step behind him, his face tense. Together, they started
out slowly across the lobby. The physician's features were as fixed as a
statue's. Petros strode ahead, opened the doors and held them for the
physician to walk through, then passed him again and threw open the
back door of the car. The physician bent and almost fell into the back.
Mehler paused in the hotel doorway till he was in, then put on his cap,
hurried across the pavement, and got in the front. Petros ran round to
the driving seat. A few seconds later they were off.

Petros drove with grim concentration. He gave all his mind to the
job, not letting himself worry about what lay ahead. He drove always
within the law – he could not risk being stopped for a motoring
offence – but fast. And fortune favoured him: traffic lights changed to
green as he approached; in every hold-up he seemed to sense the lane
in which the traffic moved off first; when he had to join main roads
other drivers stopped and beckoned him out.

In the back the physician lay unmoving, his eyes closed. Whether
he was unconscious, Petros did not know. And there was no point in
trying to find out. Mehler sat, pale and quiet, biting his nails. He and
Petros did not speak, except once when Petros gave him a brief
account of his visit to Elsa. There seemed to be nothing to say.

Before he got onto the freeway, Petros stopped for a few minutes to

181

consult the map of District 43. He looked at the road running from Township V to Township S, and at the narrow road running from it towards the south, leading to Village 152. Half way along this road was the farm. He would have to leave the freeway about forty or fifty kilometres west of the District Capital. That would take him straight to Township V. Then he looked at the map more closely. There was a secondary road which bypassed Township V and ran through a stretch of forestry land directly to Village 152. Then one could turn north and approach the farm from the south. It would mean he wouldn't have to go through the centre of Township V, and there would be far less chance of Mehler – for the physician – being seen. Moreover, that road would not be so busy as the major V to S road. He'd miss the signpost where the girl had been going to leave the message in the event of danger; but he'd never put much faith in that scheme, anyway, and had only really gone along with the plan to please her. So, as long as he remembered that he'd be approaching the stag's head tree from the 'wrong' side and it might look different, that would be the road to take. He drove on.

The new car was a double boon: not only had he been able to abandon the BFR; but this was a far more powerful vehicle – so that on the freeway he was able to keep the needle constantly round 100 km/h. The day was still grey and damp. They passed out of the 44th and into the 43rd District. When they stopped for petrol, Mehler got out and bought some bars of chocolate and cans of soft drink from a slot machine. They motored on, Petros taking his refreshment at the wheel. Still the man in the back did not stir.

It was early evening when they reached the road to Township V and pulled off the freeway. A few kilometres short of the town they came to the minor road leading direct to Village 152, and Petros turned down it. Soon, the region became more rural than any they had passed since leaving the 45th. But it was ugly, oppressive country, with few farms, mostly flat scrubland. After this they hit the first of the symmetrical, man-made pine forests, and from then on were almost continuously passing between the dark and birdless rectangles, with just occasional, dirty-looking gaps, where the fellers had clawed great gashes in the woods.

Through the forests the traffic was fairly light and the roads straight. The trouble was that they were generally too narrow to allow for passing. Several times Petros was slowed down for minutes by lorries, and at last he found himself at the tail of a minor convoy. A heavy lorry, carrying lengths of timber, was in the lead, with a van and two private cars tucked in behind it. Petros pulled out to overtake, but the road was too narrow, and he was forced to draw back. He banged on the wheel with impatience. Mehler glanced sideways at him, but didn't speak.

The lorry began to slow still further. Perhaps it was stopping altogether, then he could get past.

It did stop.

Then Petros's heart gave a leap of pure horror.

'A road block! The police!' His voice was hoarse.

'What!' Mehler jerked forward in his seat.

The man on the back seat opened his eyes, but neither of them saw him.

Sixty or seventy metres ahead, facing them, on the right, stood a police car, drawn up on the grass verge. Three uniformed and armed patrolmen were standing near it, one in the centre of the road, talking to the driver of the lorry, one apathetically peering at the load of timber, and the third standing on the verge in front of his car, his hands hooked in his gun belt, his eyes on the vehicles behind the lorry

'Turn round – quickly! Mehler spoke frantically.

'And tell them we've got something to hide? They'd come straight after us.'

The lorry trundled off. The car behind it moved up to the policeman in the road, who bent and spoke to the driver, while the second policeman moved round to the back and opened the doors. Petros's mind was racing. He said: 'I'll stay behind when the others move forward. Once they're clear I'll start slowly then suddenly accelerate. At least we'll still be going in the right direction. And they'll have to turn the car before they follow us.'

'But – what happens when you catch up with the others again? You'll never get past them on this road.'

'I'll worry about that when the time comes. It's our only chance.

183

Get that phial out. If it looks like they're going to catch us, empty it out of the window.'

'But it's the only sample in existence — '

Petros snarled at him. 'Do as I say or I'll do it myself. The Chairman's not getting hold of it. We get through or we get killed. I'll crash deliberately if necessary.'

Mehler seemed to sigh. 'Yes. All right. Sorry.'

'And be ready to set light to your notes, too, when I tell you.'

The van pulled away and the first of the cars had drawn up by the policemen. The second car moved forward and stopped behind it.

Petros put his hand in his pocket and fingered the cold, smooth butt of the revolver. He said: 'Get down when I stand on the accelerator. There'll be shooting.'

The leading car drove off. It was an eye-catching, red sports model, and it gave a deep throaty roar as it disappeared. The policeman on the verge followed it with perhaps envious eyes.

Petros and Mehler sat tense, not speaking. Suddenly they heard the rear near-side door behind them open. Momentarily they froze. Then, before they could move a voice spoke quietly.

'Do not look around. When the police call you on, stay where you are. Drive on when the road is clear. Do not stop whatever happens.' There was a slither, a bump, and the door closed softly.

Neither Petros nor Mehler was capable of speech. Petros's gaze was fixed unblinkingly on the third policeman, whose head was still turned away. From the corner of his eye he saw Mehler glance to the right.

'He's crossing the verge', Mehler hissed. 'He's dropping out of sight. There must be a ditch there. Yes — he's getting right down into it. I can't see him now.'

The police were taking their time over the second car. There seemed to be four or five men in it, and each was having to produce his identity card. The second policeman had been examining the boot. Now he closed it and moved slowly to join his colleague on the verge. They stood chatting.

The patrolman by the car handed back the last of the identity cards and straightened up. The car moved away. The policeman looked towards Petros and waved for him to come up. Petros didn't move, just sat quite still, his hands wet on the wheels, his pulse racing, his mouth dry. The policeman beckoned again, this time impatiently.

'Do something!' Mehler sounded near to hysteria.

Hurriedly Petros wound down the window and stuck his head out. 'Sorry,' he called out. 'The dam' thing's stalled. Hang on a moment, please.'

He turned off the ignition and pressed the starter button, so that the engine turned but couldn't fire. All three patrolmen were now looking towards the car. Petros continued to press the starter.

Desperately, Mehler whispered: 'They're coming, they're coming.'

As one man, the three policeman had turned and were pacing slowly towards the car. Petros drew out his gun, keeping it down by his knee.

At that moment a figure emerged from the ditch behind the policeman. Bent almost double, the physician took three steps, opened the door of the police car, and tumbled into it.

The policeman obviously heard nothing. They continued undeviatingly towards Petros and Mehler. They were barely five paces away when behind them the engine of their own car burst into life. As they swung round, the car shot forward. They saw it roaring towards them, its nearside door swinging open. They hurled themselves clear, two to the left, one to the right. The car sped between them. It swept past Petros and Mehler, who spun round in their seats to watch it. As they did so, a fusillade of shots rang out from the patrolmen.

The police car's rear window, and the window of the open door shattered almost simultaneously. And the driver's left hand, high up on the steering wheel. jerked and spurted scarlet. The car swerved, straightened, and went on. Numbed and half stupefied, Petros and Mehler sat twisted round in their seats, staring after it. Then there was a clatter of heavy footsteps near them, and the three policemen sprinted past, hopelessly chasing after their car, firing as they ran.

They ignored Petros and Mehler.

The road ahead was clear, but Petros, as though hypnotised, still watched the drama going on behind. The police car swerved again,

185

more violently this time. Mehler yelled: 'He's out of control!' The car skidded, broadside on, across the road and overturned. It seemed to roll across the ditch and, with an impact that Petros could almost feel, smashed into a tree.

Then both Petros and Mehler gave strangled gasps of horror as without warning the car bursts into flames. Within seconds it was an inferno. They watched stupidly, speechlessly, as the policemen continued to run towards it.

It was Mehler who came to his senses first. He grabbed Petros by the shoulder and forced him round. 'Drive on!' he shouted.

Petros gave a start, and threw himself at the controls. He got the car moving. The road was still clear, and he put his foot hard down.

Mehler continued to stare through the rear window for some seconds before turning slowly round to face the front again. He said quietly: 'I can't see any more.'

'He – didn't get out?'

'Don't be a fool.'

Petros couldn't speak.

Mehler said: 'Sorry. But anyway, what good would it have been if he had?'

Mehler sat slumped in his seat, his hands hanging limp, his head back, his eyes closed. Sweat was pouring from Petros, and he felt as though he had no strength left in his body. He longed to stop, to lean back like Mehler and recoup his energy. But he couldn't afford that luxury. He couldn't yet take in all that had happened. He tried to think about it. Then he tried not to.

Mehler was the first to speak. 'We were talking this morning after you left – before he was taken ill. Do you know what he asked me to do? Promise to give up control of LET to Mr Pelli – to agree to hand over my notes and the sample and leave the whole thing in his hands. He asked me just to trust him. I said no. He saved my life last night – but I wouldn't trust him. I wouldn't let myself. When he was taken ill, I'd have given anything to have been able to say yes, after all. Later, when you went to fetch the car, I had a chance to tell him I'd changed my mind – even though he was so ill. But I didn't. Now he's saved my life again. And I'll never have a chance to say it. I could live for ever thanks to him, and I refused him the one thing he asked of me.'

Petros didn't say anything.

'One thing I can do, though,' Mehler said. 'He told me Mr Pelli wants me to let you have the protection of these.' He sat up and took Berrog's papers from his pocket. 'He said the same as you – that if I put myself in Pelli's hands, I wouldn't need them. I wouldn't do that, either. But I want you to have them now.' He thrust the envelope towards Petros.

Petros shook his head without speaking.

'Don't ruin my one gesture. It's the only thing left for me to do. Please.'

Petros took the envelope and pushed it into the glove pocket. 'All right. Thanks.'

Some minutes later, he said: 'You know, apart from anything else, what he did was brilliant. It was the one thing that could have got us through. If he'd just left the car and run – given that he'd been capable of it – they'd have gunned him down before he'd gone ten metres. Even if he'd distracted them long enough for us to drive off, they'd have been after us within seconds. But as it is, not only has he prevented them following us, they can't even call in to report what's happened – the radio will never have survived the crash and the fire. It could take them half an hour to get to the nearest 'phone.'

'Do you think there'll be more road blocks?'

'I doubt it. I imagine they'd try to cover every road that runs towards the frontier – and not only the southern one, but the others as well. That'd stretch their resources a bit – especially as they're probably watching airports as well. I don't reckon they could spare more than three men on a road like this one. But just in case, you'd better set light to those Stohlmek papers. You'll never need them now, and as long as we're in danger, they're a threat to your sister.'

The clouds had cleared, the rain had stopped, and the light was better than at any time during the day. Visibility would remain good for an hour or more yet, and Petros, thinking of the border crossing, wished it had stayed overcast.

Neither of them had spoken for a long time. Mehler had slumped down in his seat again and his eyes were fixed listlessly on the dashboard. Petros was hungry and thirsty, frightened, angry and heavy-hearted, tired in body and mind.

They got to Village 152 and took the road north. It was narrow, little more than a lane, level and straight, flanked for most of its length by flat, open fields. Petros gazed fixedly ahead, searching for the last landmark of the stag's head tree.

When at last it came in sight there was no mistaking it — even approaching it from the other side. Petros pulled up by it and peered along the track opposite that led to the farm.

Mehler sat up. 'Is this it?'

'Yes.'

Petros backed, then went forward again and turned down the track. They bounced along it for three or four hundred metres and emerged in a rectangular farmyard. To their right was the farmhouse, a rambling, dilapidated building; to their left the back of a row of cowsheds. Immediately ahead was a two-storey building with double doors, probably once a stable. Over the top of the cowshed Petros could see the roof of a barn. It had been pitch dark when he was here before, but that had to be where he'd left the helicopter.

He drove on across the yard, through a gap between stables and cowsheds, and round to the left. The barn stood on the edge of a large flat field. His landing field.

Petros pulled up near the barn, jumped out, and ran across to the big doors. He fiddled with the catch, then heaved one door open and stared into the gloom.

The helicopter was still there.

Mehler, at his elbow, took a deep breath. 'I never really believed in it. It seemed too good to be true. Is it OK?'

Petros went into the barn and had a closer look. 'Nothing visibly wrong. Let's get it outside. You should find a tow rope in the corner. Make it fast to the front of the chopper. I'll back the car up.'

Then, suddenly, they both froze as from behind them there came the sound of a quiet laugh. They spun round.

Just outside the barn a man was standing, a fat, bald, middle-aged man, wearing a dark suit and a white shirt with a stiff collar. He was smiling jovially.

'I shouldn't bother to make any more preparations, gentlemen,' he said.

Petros made a grab for his gun. As he did so, two other men appeared, one each side of the first. Both wore the uniform of the security police. And both were carrying revolvers. Petros let his hand fall to his side. He looked at Mehler and gave a shrug. 'Sorry, mate.'

'It's all over, is it?'

'Afraid so.'

'Oh well, it was a nice idea while it lasted. Not your fault. No one could have done more.'

'Thanks. Come on.'

Together they walked out of the barn.

The bald man beamed at them. 'It *is* Dr Mehler, isn't it? I did wonder when my men found this magnificent machine whether it could possibly be waiting for you. When you hadn't been apprehended by lunchtime today, nor made an appearance over the border, I decided to join them out here myself to wait and see who turned up. It's been very boring. But the outcome has been well worth it.' He looked at Petros. 'You, sir, I do not recognise. All I know of you is that you are not the real, blameless Frederic Danton.'

'Oh, I'm quite a celebrity, too, in a small way. Petros is my name, Mikael Josef Petros. I'm the man who killed Kauffman.'

The bald man's mouth opened. 'Ah,' he said, and nodded slowly. 'Of course. Do forgive me. My, my, Karl Marcos *will* be pleased when he hears. He's been longing to meet you again.'

'So I imagine.'

'Now we really must be going,' said the bald man. 'We have transport laid on – garaged in that stable in the yard. One of my men will drive your car. Please come this way.'

'Don't anyone move.'

The voice came from behind the bald man, from the dark open

doorway of one of the cowsheds. It was a woman's voice, and Petros recognised it instantly. It was not the first time it had come to him unexpectedly out of the dark. His heart gave a leap of hope.

The bald man stiffened, but neither he nor any of the uniformed men moved. The girl stepped out into the light. She was wearing the same donkey jacket and jeans as before. On her feet she had mud-spattered gum boots. She was carrying a double-barrelled shotgun.

Her voice quivering with tension, she said: 'You – bald man – there's a gun pointing directly at your back. Tell your men to drop their revolvers.'

'My dear lady – whoever you are – this is a useless exercise.' His voice betrayed not a trace of emotion. 'You cannot possibly kill all three of us.'

'Maybe not. But this is a scatter gun, and you're closely bunched. I can certainly kill *you*. And wing at least one of the others. Want to risk it?'

'But if you should pull the trigger, whichever of us is left will immediately shoot your friends. So if you value their lives . . .'

Petros said: 'This is known in certain circles as a Mexican stand-off, I believe. The factor you've overlooked is that both Dr Mehler and I would prefer to be shot than go with you. So your threats carry no weight. Of course if *you* don't mind dying, either, then by all means defy her, but otherwise I should do what she says. Because I'm going to ask her to shoot if they don't drop their guns.'

'And don't think I'll be squeamish,' the girl said harshly. 'So drop them – NOW!' She shouted the last word at the top of her voice.

Still the bald man did nothing. There was sweat on the faces of the uniformed men, but he seemed unmoved. Seconds passed. The only sound Petros could hear was Mehler breathing beside him. He called out to the girl: 'Right. Shoot.'

'Drop them,' the bald man said, and two revolvers fell immediately to the ground.

'Walk away from them,' the girl ordered. The men did so. 'Are you armed?' she asked the bald man.

He nodded.

'Take out your gun – slowly – and drop it by the other two. Then

190

walk over to your boys.'

Silently, the bald man did as he was told. Petros ran and collected the three guns. He went up to the girl. 'Thank you,' he said. 'Thank you very much.'

'Pleasure.' She didn't look at him, but kept her eyes fixed on the policemen. 'Lie down on your faces,' she told them, 'arms stretched out in front of you.'

The uniformed men glanced at their chief. He hesitated, then gave a little shrug and slowly got down. The others followed suit. Petros beckoned to Mehler. He came hesitantly up, and Petros passed him one of the revolvers. He hurled another as far as he could towards the centre of the field, and handed the third to the girl, taking the shotgun from her hands. 'I'll watch them. You two tow the chopper out.'

Five minutes later the helicopter was standing in the open. Petros called out: 'Mehler — go to the stable and put the radios in their cars out of action.' Mehler nodded and hurried off. To the girl, Petros said: 'You'll find a large envelope in the glove pocket of the car. And a pair of field-glasses on the parcel shelf. Will you fetch them, please?'

'Right.'

His face nearly on the ground, the bald man spoke without looking up. 'You don't hope to get across the border in that machine, do you?'

'Never mind about our hopes.'

'You haven't a chance. It'll be suicide.'

'Shut up.'

Mehler came back. 'Done,' he said.

'Good. That's everything. Go and get in.'

Mehler ran across and scrambled aboard the helicopter.

The girl had returned and was standing by Petros's side. He took the envelope from her, and put it in his pocket. He hung the glasses round his neck. Then he gave her back the shotgun. 'Watch them till I get the chopper started up. When I'm ready to take off I'll fire a shot into the air. Back across — keep the gun on them until the very moment before you get in.'

She caught her breath. 'You're taking me with you?'

He stared at her. 'Of course. I thought that was taken for granted.'

'But I can't just leave.'

'Why not?'

'Well, people won't know what's happened to me. And – and I've got things to do.'

'If you stay the only thing you'll do is die. Probably having told them everything you know about Mr Pelli's friends under a truth drug. After they've tried to beat it out of you first, just for fun.'

'But these men haven't seen my face. I was planning to keep them on the ground and get away in your car.'

He shook his head. 'You'd never make it. It'll already have been reported that the radios in our friends' cars have gone dead. They'll have men on their way here by now. With the sort of manhunt they've got out for us, the area must be swarming with cops.'

Her face showed anguished indecision. 'I can't just leave – with nothing.'

'I know it's hard. But that's what *he's* doing.' He jerked his head towards the helicopter.

'I – I don't know.'

'Listen – there'll be nothing to stop you coming back any time you like to risk it.' Still she hesitated. 'Mehler!' Petros shouted and beckoned.

Mehler jumped down and came running back. 'What's the hold-up?'

Petros thrust the shotgun into his hands. 'Watch them' He repeated the instructions he'd given the girl. Then he grabbed her by the arm and ran her to the helicopter. 'Get in. Don't argue.' She took one look at his face and climbed up. 'Get into the back.'

She scrambled over the seats and with some difficulty squeezed herself into the luggage compartment behind them. Petros clambered up after her and sat in the pilot's seat. There was no time for any kind of examination of the helicopter. He could only hope for the best. He switched on the ignition, took a deep breath, and pressed the starter. The engine turned. He kept his hand on the button. But the engine didn't fire. He took his hand from the starter, counted ten, and tried again. This time the engine coughed twice. But that was all. He licked his lips. 'I hope you're praying,' he said over his shoulder.

'What else would I be doing.'

He pressed the starter for the third time. For three, four, five seconds, the starter motor whirred. Then the engine burst into life.

Petros gave a gasp. He revved the engine, then let it die down and tick over. 'Thank God,' he said.

In his ear, she said: 'I have.'

He ran through a hurried check of instruments and controls. Everything seemed to be functioning, the motor running sweetly. She ought to have a run-up, but there wasn't time. He pointed the revolver through the open door and fired a shot in the air.

Mehler started to walk rapidly backwards towards them, still watching the men lying on the ground. He reached the helicopter, fired both barrels of the shotgun into the air, threw it to the ground, and jumped aboard, slamming the door.

Petros's hands and feet moved in unison on the controls. The engine note grew higher. There was a second's vibration as the rotor blades battled against the dead weight below them, then the helicopter was off the ground and climbing.

Petros turned towards the south. The girl touched his shoulder and pointed. He looked back out of the window. A black saloon car was just turning into the lane leading to the farm.

'You were right,' she said. 'I wouldn't have made it. Thanks.'

Petros swore. Mehler glanced at him. 'That's bad, isn't it?'

Petros nodded grimly. 'I hoped we might get a start. But now they'll have had time to alert the border guards – and the Air Force.'

'You're going straight to the frontier? Why not make a diversion – try to cross farther to the east or west?'

'No point. They're bound to pick us up on radar, anyway. So time is the important factor. It'll be a race to get to the frontier before the Air Force can catch us.'

'How far is it?'

'About one hundred and four kilometres?'

'How long will it take?'

'I don't know. Normal top speed is 170. But we're overloaded, so we won't touch that today.' Then he said: 'I'm going to fly lower. It'll make it more difficult for them to get a sighting of us – from air or ground.'

They were passing over unbroken stretches of pine forest. Petros took the helicopter down, farther, and farther still, until they were just a few metres above the greeny-grey blur of the treetops.

He tried to keep his eyes ahead, but time and again found them drawn irresistably up to the sky. Minutes passed. They left the forests behind and started to fly over flat scrubland. Dusk was drawing in, and Petros blessed it. But it was still a little too light for comfort.

It was a long time since any of them had spoken. Petros's eyes were now locked on the horizon ahead and, unbidden, Mehler had taken over the sky-watch.

Suddenly he gave a shout and pointed to the right.

Petros followed his finger. At first he could see nothing. Then he picked out a black dot. It was at three o'clock and about twenty-five degrees above them. Rapidly it increased in size. It was a fighter. Suddenly it made a distinct change of course and came straight towards them. Petros said: 'He's spotted us.'

Tensely, they watched the fighter approaching. For an instant they could see the outline of the pilot's head. Petros waited, teeth clenched, for him to fire.

The next second he did so. They saw the tracer bullets pass harmlessly in front of them. Then he was gone.

Mehler said hoarsely: 'A warning?'

'Yes. To give us a chance to turn back.'

'W – what are you going to do?'

'Keep going.'

'And be shot down?'

'Probably. But there is just one chance. If we go back, we've got no chance at all.'

'What do you mean "one chance"?'

'I'll explain if we get through.'

'Here he comes again. From the left.'

It took every scrap of will-power he possessed, but this time Petros forced himself to keep his eyes straight ahead. Mehler continued to stare to the side. Then he threw his arms up to cover his head, the girl

194

screamed, and from the corner of his eye Petros saw a great black silent mass hurtling right at them. For a milli-second the sky was blotted out. Then there was an ear-shattering roar and they were alone again. Somehow Petros kept the helicopter steady.

Mehler shouted: 'Why didn't he shoot?'

'Just trying different tactics.' Over his shoulder he called: 'Are you all right?'

There was no reply. Mehler turned round in his seat and reached out his hand. He said: 'She's fainted.'

'Good.'

'Who is she?'

'A friend of Mr Pelli. That's all I know. She was my contact when I first arrived.'

'What was she doing at the farm?'

'I don't know.'

'Look out!' Once more Mehler pointed, this time to the right again.

Petros braced himself and prayed. Mehler sank down in his seat.

Five seconds later they were still alive. The fighter had buzzed them, fired a single burst, and flown on as before. And Petros knew they were going to get through.

He said: 'It's OK. We're safe.'

'There are still the border guards.'

'Wait and see. We're nearly there.'

He pointed ahead. In the distance could be seen the high wire fence which was the frontier. It flashed nearer. Petros saw towers with searchlights, small concrete bunkers. Then, when closer still, he could see soldiers on foot. They were staring up. None of them moved. And not a shot was fired.

The helicopter swept over the wire, over the strip of no-man's land, over the lower fence that marked the border of the free country. Two soldiers, patrolling the other side of it, looked up and one started to run. Petros gave them a wave. Then fences and soldiers were behind, and open country lay ahead. Far to the south, Paula was waiting.

The assignment was over.

16

Mehler had his head buried in his hands and his voice was muffled as he said: 'I can't believe it.' He raised his head and peered through the window into the dusk. 'It looks just the same, doesn't it?'

Petros didn't answer. He was too tired to speak. He felt no exultation, no pride. He had no feelings at all at that moment. He was just tired.

'Why didn't they fire?'

Petros made a great effort. 'Only a guess. If we'd been shot down, we'd have probably all been killed. The chopper would probably have caught fire. The drug would have been lost for ever – you dead, your notes burnt, the sample destroyed. The Chairman couldn't risk that.'

'But what good is it to him now?'

'None at the moment. But at least it is still in existence. It will continue in existence. So there's still a chance he might one day get supplies himself. That's better than no chance at all. It'll give him something to scheme for and dream about. Once we'd got into the air with your notes and the sample in our possession, we were safe. I didn't realize it at the time – though I should have done. That buzzing was just bluff.'

Mehler nodded slowly. 'It makes sense. And I suppose he *will* get supplies, too – later, when it does go on the open market.'

'Let's hope he's dead by then.'

There was a stirring behind them. Mehler turned round in his seat and smiled. 'Welcome back.'

The girl sat up. 'Where are we? What's happened?'

'We crossed the frontier two minutes ago.'

'No! Really? Gosh, that's wonderful!' She got onto her knees and leaned forward between them. 'Where do we land?'

'On the first piece of level ground I see near a quiet road. And quickly – before it gets quite dark.'

'Then what?' Mehler asked.

'Get away from this machine before the police reach it. Our crossing will have been reported by now, so we mustn't waste time.'

'But – we don't have to be afraid of the police in this country, do we?' Mehler sounded suddenly alarmed.

'No, no, don't get me wrong. If they did pick us up, they'd be very kind. But there'd be an awful lot of red tape to go through – interviews and form-filling, and they'd probably isolate us in a big country house for weeks while they checked out our stories. It would be a very comfortable country house, mind you, but I just want to bypass all that.'

'Then what is the plan?'

'I take you to my place make a 'phone call, and then wait for Mr Pelli or one of his friends to turn up. After that my job's over. You'll be in Mr Pelli's hands.'

Petros put the helicopter down in the corner of a field near a country road, out of sight of any building. It was now almost dark, but he had just enough light. The corner was screened by a small clump of trees, and he thought there was a good chance the helicopter would remain undiscovered until the morning.

After he'd switched off the engines they all sat in silence for some seconds, revelling in the peace and stillness.

Then Mehler said: 'Now what?'

'We walk.'

'Where?'

'To the nearest town. I saw lights about ten kilometres to the east before we landed. Then we'll try to find a taxi driver who'll take us to my home.'

'Where's that?'

He told them, and Mehler said: 'It'll cost a bit to go that distance by taxi.'

'I know. But I don't want to stay in this vicinity a minute longer than we've got to. That's quite a small town, I think. It's unlikely there'll be a train or coach tonight, and even if there were, I haven't got a single copper of local money on me – nor will there be anywhere open where I could change this' – he tapped his hip pocket. 'But with a taxi, you don't have to pay till the end of the journey. And my wife and I always keep some cash at the apartment for emergencies.'

'There wouldn't be a chance of something to eat, would there?' the girl said.

For the last few hours Petros hadn't had time to think of food, but now he realized how desperately hungry he was. The slot machine chocolate had been a long time ago.

Mehler said: 'Frankly, I don't think I can face a ten kilometre walk on an empty stomach.'

'I'm afraid you've got to try. If we should be lucky enough to find a bar open when we get to the town, I'll have a go at flogging the binoculars – though it will be late and, as I said, I think it's only a small place. All we can do is hope for the best. Come on.'

The girl said: 'Is this box to be left here?'

'What box?'

'This cardboard carton. Do you want to leave it or take it with you?'

'I don't know what you're talking about.' He turned round, switched on the interior light, and stared at the box. 'I've never seen it before.'

'Shall I open it?'

'Yes.'

She pulled up the flaps, then gave a little cry. 'Food!'

'What?'

She started to pull things out of the box. 'A tin of ham. Some cracker biscuits. Apples. Another tin – butter – real butter! And some bottles: beer – and Coca-Cola. I've heard of this, but I've never tasted it.'

Petros stared at the stuff in amazement. 'Mr Pelli or Alex must have put it there in case of emergency before I started out and then

198

forgotten to tell me.'

'Who cares where it came from?' Mehler said. 'Let's eat.'

'We ought to get away from the helicopter first.'

'What – and eat in the dark, under a hedge, surrounded by cattle? No, let's have it in comfort. Frankly, I'd rather risk getting picked up by the police than go a step without eating first.'

'I'm with you,' the girl said.

Petros gave in.

In addition to the food and drink the box contained a can and bottle opener, knives, and plastic plates and beakers.

And, in the very bottom, was a well-filled envelope. The girl passed it to Petros without a word. He opened it. 'Money,' he said. He rapidly counted it. 'There should be enough here to take us all the way – by whatever means we go.'

Ten minutes later they were all feeling better. Petros was still desperately tired and didn't feel like talking. But Mehler and the girl were soon chatting animatedly.

Suddenly, Mehler said: 'By the way, we don't know your name.'

She looked a little shy. 'It's Greta. Greta Enderman.'

'My name's Thomas Mehler.'

They shook hands solemnly.

Petros said: 'He's a very famous scientist.'

She looked questioningly at Mehler. 'Are you?'

'Not really famous yet – just brilliant.'

Petros said: 'And you both heard me tell my real name at the farm.'

There was an awkward silence, then Mehler said: 'Yes. It was – quite a surprise.'

Greta said hurriedly: 'He must have had good reason for what he did. Mr Pelli would never have chosen him if he hadn't been all right.'

'Good heavens,' Mehler said, 'I'm not judging anybody.'

'Thanks,' Petros said gruffly. 'Yes, I did have good reason. Perhaps I'll be able to explain one day.'

Mehler said to Greta: 'Now perhaps you'll tell us by what miracle you happened to be at the farm.'

She bit into an apple and crunched it up, before saying: 'I promised

199

Mr Petros I'd try to keep an eye on the chopper. I went for the third time early this morning. I decided it would be safer if my van wasn't seen near there, so I left it a few kilometres away and cut across country. I took the shotgun in case I had a chance to get a rabbit. There was nobody there when I arrived. I checked the helicopter, and I was just going to leave when I heard a car coming along the track.' She glanced at Petros. 'I thought for a minute it might be you. So I got out of sight and waited. It was those two uniformed policemen. They started to search.'

'How come they didn't find you?' Petros asked.

'They didn't know the farm as well as I do. There are all sorts of odd hidey-holes I know of. I lived there once, you see.'

Petros gave an exclamation of surprise. 'You did? I had no idea.' Then he nodded thoughtfully. 'I see. That explains a lot. Sorry — please go on.'

'Well, I managed to keep one step ahead of them, though they got pretty close to me at times. I gathered from odd things they said that they were not particularly suspicious of the farm; they were just part of a team searching the whole area. Then they found the chopper and got very excited. They must have radioed in to report, because then they just hung around until the bald man arrived. He spent a long time messing around in the barn with the helicopter. Then they hid themselves in various places, and I guessed you must be on your way and they were going to wait for you. I wanted to get away and leave a warning for you by the signpost, as we arranged.'

Petros opened his mouth to say something. Then he changed his mind.

She went on: 'The trouble was that I couldn't get down the track to the road without being seen. The only way I could get clear was across the fields in the opposite direction. And if I did that, I knew I might miss you — you'd pass the signpost before I had a chance to double back to it and leave the warning. So I decided the best thing to do was wait about and try to help after you arrived. That must have been about four or five hours before you eventually got there.'

Mehler said: 'You were there all that time with nothing to eat! You must have been starving.'

200

Almost apologetically, she said. 'I had a few candies.' Then: 'You know the rest.'

Petros said: 'I can't begin to say how grateful we are. You saved our lives, there's no doubt about that.'

'You were great,' Mehler said simply.

In spite of the dim light they could see her blush. Petros said quickly: 'I'm afraid your family will be getting very worried about you by now.'

She shook her head. 'I haven't any family.'

'You don't live in that house alone, surely?'

'No, but they're not my family. My parents and sister died ten years ago. In the mystery epidemic. I was fourteen. I've been living with distant relatives of my mother ever since. They've been very kind. But I've never really been one of the family. They won't be sorry to be rid of me. They're not friends of Mr Pelli, you see. In fact, they're extremely loyal to the government. That makes a difference.'

'Then what on earth persuaded them to put me up that night? Who did they think I was?'

'They didn't know anything about it. They were away for a week. I shouldn't have been able to help you if they'd been around. But they left me to look after the place. It worked out awfully well. They actually said I could have a friend to stay. So even if they'd found out about you they could hardly have complained, could they?'

They'd eaten all the food, except for a few apples, which they stuffed into their pockets. Then they got out and started to walk. The last traces of daylight had now gone. It was a dry, mild night, with a nearly-full moon giving ample light for them to see their way. They tramped on in silence, along the quiet country roads.

Petros had decided to stick to his original plan of taking a taxi home. There would almost certainly be a long wait for a train or coach – and probably a change half-way. Besides, when they did finally find transport, he wanted to sit in a comfortable seat and sleep until he was right outside his own home.

He had been tired before leaving the helicopter, and they hadn't gone far before he was overtaken by an exhaustion more complete than he'd ever experienced. He was wearier than he would have thought it possible to be. The forty-plus hours since he had left the caravan on the Thursday morning to drive the hire car to the lay-by had been a time of virtually non-stop activity – including hours of walking over rough terrain, several long drives, and a helicopter flight – continuous danger, and unceasing responsibility for the lives of others. He had had just four hours in bed. Now the final stage was nearly too much for him. By the time they reached the outskirts of the town he was in a semi-trance, stumbling along, being guided and half-supported by the others.

At last they came to a telephone kiosk. During the talk over their meal it had transpired that neither Mehler nor Greta spoke more than a few words of the language, so Petros had to force himself awake to do the telephoning. He had no small change, only notes, so had to go via the operator and reverse the charges.

The first taxi company he rang wouldn't take on a trip of such a long distance. He tried a second firm and was lucky.

They waited by the kiosk, Petros leaning up against it, virtually asleep on his feet, until the car arrived. Then the driver wanted to see their money in advance. Petros, his head spinning, gave him the envelope. He counted the notes carefully, and kept them waiting while he did some laborious calculations to check that the money would cover the fare. Only then did he agree to start the journey. They almost fell into the back, Greta in the middle, Petros now craving rest like a drug addict craving a shot. He sank down into the corner, kicked off his shoes, lay back, and was asleep before the driver was out of bottom gear.

He was brought back from a deep abyss of sleep by a repeated shaking of his shoulder. He gave a groan and opened his eyes to thin early morning sunlight.

Greta said: 'I think we're there.'

Petros sat up with a jerk and blinked around him. The taxi was parked outside Riendett House. The street was already busy with traffic. Petros struggled into his shoes, opened the door, and got stiffly out. Mehler and Greta scrambled out after him. He paid the hefty fare and the driver drove off. Petros looked up to the windows of his flat. The curtains were drawn. He glanced at his watch. No, of course, Paula wouldn't be up yet. 'Right,' he said, 'come on in and meet my wife.'

They hurried across the forecourt, past the modernistic sculptures, Mehler and Greta staring at them. In a wondering voice, she said: 'You really live here? You must be terribly rich.'

He laughed. 'It's quite modest by standards here, I assure you.'

They entered the building, receiving curious glances from several people leaving early for work. It wasn't surprising: all three were grubby and dishevelled, Petros and Mehler unshaven, Greta in her donkey jacket, jeans, and gumboots.

On the way up in the lift Petros rubbed his eyes and shook his head. He felt awful. Greta said: 'That was quite a sleep you had. You didn't stir.'

'What about you two?'

'We slept for a bit,' Mehler said, 'but since it got light we've just been looking out of the windows.'

'Isn't it lovely here?' Greta said. 'All so clean and white.'

'Yes, it struck me like that when I first arrived, I remember.'

The lift stopped and the doors opened. There were more people outside, waiting to go down, and more surprised looks to face. Petros led his companions hurriedly along the corridor. He could hardly wait to see Paula's face when she opened the door. He almost ran the last few paces and gave a long ring on the bell. There was silence, and he rang again, four or five staccato, triumphant rings. He imagined Paula sitting up in bed, looking at the clock, remaining motionless for seconds, fearful of bad news, then leaping out and running to the hall. He gave another peal on the bell. Still all was quiet within the flat. He bent down and called through the letter box.

'Paula! Darling, it's me.'

Nothing.

Petros felt the first stirrings of unease. He put his eye to the letter-box, but all this told him was that there was nobody in the hall and that the doors leading off it were closed. He straightened up.

Mehler and Greta were looking anxious. Greta said: 'She wouldn't have expected you back yet, would she?'

He shook his head.

'Well, mightn't she have gone to stay with a friend, or something? Perhaps she didn't like being here without you.'

'It's possible.'

Mehler asked: 'Can you get in?'

'I'll have to get the pass key from the janitor.'

They accompanied him to the ground floor. The janitor knew nothing about Paula being away; but as he apparently didn't know Petros had been away, this meant little. They hurried back upstairs and Petros opened the front door. In the sitting-room everything was tidy and normal. He went into the bedroom – and stopped short.

The bed hadn't been made.

Then Petros knew real fear. It was inconceivable that Paula would go away leaving an unmade bed. He carried out a hurried search of the room, then sank slowly down onto the bed, his heart pounding. Paula did not have a great many clothes, and he was virtually certain that all her coats, suits, dresses, and shoes were present. So were her handbags and her small travelling-case. But there was no sign of a soiled nightdress – nor of the light-weight dressing-gown she had been wearing this summer. Petros got slowly to his feet and returned to the sitting-room.

Mehler and Greta were standing close together in the centre of the room, looking worried and ill at ease. They both stared at him with raised eyebrows. He explained the situation.

'What are you going to do?' Mehler asked. 'Ring Mr Pelli?'

'I can't. I don't know the number.'

'But I thought you said – '

'I know. But there were two numbers to memorize – this one, and the other emergency number, the one I rang to get help when you were unconscious. I memorized that one; but I wouldn't need this one until I got back, and so that I shouldn't get them mixed up, Paula said *she'd* memorize it instead. I've no idea what it is.'

'Might she have written it down somewhere?'

'No, he asked us not to write them down. That's why we had to commit them to memory.'

'I see. So what *are* you going to do?'

Petros shook his head helplessly. He simply couldn't get his mind to work. For a minute there was silence. Mehler coughed. Petros pulled himself together. 'I'd better make some coffee. Perhaps I'll be able to think then.'

'May I do it?' Greta asked.

'What? Oh, there's no need – '

'Please. I'd like to.'

'Well, all right. Thanks. The kitchen's through there.'

She went out. Mehler said: 'Don't you know anyone else who's in touch with Pelli?

'One. But I've no idea how to reach him, either.'

'What about Julius? Wouldn't he be able to help?'

'He knows no more about Mr Pelli's organization than I do. I asked him. It was always Mr Pelli who made contact with him.'

With a fierce, urgent clamour, seeming louder than it had ever been before, the front door bell rang.

Petros's heart gave a leap. He swung round and looked stupidly towards the hall. Then he jumped to his feet and rushed out. He jerked the door open. A tall, fair-haired, good-looking young man was standing outside. He smiled. 'Mr Petros?'

'Yes.'

'My name is Loeb. I am a colleague of Mr Pelli.'

Petros said: 'My wife. Do you know – ?'

Loeb raised a hand. 'She is safe and well, Mr Petros.'

An immense wave of thankfulness swept over Petros. He swayed and had to put his hand against the wall to steady himself.

He drew a deep breath. 'Where is she? Why isn't she here?'

'I'll explain everything. May I come in?'

'Yes, of course. I'm sorry.'

He stood aside and Loeb came into the hall. Petros closed the door and turned to see Mehler and Greta standing, staring at them anxious-faced. He realized they probably wouldn't have been able to understand anything that had just been said.

'It's all right,' he said, switching back to his native language again.

205

'This gentleman's a colleague of Mr Pelli. He says my wife's OK.'

Greta gave a big smile. Mehler said: 'Thank heaven for that.'

They all went into the sitting-room. Petros introduced Loeb to Mehler and Greta, then, still in his own tongue, asked: 'Where is my wife, please?'

In the same language, Loeb said: 'It is long story. In my — my Department we thought it most safe if Mrs Petros was moved — perhaps danger from the enemies.' He spoke slowly, with a thick accent, and seemed to be groping for words. He smiled at Greta. 'I am sorry. I speak your language very badly. Quicker if I speak my own. Please?'

'Oh yes, of course. I'll go and finish getting the coffee.' She turned to Mehler: 'You might as well come and help me. There's no point in your staying here. You can't understand any more than I can.' She went out.

Mehler said: 'One thing first.' He looked at Loeb. 'Have arrangements been made for me? For me to carry on my work — for my discovery to be developed?'

Loeb listened intently. 'All things are ready for you, Doctor Mehler,' he said.

'Good. I was sure they would be. Petros can pass on the details later.' He went out and turned towards the kitchen.

Loeb waited a few seconds, then looked at Petros and spoke quietly in his own tongue again. 'Now, Mr Petros, don't be alarmed at what I'm going to say. As I told you, your wife is safe and well. And she's not far away. But I didn't tell you the strict truth just now.'

Petros stiffened. 'What do you mean?'

'I'm not a colleague of your Mr Pelli. Quite the opposite. In fact, I *am* one of the enemy. It is my friends who are holding your wife. We just want Mehler back, that's all — without any fuss or struggle. Co-operate and your wife will be returned to you as good as new.'

Petros emptied the cognac glass and put it down with a hand that hardly shook at all.

'What do you want me to do? Why don't you just take him? I'm sure you've got help close at hand. Professionals. Armed. We couldn't put up much of a fight.'

'We've been told not to risk hurting Mehler. So we don't want a fight – quite apart from the noise. We could perhaps drug him without his knowledge. But even that might be dangerous in view of his illness – and we'd have the additional problem of getting an unconscious man down to the car in broad daylight. If we have to do it that way, we shall. But we'd rather avoid it. We want him to walk out of here of his own free will. Therefore, he must not have the slightest suspicion of who I really am. We knew I wouldn't fool you for long. We don't know enough about this man Pelli and his organization. You'd be bound to catch me out. But Mehler apparently trusts you. If you tell him I'm genuine, he'll go with me happily. So don't even hint I'm not one of Pelli's men. If Mehler has any doubts, you quash them. Tell him you know I'm genuine. I don't care how you convince him. But do it.'

'How do I know my wife is still alive? How do I even know you've got her at all?'

Loeb reached into his pocket and brought out a small square object. He held it out. Petros took it and saw that it was a tape recorder.

'Turn it on,' Loeb said. 'That switch at the side.'

With a sick gnawing in his stomach, Petros did so. For a few seconds the tape was silent, then he picked out the sound of breathing. Next, a man's voice spoke: 'Now, don't be silly, Mrs Petros. Refusing to talk will do no one any good.' Still there was silence. The man seemed to sigh. 'Mrs Petros, do you really want your husband to think you're dead?' Another pause, followed by: 'Very well. We shall have to use some persuasion. Roll her sleeve back.'

There were some indefinable scuffling noises before Petros heard a woman's voice. 'What are you going to – '

She broke off sharply, as though realizing suddenly that she was co-operating. The voice was Paula's.

'Ah!' The man sounded pleased. 'Speech. But not quite enough, I'm afraid. Your husband must be in no doubt the voice is yours. So just a few more words, please.'

Again there was silence for about five seconds before the man said: 'Very well.'

There came the sound of breathing once more, a rustling noise suggestive of suppressed movement – and a short, sharp scream. Then Paula's voice: 'No, no – please, not again! Oh, damn you!' This was followed by the sound of sobbing and the man's voice:

'That's enough.'

The tape went silent. 'That was just a fleeting pain she was experiencing,' Loeb said. 'A cigarette on her arm – no permanent damage done. I'm sorry about it. I was not personally responsible. But I hope it's convinced you.'

There was a pounding in Petros's head and the room went dark. He was within an ace of hurling himself on Loeb. A look of alarm appeared in Loeb's eyes and his right hand started to reach inside his coat.

Then the spell was broken.

The door opened and Greta marched in, carrying a large coffee pot. Mehler was at her heels, bearing a tray. Greta said brightly: 'I managed to find everything.'

Petros made a supreme effort of will. He let his hand fall to his side and sank down into the nearest chair, pushing the recorder out of sight behind it. He heard the others uttering banalities, heard his own voice answering, took a cup of coffee from Greta and started to drink it.

It was the heat of the drink that brought him back to comparative normality. The others were all sitting round, cups of coffee in their hands. Greta, he noticed inconsequentially, had taken off her boots and was in her stockinged feet. He became aware that stilted conversation was proceeding. They had apparently been talking about Mr Pelli.

'Yes,' Loeb was saying, 'he is a fine administrator. It is a privilege to work under him.'

'I suppose he'll be retiring shortly now,' Greta said.

'Well, yes, sooner or later. I do not know exactly when.'

'Do you have any idea who might replace him?'

Loeb gave a shrug. 'Who can say? There will be strong competition. Much twisting of arms – much – what is the phrase? – wire pulling. I would not forecast.'

He finished his coffee, put down the cup, and said: 'Thank you. That was very nice.' He stood up, turned to Mehler, and said: 'Now Doctor, if you are ready, perhaps you will come with me.' Then switching languages again, he said: 'Please tell Dr Mehler that the country's most eminent scientists are waiting to talk to him, and that we have accommodation and full scientific facilities laid on.' He waited, his eyes fixed on Petros.

Petros translated the words.

Mehler got to his feet. Then Greta spoke. Very quietly. 'Don't go with him.'

Mehler's eyes narrowed. 'Why not?'

'He's a phoney. He's no more a friend of Mr Pelli than the bald man was. He's one of Them.'

There was a dead silence.

Then, from Mehler: 'Petros, is that true?'

'It's true.' It was Loeb who answered. He was on his feet with a gun in his hand.

'I'm sorry,' Petros said. 'They've got my wife. They're threatening to kill her if you don't go with them.'

'So now-you know.' Loeb backed to the wall, from where he could cover all three of them. 'How did you spot me?'

Greta shrugged. 'Several things. You weren't consistent in your speech. You were talking to us quite fluently at times towards the end. But chiefly all that nonsense about Mr Pelli retiring and there being competition for his job. No real friend of his could talk like that.'

'I'll bear it in mind next time. Now, Dr Mehler, let's get moving, shall we?'

'Not a chance.'

'Look, I'm warning you – '

'You have no hold over me at all,' Mehler said. 'It's no good your threatening Mrs Petros's life. She means nothing to me. And I'm quite sure you've been told not to harm me. So how are you going to make me come?'

He took three quick steps to the window and flung it open. 'I'll jump sooner than let you knock me on the head or stick a needle in me.' He glanced out. 'There's a policeman down there. He's on crossing duty, so he'll be there for some time. Which means it wouldn't even be necessary for me to jump. Take one step towards me, and I'll call him. I know the words for "Help" and "Police". So it's your move.'

As Mehler had moved, Loeb had kept his gun trained on him. Petros could still feel the bulge of his own revolver in his pocket. But Loeb's eyes were flicking to and fro rapidly between the three of them, and it was impossible to make a move. Mehler was the only one whom Loeb had been ordered not to harm.

Now Loeb suddenly swung the muzzle of the gun to point at Greta. She went pale, but didn't speak.

'What about the girl? Are you quite indifferent to what happens to her, too?'

'No. But you won't shoot her. What earthly good would it do you? You'd be wanted for murder, as well as kidnapping. And I'd immediately yell for the policeman. You might get away. But you couldn't take me with you. Nor could you silence me. You're not allowed to hurt me, remember. I could give a very accurate description of you to the police. What's more, you've left your prints in several places in this room. Once they're circulated by Interpol your value to your Department as a foreign agent will be precisely nil. If you succeed in getting home, they might keep you on for internal assignments. But I doubt it. They won't be very pleased that all the money and time they've spent training you has gone down the drain. Nor that you've bungled this assignment. So if I were in that situation I wouldn't be looking forward to reporting back to my HQ. I've lived in close contact with colleagues of yours, Loeb. They've talked to me about the Department. And I rather gather your chiefs are not fond of failures.'

Petros could see the sweat on Loeb's forehead. He marvelled at Mehler's coolness and powers of logical argument under pressure. It was time to add his own contribution.

'Something else,' he said. 'The government would be far from pleased about the bad publicity they'd get. I know for a fact your Department were ordered to avoid any action that would harm the

210

country's image. Doctor Mehler is a world-famous scientist. When he talks about kidnapping and murder he'll be believed. And the country's going to get another very bad press. Whose fault will it be, Loeb? Who's going to carry the can?' He paused, then added: 'Of course, there is a way out for you.'

'What do you mean?'

'You can walk away from the whole business. Clean. We won't call the cops or report your involvement in this to anybody. You'll have failed in this one assignment. But the blame won't fall exclusively on you, you'll still be usable as a foreign agent – and there'll be no bad publicity.'

'Go on. I'm listening.'

'Put your gun away first. You're not going to use it.'

Loeb hesitated, then slowly lowered his automatic and returned it to his shoulder holster. With a shifting of feet and a letting out of breath, the tension immediately eased.

'Well?' Loeb said.

'Suppose your ruse had succeeded and you'd left here with Dr Mehler, who believed you were an associate of Mr Pelli: what was the plan then?'

'I should have taken him to the place where your wife is being held – hoping to keep up the deception as long as possible – and there handed him over to somebody else.'

'Is there anybody working with you?'

'Yes. He's outside in the car?'

Greta broke in: 'A blue Saab?'

'That's right.'

'I noticed him when we arrived,' she said. 'Just sitting in his car, waiting.'

'After you'd delivered Dr Mehler, what would have happened to my wife?'

'She would have been handed over to me in exchange for him. I would have driven her out to the country and put her down somewhere near a telephone.'

'What would have been done with Dr Mehler then?'

'He would have been taken back home. I don't know how or

211

when. That would not have been my responsibility.'

'Just how much do you and your immediate circle know about this affair – and about Doctor Mehler?'

'Only that he's made an important scientific discovery and defected with it.'

'You don't know what it is?'

'Some sort of drug. That's all.'

'How did you know he'd been ill?'

'Your movements Thursday were traced. Apparently a woman saw you taking him unconscious from a caravan.'

'How did you know I'd be bringing him here?'

'You all talked rather too much last night.'

'What do you mean?'

'In the helicopter. It had been bugged. Every word you said while you were in it was picked up.'

Grea gave a gasp and Mehler said: 'Sorry, Petros. You were right. We should have got away from the chopper before having supper.'

Petros said: 'Why on earth did they do that? They weren't *planning* to let us get away.'

'No. But they didn't know who was going to turn up. They weren't sure it was waiting for Doctor Mehler. There are people whom it would pay us to let escape, if by so doing we could listen to their conversation for a while. It might have been standing by for one of them. Besides, it's an automatic thing: we're taught always to play safe and plant a mike.'

Mehler said: 'This is immaterial. *Why* they planted it isn't important – only that they did.'

'I know. Sorry.' To Loeb, he said: 'So after we'd revealed our destination, somebody came here and picked up my wife, while you were told to wait for us to arrive and then make the contact.'

'Right.'

'You saw us pull up in the taxi?'

'Yes.'

'Had either of you ever seen Dr Mehler or me before?'

'No.'

'You simply had our descriptions to go by?'

'That's right.'

'But you weren't close to us, were you?'

'About fifty metres away.'

'We must look quite alike from that distance. How did you know which was which?'

'Clothes. We were told by our men at the farm that you were wearing a tweed jacket, and he a black blazer and a cap.'

'And neither of you saw our faces clearly?'

'No.'

'What was behind that charade about the language?'

'That was my own idea – at the last minute, on my way up in the lift. I had to think of some way of speaking to you alone. I thought these two would stay and take part in the conversation if they could understand it, but that if they couldn't they might go out and leave us alone. It worked.'

Loeb now seemed positively eager to co-operate. He was watching Petros with an anxious expression. 'Well?' he said impatiently.

'Where are they holding my wife?'

'I'm not telling that until I know what you're planning.'

'I don't mean the exact place – just what sort of building?'

'It's not a building – it's a boat.'

'What kind of boat?'

'A cabin cruiser.'

'How many men guarding her?'

'I don't know, exactly. Two or three.'

'Right,' said Petros, 'this is what we do.'

17

Ten minutes later Petros, Mehler, and Greta emerged with Loeb from Riendett House. They walked slowly across the forecourt, chatting amicably. At the pavement they paused. Loeb raised an arm and beckoned. The blue Saab moved up the street and stopped by them. Loeb opened the rear door. 'Here we are, Doctor.'

'Thank you. Well, good-bye, Petros. Many thanks for all you've done.'

'I won't say it's been a pleasure, Dr Mehler. But I'm glad it worked out.'

They shook hands. Then: 'Good-bye, Greta. Thank you very much for all your help, too. I don't think we would have made it without you.'

'It was quite exciting,' said Greta. 'Good-bye, Dr Mehler.' She held out her hand also.

'I hope to meet you both again very soon.'

He tipped his cap, bent down and got into the car. Loeb got in next to him, slammed the door, and the car pulled out into the centre of the road and accelerated away. Greta waved, there came a wave in return from the back of the car, and in a few seconds it was lost in the heavy rush-hour traffic.

The car weaved its way through the city streets. It was making towards the older, poorer part of the city. Towards the docks. The two men in the back made polite, formal conversation. Loeb pointed out the occasional notable building or famous landmark.

And Petros — dressed in Mehler's blazer and cap — nodded, and expressed interest, and commented favourably on the climate, and the architecture, and the clean streets. His hand in his pocket was tightly gripping the butt of his gun. His eyes were mainly on the man behind the wheel, a burly figure with a red neck and close-cropped gingery hair. According to Loeb, this man was not merely a driver, but his own immediate superior. It was important they said nothing which would give him any inkling of the truth.

Petros hadn't liked leaving Mehler and Greta unguarded. But as long as the enemy believed they had the real Mehler; and so long as Mehler and Greta stayed in the flat with the door locked and didn't answer to anyone, there should be no danger. Perhaps it had been an unnecessary risk for them to come downstairs when he left but on the other hand, it would have been unnatural for 'Petros' not to see 'Mehler' off. Moreover, both Mehler and Greta were armed – and on their guard.

Gradually the streets they were passing through changed in character, the shops, cafés, and people on the pavements became more cosmopolitan. Shortly, Petros started to see cranes, warehouses, funnels, and the glint of water. Then they were on the docks proper. The car kept going. It left behind the deep-water berths and the big ships. They were soon in a remote corner of the dock, with only small craft in sight.

The car stopped. Petros looked around. They were on a narrow quayside. To their right towered the backs of great windowless bonded warehouses. On the left was a small shallow harbour. On the far side of the harbour a number of light craft, mostly of the cabin cruiser type, were berthed. The water was too low for him to see if any were moored on the near side, over the edge of the harbour wall nearest to them.

Now it was crucial to show no sign of suspicion. Though to seem a shade puzzled would be natural.

'Why have we stopped?'

'This is as far as we go by road. The next stage is by boat.'

'Oh?' He made his voice sound surprised.

'Yes. We are taking you to a completely safe place – an island off the coast.'

'I see.' He hesitated a moment. 'Well, if you say so. I'm in your hands.'

The driver had got out, and now he opened Petros's door and stood holding it. Petros got out. Loeb followed him.

'This way, sir. The boat's just over the side.'

Loeb made his way towards the quayside. Petros followed him, and the driver fell in a pace or two behind Petros and slightly to his right.

Petros drew a deep breath, tensed himself, then without the slightest warning, took three rapid steps to his right, and spun round, revolver in hand.

The driver's face changed. He made an instinctive grab for his own gun.

'Hold it!' Petros barked the words, and the driver froze.

'Dr Mehler!' Loeb's voice carried a note of carefully simulated bewilderment. 'What on earth – ?'

'I'm not Mehler, you fool! I'm Mikael Petros.'

'You bloody idiot!' The driver spat the words at Loeb.

Loeb's voice came in a gasp. 'He said he was Mehler. The other said he was Petros. How was I to know?'

'It was a mistake to send somebody who didn't know what Mehler looked like,' Petros said. 'Didn't it occur to anybody that Mehler and I might anticipate an attempt to get him back – and change clothes? Now, that's enough talk. Turn round. Walk towards the quayside.'

Neither of them moved.

Petros's finger tightened on the trigger. 'I'm warning you, I'll use this. And I'll shoot to kill to save my wife. I'm not bluffing. So walk.'

For a second longer it seemed the driver would defy him. Then he turned and walked. Loeb followed.

They approached the quayside. Petros lowered his gun to his pocket, keeping his hand on it, and peered over the side. He saw a shabby, ten-metre cabin cruiser bobbing on the water, the roof of its cabin about a body length below the top of the quay. Its stern was about twelve metres from them and it was made fast to a mooring ring fixed near a flight of steps cut into the harbour wall.

As he looked, the cabin door started to open.

Petros turned, took one step towards Loeb and pushed him with all his strength. Loeb went flying over the side of the quay.

Before he'd hit the water, Petros had his gun out again, and as the driver swung round Petros clipped him across the jaw with the barrel. He fell as though shot through the heart.

Petros sprinted along the quay and took a flying leap over the side.

He landed with a tremendous thud in the well of the boat, two metres from the cabin door, and fell forward on his hands and knees. The boat pitched and rolled under his impact. He saw the startled face of a figure framed behind the half-open door sway sideways as the boat moved. Petros stood up, steadied himself, and threw all his weight at the door. He felt it meet the momentary resistance of the other's body, then there was a cry, and the door swung freely inwards. Petros jumped again, straight through the doorway.

The light was dim, but he could see a form sprawling on the floor at the bottom of a short flight of steps. He landed feet together on the man's chest. He heard bones crack, and the man screamed.

At the far end of the cabin, a second man was standing gun in hand. Petros dived towards him, firing as he did so. The man staggered back against the bulkhead and sank to the floor. The gun dropped from his hand and slid across the floor out of his reach.

Petros rose slowly to his feet. The second man was sprawled against the bulkhead, a hand clasped to his shoulder, blood seeping through his fingers, his face screwed up in pain.

'Don't – don't shoot.' He jerked the words out.

But Petros ignored him. His eyes were on the figure lying on the bunk.

It was Paula. She was wearing her dressing-gown, nightdress and slippers, was bound hand and foot, and gagged. But her eyes were open and were fixed on Petros, big with wonder. He tucked his gun in his belt and stepped across to her.

'Darling. Thank God.'

Casting frequent glances over his shoulder at the men on the floor, he quickly undid her gag. When he removed it, she tried to speak, but all she could get out was 'Oh, Mikael.'

'Don't talk,' he said.

For several seconds he wrestled unsuccessfully with the knots. He didn't have a knife on him. He looked round the cabin, but couldn't see one.

'Sorry, darling,' he said. 'They'll have to wait.' He bent down and lifted her up, turned, and went to the steps. Neither of the men on the floor made any attempt to stop him. They seemed to have lost interest in the proceedings.

On deck he carried Paula to the side and, with some difficulty, clambered over the side and onto the stone step. As he went up them he looked back and saw Loeb pulling himself over the gunwale on the far side.

Petros ran stumbling to the Saab, dumped Paula onto the passenger seat, ran round to the driver's side, and got in. Near the quayside the ginger-haired man was just starting to get shakily to his knees. Petros started the engine and drove off.

He didn't know whether to be glad or sorry he hadn't killed any of them.

Paula said: 'There's not a lot to tell, really. I don't know what time it was — about four, I suppose. I was fast asleep, anyway, when the door-beel went. I did ha⌐ ⌐e sense to call out and ask who it was. But a voice said he was from Mr Pelli, with a message about you, and like a fool I didn't stop to think, but just threw the door open. There were two men there.'

'Which two?'

'The two on the boat — the one you landed on and the one you shot. They grabbed me and shoved a cloth over my mouth. Chloroform, I suppose. Anyway, I blacked out. When I woke up, I was lying on the bunk, tied up and gagged. Then I just lay there while they came and went. It was more boring than anything else. That's all.'

'That's not all. I heard the recording.'

'Oh, that.' She gave a shaky laugh. 'I'm sorry about that. I tried not to say anything. But it was nothing really. The mark'll be gone in a day or two.'

'Who did it?'

'The one you jumped on. He was the leader.'

'I should have put a bullet through his head before I left.'

'Oh no, Mike. You'd already hurt him far more than he hurt me. I should think he'll be a long time getting over that.'

'Good.'

They were on their way back home. A safe distance from the docks he'd stopped and got the ropes off her. Then they'd both had a drink of cognac from a hip flask he'd filled before leaving the flat. During this time their talk had tended to be incoherent, repetitive, and emotional, but after he'd driven on they'd both been more composed, and he'd insisted on hearing what had happened to her.

'Now it's your turn,' she said.

'It'll take too long to go into details now. I got Mehler out. He's at the flat now with a girl who helped us. He's brought a sample of the drug with him. We've got Berrog's papers. And Mehler's given them to me.'

She gave a gasp of excitement. 'You've done it all!'

'Just about.'

'Oh, Mike, how wonderful.'

'Yes, it's – a relief.'

'Well, you can't stop there. You must tell me more.'

So he told her as much as there was time for. But he didn't mention the incident at the road block. That could keep.

He parked the Saab outside Riendett House. They got out and, arms round each other, crossed the forecourt and entered the building. There were many more people about now than earlier, and most of them stared openly at the haggard, unshaven man and the bedraggled woman in dressing-gown and slippers. But Petros didn't care. He was getting used to it. They went up in the lift and hurried along the corridor towards their flat. Then Petros stopped dead.

The front door of the flat was ajar.

A black cloud of sheer despair enveloped him. He whispered: 'Oh no. The fool. The damn fool. I told him to lock the door and not to open it to anybody.'

Paula gripped his arm tightly.

He could hardly bring himself to walk the last few steps. If they'd got Mehler after all . . . And if they'd got Berrog's papers . . . He and Mehler had emptied their pockets when they'd changed coats, and he'd locked the papers in a drawer. He'd thought they'd be safer there than in his pocket when he went with Loeb . . . He went slowly through the door, Paula at his heels. All was quiet and still. He turned his head and breathed into her ear: 'Stay in the hall.' Then he took out his gun and stepped quickly through the open door of the sitting-room.

'You *have* been a long time,' said Greta.

'Yes, we were getting quite worried,' Mehler added.

They were sitting side by side on the settee. Petros stared at them speechlessly, relief battling with anger in his mind. At last he let anger win.

'You stupid idiots! What do you think you're playing at – sitting here like a couple of sacrificial goats with the front door wide open?' His voice rose to a shout. 'And where did you get those clothes?'

For he suddenly realized that they'd both changed. Mehler had on a smart grey suit, with a clean shirt and tie; he'd combed his hair and shaved. Greta was wearing a wine red two-piece, with a white blouse and high-heeled shoes; she too had attended to her hair and had applied some discreet make-up.

'They left the door open because I told them to. And the clothes are a present from me. Though to sit there quietly waiting for you was Greta's idea.'

Petros swung round towards the voice.

From a deep armchair in the corner of the room, Mr Pelli rose and walked forward. Petros closed his eyes and slowly expelled his breath in sheer relief. Then he opened his eyes. 'Am I glad to see you, sir!'

'I am glad to see you, Mikael? Is Paula all right?'

'Yes – ' Petros suddenly remembered he'd left her in the hall. He turned. 'Darling,' he called, 'come on in.'

There was no answer.

'Don't be alarmed,' Mr Pelli said. 'She has not been kidnapped again.'

'She peered round the door for a second after you came in,' Greta said. 'I imagine she's making herself presentable.'

'I am very sorry she had to go through that experience.' Mr Pelli said. 'One has to be constantly on guard against impersonations of my friends by the other side. But perhaps when you have all known me as long as Greta has you will be able to recognize imposters.'

Greta looked embarrassed. 'He just didn't ring true,' she said.

'But now, Mikael, you need no longer fear for yourself or your wife,' Mr Pelli said. 'The four men you have just routed comprise virtually the Chairman's entire strength in the city at present.'

Startled, Petros said: 'You know about what's happened?'

'Yes. You were followed – although there was no opportunity to contact you. The incident on the dockside was watched and reported to me.'

'Mr Pelli told us all about it almost as soon as he arrived,' Mehler interjected. 'Didn't you see his man?'

'No. I didn't see anyone apart from the other side.'

'I assure you help was not far away if you had wanted it and looked for it,' Mr Pelli said. 'Happily, you succeeded on your own, but if you had been a little less impetuous, the rescue could have been effected with less risk.'

'Wasn't it all a strangely inefficient effort for that department, sir?' Mehler asked him. 'It seems to have been full of loopholes.'

'That was unavoidable. It was merely a last desperate attempt on the part of the government to get you back. The local men were ordered to do their utmost – yet not to harm you. They had little time and few resources. They could only improvise. And their plan came close to working. Fortunately, all has ended satisfactorily for you both, and long before they can re-muster or be reinforced you will be in a safe place and the Chairman will have been warned of the consequences should any harm befall Mikael or his wife.' He turned back to Petros. 'Thomas has just told me that he has given you the Berrog papers. I shall need them if I am to send copies to the Chairman.'

'Oh yes, of course.' Petros fetched the envelope from the drawer where he'd left it and handed it to Mr Pelli.

'Thank you. Will you have them back afterwards, or shall I keep them safe for you?'

'You keep them, please.'

221

'As you wish.' He put the envelope in his pocket unopened. Then he said: 'Well, my friend, you have carried out your assignment with complete success. Congratulations – and thank you.'

'Hardly with complete success, sir,' Petros said quietly. 'I suppose – you have been told about – what happened at the road block.'

Mr Pelli bowed his head. He seemed about to speak, but Mehler got in first, addressing Petros: 'That doesn't detract from your success. His death wasn't your fault. It was mine. I brought about my own sickness. If I hadn't the doctor would be alive today. He gave his life for me. I know that.'

'In the end he gave his life for both of us,' Petros said. He turned back to Mr Pelli. 'It was one of the two bravest acts I've ever seen. I believe he was very close to you, sir, wasn't he?'

For the first time since Petros had known him Mr Pelli looked away. He spoke in a curiously flat voice. 'You don't know, do you?'

Suddenly, Petros felt a stab of alarm. 'Know what, sir?' he asked sharply.

Long seconds passed. Then: 'That you are speaking of my son,' said Mr Pelli.

Petros whispered: 'Oh no.' He tried to say something else, but it just wouldn't come. At last he forced words out: 'What can I say? I didn't know.'

'Nor me.' Mehler sounded stunned. 'I hadn't a clue. I'm desperately sorry.'

'You are both quite sure he is dead?' Mr Pelli asked.

They glanced at each other, neither wanting to answer. This time it was Mehler who eventually spoke first. 'There can't by any doubt, I'm afraid. Nobody could have lived through it.'

Petros said: 'I agree.'

Mr Pelli looked from one of them to the other. Then: 'Suppose I were to tell you it has been reported he is alive?'

They stared at him. Petros said: 'Reported? By whom?'

'By some who claim to have been eye-witnesses. I cannot say who they are. The messages so far have been fragmentary and unconfirmed.'

Very quietly, Mehler said: 'I'm afraid your hopes have been raised groundlessly. I saw it all. He is dead.'

Mr Pelli looked at Petros. 'Mikael?'

Petros hesitated. He said slowly: 'The car door was open. The car overturned and rolled over the ditch. He could conceivably have been thrown out into the ditch and escaped both the crash and the fire. Then he might have stayed in the ditch until the police had gone. The only injury we know of was the wound in his hand. The attack he was suffering from could have passed . . .'

'Oh, come on!' Mehler exclaimed. 'Do you really think that's what happened?'

'No, I don't. But it is just possible.'

'It's not. Not the way that car was rolling. We'd have seen if he'd been thrown out. No, I'm sorry to keep saying it, sir, but short of a miracle your son is dead.'

'And you don't believe in miracles. Thomas?'

'No, sir, I don't.'

'And you, Mikael?'

Petros didn't reply immediately. When he did so it was with a question. 'Are you telling me you think I'd be right to believe he's alive, sir?'

Mr Pelli sighed. 'It is true the weight of probability is against his being so,' he said heavily. 'A trained scientist says it is impossible. The report of the other eye-witnesss is isolated and unsubstantiated. Yet the source of the report has proved reliable in other matters.'

Petros said: 'I see. Well, in that case I suppose we'll just have to wait – and hope. No doubt we'll learn what happened fairly soon.'

'Do not depend on that. Merely communicating with my friends across the frontier has been growing ever more difficult. Security is sure to be tightened still further from now on. So long as the present regime is in power, actually to cross may well be impossible.'

'Then all I can say is that I'm prepared to keep an open mind. I accept that he could be alive. Beyond that I can't go. But whatever the truth, the fact still remains that he did willingly sacrifice himself. When the crunch came he knew that if Mehler and I were to escape he had to draw the enemy's attention to himself. That is what he did. His action isn't in any way devalued if by some miracle he is alive.'

223

Mehler said: 'That's quite true. But I'm afraid I still maintain he couldn't have escaped. Unless he comes back and I actually see him I've got to say he's dead. He gave his life for me. And I want to do something in return.'

From one pocket he took the glass phial, and from inside his coat the manilla folder. He held them up with an air of pride. 'LET is yours, sir. I'm giving you full rights in it – full control over its production and use. We can have papers drawn up to make it legal. There's just one condition: I promised Petros that he and his wife would be among the first to get supplies once it's in production. I know you'll honour that.' He held the phial and the folder towards Mr Pelli.

But Mr Pelli didn't take them. 'There are no conditions, Thomas.'

Mehler looked a shade embarrassed. 'I'm sorry, sir. I didn't mean I wanted it written into the contract. Your verbal promise will do, of course.'

'I can make no such promise.'

'Oh, but surely Petros has earned the right – '

'Mikael has earned the right to those things I promised him if he succeeded in his mission. Those he will receive. Access to this drug was not among them.'

'Are – are you saying you'd withhold supplies from Paula and me?' Petros's voice was incredulous.

'From you – and from all mankind.'

Petros went cold. 'What do you mean?'

'If I am given the freedom to do so, I shall destroy that sample and those notes.'

Mehler gaped at him. 'You can't mean it!'

'I do mean it. Unwittingly, you have discovered something which, if it continues in existence, will bring untold misery to the world.

'But – I don't understand. I thought – Petros made me think – you wanted to develop it for the good of everybody.'

'By no word or deed or inference did I indicate so. I said only that my wish was to prevent the Chairman gaining possession of it.'

'But we've done that! Why do you want to destroy it?' Mehler seemed utterly dazed.

'Thomas, you have no conception of the vast cost which would be incurred in making your discovery available to all but a handful of men. Money, time, skill sorely needed for other work would have to be diverted to its development. And during that time men and women would kill and steal and fight and cheat and send armies into battle to obtain such meagre supplies as were available. The leaders of the world would subjugate all else to obtaining and keeping supplies themselves. Do you wish to multiply the suffering and hardship that already exists in the world?'

Mehler's face was white. He stood unmoving, the phial and the folder still clasped in his hands. He said: 'I did anticipate there would be some trouble – at first. But surely, there'll be a way round it. Think of the long-term benefits!'

'There is no way round it. And there are no long-term benefits. For I have mentioned only part of the evil. Have you done any research at all into the effects of the drug on the human mind and personality – given that the time came when it became freely available to all who wanted it?'

'No, of course not. I'm not a psychologist. No doubt some people would have problems adjusting to a virtually endless life. A lot of re-education would be necessary. But that would all be outweighed by the – the sheer wonder of it.'

'It would be horrible.'

It was Paula who spoke from the doorway. As they turned, she came forward into the room. She had washed, brushed her hair, and dressed in a simple grey cotton dress.

She spoke to Mehler. 'I'm with Mr Pelli. I've hated the idea from the start. One would go through life terrified one was going to be stricken down by some deadly disease – they'll never master every disease – or killed in an accident.'

'But that's crazy! You could have an accident or get ill now – or any time.'

'I know. And isn't it the fact that your life is naturally limited anyway that prevents you worrying too much about it? "*Oh well, we've all got to go sometime*". Isn't that what we say? But if we know that our lives will go on for ever – *if we're lucky* – aren't we going to

225

be much more frightened of losing them? They're going to be so much more valuable than they've ever been before. I mean, I'd be much more upset at losing my purse if it was stuffed with notes than if there were just one or two in it, wouldn't I? I'm sorry, but I think your drug will produce a race of hypochondriacs and cowards.'

Mehler's expression was a confused combination of bewilderment, anger, disappointment – and the first stirrings of doubt. With no answer for Paula, he looked round, seeking support. His eyes alighted on Greta, who all this time had been sitting quietly on the settee, drinking in every word that was said. 'Do you agree with them?'

She looked alarmed. 'I'm afraid I don't really understand. You've invented something that will make people live for ever?'

'I'm sorry. I was forgetting you didn't know. Not quite for ever, yet. But near enough.' He held up the phial. 'Regular injections of this would mean that you could live for two hundred and fifty or three hundred years. Eventually it might be improved, so that your life theoretically need have no end.'

Her eyes widened. 'But where on earth would you put everybody?'

'Well, obviously there'd have to be strict population control.'

'You mean you'd have to stop having children – by law?'

'Not everybody. But the vast majority.'

She said: 'A world without children. No fairy tales or Santa Claus. I don't think I'd like that.'

Quietly, as if thinking aloud, Mr Pelli said: 'A world without innocence. A world without the old to revere or the young to protect. A world without families. A world of old, tired, inflexible minds, barren of new thought. A world of eyes which have seen everything, bodies which have experienced everything. A world where the seeking of new sensations will be the only escape from intolerable boredom. A world with ample time for everything, and in which, as a result, little of real importance will ever be done. A world in which men will never need to face eternal truths. Or so they will come to believe.'

Mehler gathered his resources. 'What if I say I won't give you the drug on your terms, that I'm going ahead with its development? You couldn't stop me.'

'I could stop you, Thomas. But have no fear: I promise you I will never do so. If you do give me that answer, it will mean simply that I have failed. And a very great evil will be released on the world.'

Mehler looked like a man with his back to the wall. He seemed to grope for words. 'Well – would you be willing to compromise – to accept that you've lost, and work with me to help minimize those evils which you think you foresee?'

'No. It is all or nothing, Thomas. Renounce the drug, accept my terms, and I can see that you have a home, freedom, safety, and a lifetime of satisfying and rewarding work. But decide instead that you cannot give it up, and you will go your own way without help from me. You will not see me or hear from me again.'

Mehler looked away. There was a hunted expression in his eyes. Petros was racked between hopes: he wanted the drug so much himself; yet the decision Mehler now had to make irresistably suggested one he himself had faced nearly five years before. Renunciation and commitment had been asked of him, too. He had responded to the appeal. At times since he had regretted his decision.

But only rarely. And never for long. To his surprise, he found himself willing Mehler to give in.

Suddenly, Mehler dropped the phial and the folder onto the settee and turned towards the door. 'I must be alone,' he said, and his voice was harsh. 'I've got to think.'

Mehler went out of the room, and a moment later they heard the front door slam. Petros gave Mr Pelli an anxious look. 'Surely we shouldn't let him be out there alone?'

'He will be watched.'

Greta said: 'Can I go with him, sir?'

'Yes. But let him be on his own a while first.'

She nodded and followed Mehler out of the flat.

Mr Pelli walked slowly across to a chair and sat down. Petros and Paula both did the same. For two or three minutes it was as though nobody wanted to talk.

At last Paula said: 'What do you think he will decide?'

'I believe he will accept the truth of what we said when he has considered it. The arguments we put to him were not ones he had met

227

before. Naturally, they were a shock. But he is an honest man. He will recognize the truth.'

'Yes, for the moment, perhaps. What I don't see is how you can guarantee that he won't go back on his decision later on. I mean, over the years surely there'll be terrific temptations for him to start again – to publish his findings. Especially as he finds himself getting older and knows that he could have the means of extending his own life.'

'Yes, of course there will be temptations.'

'What can you do about them?'

'Merely talk to him, and see that others talk to him, if ever it seems that his resolve is weakening.'

'And you think that will be adequate?'

'I can only trust it will be.'

'I fancy the young lady who just went out might be a help in that respect.'

'Yes, if he should waver. But I feel that once he is convinced he will remain steadfast.'

'I suppose the Chairman will always be trying to get him back, too,' Petros said.

'Undoubtedly.'

'But you think you can keep him safe?'

'Yes, as long as he wishes to remain safe. The Chairman shall never get Thomas back against his will. I have promised that.'

Petros picked up the phial. 'So this is all there may ever be of the elixir of life.'

'Are you very disappointed?'

'Yes, sir.' He put the phial back down. 'After all, it's not every day one loses the chance of everlasting life.'

'You have lost nothing. Nothing has been taken from you. It is merely that you are going to be offered no uncertain means of multiplying the precarious years you spend on this earth. That would not be real everlasting life. That is not your – or any man's – true destiny.'

'Tell me – apart from wanting to give me a chance to get the Berrog papers, why did you send *me* to get Mehler? You seem to have so many friends there. Surely one of them could have done the job?'

'None so satisfactorily. None who could have flown Thomas out

228

of the country. There are those among them who could perhaps have made the first approach to him, and later escorted him to the border. Whether any of them would have been capable of engineering the actual escape from his guards, I doubt. And they would have been putting themselves in great peril – without being in a position to seek safety by fleeing the country for ever, as you were able to do. All my friends there have their own responsibilities.'

'I see. So you really needed me?'

'Most certainly.'

Petros was thoughtful for a moment. Then he said: 'Oh, speaking of fleeing the country: about the helicopter.' He described roughly where he'd left it, and added: 'I hope Alex won't have any trouble getting it back.'

'I shouldn't worry about that. It is somebody else's concern.'

Paula said: 'By the way, there's a car outside belonging to the other side. What had we better do about that?'

'Nothing. Give me the key to it. I will ask Alex to drive it back to the dock, leave it there locked, and send the ley to you. If the other side want it they can easily obtain a duplicate key. I suggest you go to the docks in two or three days. You will I expect, find that their boat has gone, but that the car is still there. Drive it to a police station and, if its loss is not reported to the police within a month, you can claim it as an abandoned car. The law of the land allows you to do that. It will then be yours.'

Petros stared. 'Really? Why, that's great. Thank you very much.'

Paula said: 'That's almost worth being kidnapped for.'

Then Petros reached into his hip pocket and brought out his wad of banknotes. 'This is left out of what you gave me.'

'It's your money, Mikael. I gave it to you. If you made a profit on the assignment, that's to your advantage. I suggest you take Paula for a holiday on it. I believe her term ends next month.'

A short time later there was a ring at the front door. Paula went to answer it. Mehler came back into the sitting-room, followed by Greta. His face expressionless, he crossed to the settee, picked up the

229

phial and the folder, and handed them to Mr Pelli.

'I owe my life to you and your son. So I can't refuse you these. Destroy them if you wish. But the secret is still in my head. And I'm not promising anything. I need more time to think. Can I have those things you offered on these terms?'

'Indeed you can. Come with me now to a safe place I have had made ready. Your friend Julius will meet you there. Talk with him and with others. Reflect. And then decide. I have no power to keep you there against your will. You will be free to do what you wish at any time.'

Mehler bowed his head in acceptance. 'Very well. Thank you.'

Mr Pelli handed the folder back to him. 'I would like you to destroy these yourself,' he said.

For a second or two Mehler stood unmoving, the folder in his hand. It seemed he was going to refuse. He looked Mr Pelli straight in the eyes. Then, unexpectedly, he smiled. He opened the folder, ripped the sheets from it, took a box of matches from his pocket, struck one, and set light to the papers. While they first flickered, then blazed in his hand he crossed to the window and opened it. When the papers had burned down nearly to his fingers he put his arm outside the window and released them. They floated up and away, breaking into a thousand tiny black fragments. Mehler closed the window and turned round. His face was white, But his expression was not one of defeat.

Mr Pelli still had the phial of pink liquid in his hand. Now he turned to Petros and held it out to him. 'Will you dispose of this, Mikael?' he said.

Petros took it. He hesitated for a moment, then turned and left the room. He walked to the kitchen, went to the sink, and took the stopper from the phial. He held the phial up and looked at it. On a shelf over the sink was a small empty bottle. Petros picked ut up. He paused, the phial in one hand, the empty bottle in the other. He looked over his shoulder. No one had followed him. He was quite alone. He raised both hands to eye level. For fully ten seconds he stood, quite still.

Then he gave a sigh, put the bottle back on the shelf, and quickly, trying not to think about what he was doing, emptied the phial down the sink. He ran the tap and washed all remnants of the pink liquid away. He thoroughly rinsed the phial and the stopper, then returned to the sitting-room. All eyes were on him as he entered. Without a word he handed the empty phial to Mr Pelli.

'Thank you, Mikael.'

Petros went across to stand beside Paula. She took his hand and gave it a squeeze.

Mr Pelli turned his eyes on Greta, who was standing just inside the doorway. 'Come here, my dear.'

She came forward.

'You look troubled, Greta.'

'Do you think I did the right thing in coming in the helicopter with them, sir? I didn't know what to do.'

'Yes, I think you did quite right. I am sure one day you will return home. But not yet. In fact, you can be very useful to me here – if you are willing.'

'I – I'm willing. What do I have to do?'

'Come with Thomas and me – to the safe place I mentioned. I have work you can do there. Does that appeal to you?'

Greta's face lit up. 'Oh, yes!'

'Good. Then let us leave now. It is time Mikael and Paula had some time alone.'

As the others went into the hall Mr Pelli drew Petros aside. 'Regarding that new job I promised you: there will be a letter waiting for you when you return from holiday. It will invite you to call on a certain man. Do so. I believe you will find the meeting of interest.'

Mehler stuck out his hand. 'Good-bye. Thanks for everything. Sorry I wasn't able to keep my promise about the drug. And for what I said to Loeb about your wife's safety not being important to me. I was only calling his bluff. I would have gone with him, rather than let them kill her. At least, that's what I like to think.'

'I'm sorry I let you believe he was genuine,' Petros said. 'I was just playing for time. I wouldn't have actually let you go with him. At least, that's what I like to think.'

Paula, who'd been listening, gave Greta the ghost of a wink over Petros's shoulder. 'Oh, I see,' she said. 'And if it hadn't been bluff, I'd have ended up dead. Thank you so much, darling.'

'I didn't think you'd mind,' Petros said. 'After all, we've all got to go sometime, haven't we?'